MARGARET MILLAR (1915–1994) was the author of 27 books and a masterful pioneer of psychological mysteries and thrillers. Born in Kitchener, Ontario, she spent most of her life in Santa Barbara, California, with her husband Ken Millar, who is better known by his nom de plume of Ross Macdonald. Her 1956 novel *Beast in View* won the Edgar Allan Poe Award for Best Novel. In 1965 Millar was the recipient of the *Los Angeles Times* Woman of the Year Award and in 1983 the Mystery Writers of America gave her the Grand Master Award for Lifetime Achievement. Millar's cutting wit and superb plotting have left her an enduring legacy as one of the most important crime writers of both her own and subsequent generations. Her *Vanish in an Instant* and *The Listening Walls* are also available or forthcoming from Pushkin Vertigo.

PRAISE FOR MARGARET MILLAR AND HER WORK

"In the whole of crime fiction's distinguished sisterhood, there is no one quite like Margaret Millar"

GUARDIAN

"One of the most original and vital voices in all of American crime fiction"

LAURA LIPPMAN, AUTHOR OF *SUNBURN*

"She has few peers, and no superior in the art of bamboozlement"

JULIAN SYMONS, *THE COLOUR OF MURDER*

"Mrs Millar doesn't attract fans, she creates addicts"

DILYS WINN

"She writes minor classics"

WASHINGTON POST

"Very original"

AGATHA CHRISTIE

A Stranger in My Grave

PUSHKIN VERTIGO

MARGARET
MILLAR

Pushkin Press
71–75 Shelton Street
London WC2H 9JQ

A Stranger in My Grave © 1960 The Margaret Millar
Charitable Remainder Unitrust, u/a 4/12/82

First published by Random House in New York, 1960

First published by Pushkin Press in 2019

1 3 5 7 9 8 6 4 2

ISBN 13: 978-1-78227-573-2

Designed and typeset by Tetragon, London
Printed and bound by CPI Group (UK) Ltd, Croydon CRO 4YY

www.pushkinpress.com

This book is dedicated, with
affection and admiration, to
Louise Doty Colt

THE GRAVEYARD

*My beloved Daisy: It has been so many years since I have seen
you...*

The times of terror began, not in the middle of the night when
the quiet and the darkness made terror seem a natural thing, but
on a bright and noisy morning during the first week of February.
The acacia trees, in such full bloom that they looked leafless, were
shaking the night fog off their blossoms like shaggy dogs shaking
off rain, and the eucalyptus fluttered and played coquette with
hundreds of tiny gray birds, no bigger than thumbs, whose name
Daisy did not know.

She had tried to find out what species they belonged to by consulting the bird book Jim had given her when they'd first moved
into the new house. But the little thumb-sized birds refused to stay
still long enough to be identified, and Daisy dropped the subject.
She didn't like birds anyway. The contrast between their blithe
freedom in flight and their terrible vulnerability when grounded
reminded her too strongly of herself.

Across the wooded canyon she could see parts of the new hous-
ing development. Less than a year ago, there had been nothing
but scrub oak and castor beans pushing out through the stubborn
adobe soil. Now the hills were sprouting with brick chimneys
and television aerials, and the landscape was growing green with
newly rooted ice plant and ivy. Noises floated across the canyon
to Daisy's house, undiminished by distance on a windless day:
the barking of dogs, the shrieks of children at play, snatches of

music, the crying of a baby, the shout of an angry mother, the intermittent whirring of an electric saw.

Daisy enjoyed these morning sounds, sounds of life, of living. She sat at the breakfast table listening to them, a pretty dark-haired young woman wearing a bright blue robe that matched her eyes, and the faintest trace of a smile. The smile meant nothing. It was one of habit. She put it on in the morning along with her lipstick and removed it at night when she washed her face. Jim liked this smile of Daisy's. To him it indicated that she was a happy woman and that he, as her husband, deserved a major portion of the praise for making and keeping her that way. And so the smile, which intended no purpose, served one anyway: it convinced Jim that he was doing what at various times in the past he'd believed to be impossible—making Daisy happy.

He was reading the paper, some of it to himself, some of it aloud, when he came upon any item that he thought might interest her.

"There's a new storm front off the Oregon coast. Maybe it will get down this far. I hope to God it does. Did you know this has been the driest year since '48?"

"Mmm." It was not an answer or a comment, merely an encouragement for him to tell her more so she wouldn't have to talk. Usually she felt quite talkative at breakfast, recounting the day past, planning the day to come. But this morning she felt quiet, as if some part of her lay still asleep and dreaming.

"Only five and a half inches of rain since last July. That's eight months. It's amazing how all our trees have managed to survive, isn't it?"

"Mmm."

"Still, I suppose the bigger ones have their roots down to the creek bed by this time. The fire hazard's pretty bad, though. I

12

hope you're careful with your cigarettes, Daisy. Our fire insurance wouldn't cover the replacement cost of the house. Are you?"

"What?"

"Careful with your cigarettes and matches?"

"Certainly. Very."

"Actually, it's your mother I'm concerned about." By looking over Daisy's left shoulder out through the picture window of the dinette, he could see the used-brick chimney of the mother-in-law cottage he'd built for Mrs. Fielding. It was some 200 yards away. Sometimes it seemed closer, sometimes he forgot about it entirely. "I know she's fussy about such things, but accidents can happen. Suppose she's sitting there smoking one night and has another stroke? I wonder if I ought to talk to her about it."

It was nine years ago, before Jim and Daisy had even met, that Mrs. Fielding had suffered a slight stroke, sold her dress shop in Denver, and retired to San Félice on the California coast. But Jim still worried about it, as if the stroke had just taken place yesterday and might recur tomorrow. He himself had always had a very active and healthy life, and the idea of illness appalled him. Since he had become successful as a land speculator, he'd met a great many doctors socially, but their presence made him uncomfortable. They were intruders, Cassandras, like morticians at a wedding or policemen at a child's party.

"I hope you won't mind, Daisy."

"What?"

"If I speak to your mother about it."

"Oh no."

He returned, satisfied, to his paper. The bacon and eggs Daisy had cooked for him because the day maid didn't arrive until nine o'clock lay untouched on his plate. Food meant little to Jim at break-fast time. It was the paper he devoured, paragraph by paragraph,

13

eating up the facts and figures as if he could never get enough of them. He'd quit school at sixteen to join a construction crew.

"Now here's something interesting. Researchers have now proved that whales have a sonar system for avoiding collisions, something like bats."

"Mmm." Some part of her still slept and dreamed: she could think of nothing to say. So she sat gazing out the window, listening to Jim and the other morning sounds. Then, without warning, without apparent reason, the terror seized her.

The placid, steady beating of her heart turned into a fast, arrhythmic pounding. She began to breathe heavily and quickly, like a person engaged in some tremendous physical feat, and the blood swept up into her face as if driven before a wind. Her forehead and cheeks and the tips of her ears burned with sudden fever, and sweat poured into the palms of her hands from some secret well.

The sleeper had awakened.

"Jim."

"Yes?" He glanced at her over the top of the paper and thought how well Daisy was looking this morning, with a fine high color, like a young girl's. She seemed excited, as if she'd just planned some new big project, and he wondered, indulgently, what it would be this time. The years were crammed with Daisy's projects, packed away and half forgotten, like old toys in a trunk, some of them broken, some barely used: ceramics, astrology, tuberous begonias, Spanish conversation, upholstering, Vedanta, mental hygiene, mosaics, Russian literature—all the toys Daisy had played with and discarded. "Do you want something, dear?"

"Some water."

"Sure thing." He brought a glass of water from the kitchen. "Here you are."

14

She reached for the glass, but she couldn't pick it up. The lower part of her body was frozen, the upper part burned with fever, and there seemed to be no connection between the two parts. She wanted the water to cool her parched mouth, but the hand on the glass would not respond, as if the lines of communication had been broken between desire and will.

"Daisy? What's the matter?"

"I feel—I think I'm—sick."

"Sick?" He looked surprised and hurt, like a boxer caught by a sudden low blow. "You don't look sick. I was thinking just a minute ago what a marvelous color you have this morning—oh God, Daisy, don't be sick."

"I can't help it."

"Here. Drink this. Let me carry you over to the davenport. Then I'll go and get your mother."

"No," she said sharply. "I don't want her to—"

"We have to do something. Perhaps I'd better call a doctor."

"No, don't. It will all be over by the time anyone could get here."

"How do you know?"

"It's happened before."

"When?"

"Last week. Twice."

"Why didn't you tell me?"

"I don't know." She had a reason, but she couldn't remember it. "I feel so—hot."

He pressed his right hand gently against her forehead. It was cold and moist. "I don't think you have a temperature," he said anxiously. "You sound all right. And you've still got that good healthy color."

He didn't recognize the color of terror.

15

Daisy leaned forward in her chair. The lines of communication between the two parts of her body, the frozen half and the feverish half, were gradually re-forming themselves. By an effort of will she was able to pick up the glass from the table and drink the water. The water tasted peculiar, and Jim's face, staring down at her, was out of focus, so that he looked not like Jim, but like some kind stranger who'd dropped in to help her.

Help.

How had this kind stranger gotten in? Had she called out to him as he was passing, had she cried, "Help!"?

"Daisy? Are you all right now?"

"Yes."

"Thank God. You had me scared for a minute there."

Scared.

"You should take regular daily exercise," Jim said. "It would be good for your nerves. I also think you haven't been getting enough sleep."

Sleep. Scared. Help. The words kept sweeping around and around in her mind like horses on a carousel. If there were only some way of stopping it or even slowing it down—*hey, operator; you at the controls, kind stranger, slow down, stop, stop, stop.*

"It might be a good idea to start taking vitamins every day."

"Stop," she said. "Stop."

Jim stopped, and so did the horses, but only for a second, long enough to jump right off the carousel and start galloping in the opposite direction, *sleep* and *scared* and *help* all running riderless together in a cloud of dust. She blinked.

"All right, dear. I was only trying to do the right thing." He smiled at her timidly, like a nervous parent at a fretful, ailing child who must, but can't, be pleased. "Listen, why don't you sit there quietly for a minute, and I'll go and make you some hot tea?"

"There's coffee in the percolator."

"Tea might be better for you when you're upset like this."

I'm not upset, stranger. I'm cold and calm.

Cold.

She began to shiver, as if the mere thinking of the word had conjured up a tangible thing, like a block of ice.

She could hear Jim bumbling around in the kitchen, opening drawers and cupboards, trying to find the tea bags and the kettle. The gold sunburst clock over the mantel said 8:30. In another half hour the maid Stella would be arriving, and shortly after that Daisy's mother would be coming over from her cottage, brisk and cheerful, as usual in the mornings, and inclined to be critical of anyone who wasn't, especially Daisy.

Half an hour to become brisk and cheerful. So little time, so much to do, so many things to figure out. *What happened to me? Why did it happen? I was just sitting here, doing nothing, thinking nothing, only listening to Jim and to the sounds from across the canyon, the children playing, the dogs barking, the saw whirring, the baby crying. I felt quite happy, in a sleepy kind of way. And then suddenly something woke me, and it began, the terror, the panic. What started it, which of those sounds?*

Perhaps it was the dog, she thought. One of the new families across the canyon had an Airedale that howled at passing planes. A howling dog, when she was a child, meant death. She was nearly thirty now, and she knew some dogs howled, particular breeds, and others didn't, and it had nothing to do with death.

Death. As soon as the word entered her mind, she knew that it was the real one; the others going around on the carousel had been merely substitutes for it.

"Jim."

"Be with you in a minute. I'm waiting for the kettle to boil."

17

"Don't bother making any tea."

"How about some milk, then? It'd be good for you. You're going to have to take better care of yourself."

No, it's too late for that, she thought. *All the milk and vitamins and exercise and fresh air and sleep in the world don't make an antidote for death.*

Jim came back, carrying a glass of milk. "Here you are. Drink up."

She shook her head.

"Come on, Daisy."

"No. No, it's too late."

"What do you mean it's too late? Too late for what?" He put the glass down on the table so hard that some of the milk splashed on the cloth. "What the hell are you talking about?"

"Don't swear at me."

"I have to swear at you. You're so damned exasperating."

"You'd better go to your office."

"And leave you here like this, in this condition?"

"I'm all right."

"O.K., O.K., you're all right. But I'm sticking around anyway." He sat down, stubbornly, opposite her. "Now, what's this all about, Daisy?"

"I can't—tell you."

"Can't, or don't want to? Which?"

She covered her eyes with her hands. She was not aware that she was crying until she felt the tears drip down between her fingers.

"What's the matter, Daisy? Have you done something you don't want to tell me about—wrecked your car, overdrawn your bank account?"

"No."

18

"What, then?"

"I'm frightened."

"Frightened?" The word displeased him. He didn't like his loved ones to be frightened or sick; it seemed to cast a reflection on him and his ability to look after them properly. "Frightened of what?"

She didn't answer.

"You can't be frightened without having something to be frightened about. So what is it?"

"You'll laugh."

"Believe me, I never felt less like laughing in my life. Come on, try me."

She wiped her eyes with the sleeve of her robe. "I had a dream."

He didn't laugh, but he looked amused. "And you're crying because of a *dream?* Come, come, you're a big girl now, Daisy."

She was staring at him across the table, mute and melancholy, and he knew he had said the wrong thing, but he couldn't think of any right thing. How did you treat a wife, a grown woman, who cried because she had a dream?

"I'm sorry, Daisy. I didn't meant to—"

"No apology is necessary," she said stiffly. "You have a perfect right to be amused. Now we'll drop the subject if you don't mind."

"I do mind. I want to hear about it."

"No. I wouldn't like to send you into hysterics; it gets a lot funnier."

He looked at her soberly. "Does it?"

"Oh yes. It's quite a scream. There's nothing funnier than death, really, especially if you have an advanced sense of humor." She wiped her eyes again, though there were no fresh tears. The heat of anger had dried them at their source. "You'd better go to your office."

"What the hell are you so mad about?"

"Stop swearing at—"

"I'll stop swearing if you'll stop acting childish." He reached for her hand, smiling. "Bargain?"

"I guess so."

"Then tell me about the dream."

"There's not very much to tell." She lapsed into silence, her hand moving uneasily beneath his, like a little animal wanting to escape but too timid to make any bold attempt. "I dreamed I was dead."

"Well, there's nothing so terrible about that, is there? People often dream they're dead."

"Not like this. It wasn't a nightmare like the kind of dream you're talking about. There was no emotion connected with it at all. It was just a *fact.*"

"The fact must have been presented in some way. How?"

"I saw my tombstone." Although she'd denied that there was any emotion connected with the dream, she was beginning to breathe heavily again, and her voice was rising in pitch. "I was walking along the beach below the cemetery with Prince. Suddenly Prince took off up the side of the cliff. I could hear him howling, but he was out of sight, and when I whistled for him, he didn't come. I started up the path after him."

She hesitated again. Jim didn't prompt her. It sounded real enough, he thought, like something that actually happened, except that there was no path up that cliff and Prince never howled.

"I found Prince at the top. He was sitting beside a gray tombstone, his head thrown back, howling like a wolf. I called to him, but he paid no attention. I went over to the tombstone. It was mine. It had my name on it. The letters were distinct, but weathered, as if it had been there for some time. It had."

"How do you know?"

"The dates were on it, too. Daisy Fielding Harker, it said. Born November 13, 1930. Died December 2, 1955." She looked at him as if she expected him to laugh. When he didn't, she raised her chin in a half-challenging manner. "There. I told you it was funny, didn't I? I've been dead for four years."

"Have you?" He forced a smile, hoping it would camouflage his sudden feeling of panic, of helplessness. It was not the dream that disturbed him; it was the reality it suggested: someday Daisy would die, and there would be a genuine tombstone in that very cemetery with her name on it. *Oh God, Daisy, don't die.* "You look very much alive to me," he said, but the words, meant to be light and airy, came out like feathers turned to stone and dropped heavily on the table. He picked them up and tried again. "In fact, you look pretty as a picture, to coin a phrase."

Her quick changes of mood teased and bewildered him. He had never reached the point of being able to predict them, so he was completely unprepared for her sudden, explosive little laugh. "I went to the best embalmer."

Whether she was going up or coming down, he was always willing to share the ride. "You found him in the Yellow Pages, no doubt?"

"Of course. I find everything in the Yellow Pages."

Their initial meeting through the Yellow Pages of the telephone directory had become a standard joke between them. When Daisy and her mother had arrived in San Félice from Denver and were looking for a house to buy, they had consulted the phone book for a list of real-estate brokers. Jim had been chosen because Ada Fielding was interested in numerology at the time and the name James Harker contained the same number of letters as her own.

In that first week of taking Daisy and her mother around to look at various houses, he'd learned quite a lot about them. Daisy had put up a great pretense of being alert to all the details of construction, drainage, interest rates, taxes, but in the end she picked a house because it had a fireplace she fell in love with. The property was overpriced, the terms unsuitable, it had no termite clearance, and the roof leaked, but Daisy refused to consider any other house. "It has such a darling fireplace," she said, and that was that.

Jim, a practical, coolheaded man, found himself fascinated by what he believed to be proof of Daisy's impulsive and sentimental nature. Before the week was over, he was in love. He deliberately delayed putting the papers for the house through escrow, making excuses which Ada Fielding later admitted she'd seen through from the beginning. Daisy suspected nothing. Within two months they were married, and the house they moved into, all three of them, was not the one with the darling fireplace that Daisy had chosen, but Jim's own place on Laurel Street. It was Jim who insisted that Daisy's mother share the house. He had a vague idea, even then, that the very qualities he admired in Daisy might make her hard to handle at times and that Mrs. Fielding, who was as practical as Jim himself, might be of assistance. The arrangement had worked out adequately, if not perfectly. Later, Jim had built the canyon house they were now occupying, with separate quarters for his mother-in-law. Their life was quiet and well run. There was no place in it for unscheduled dreams.

"Daisy," he said softly, "don't worry about the dream."

"I can't help it. It must have some meaning, with everything so specific, my name, the dates—"

"Stop thinking about it."

"I will. It's just that I can't help wondering what happened on that day, December 2, 1955."

"Probably a great many things happened, as on any day of any year."

22

"To me, I mean," she said impatiently. "Something must have happened to *me* that day, something very important."

"Why?"

"Otherwise my unconscious mind wouldn't have picked that particular date to put on a tombstone."

"If your unconscious mind is as flighty and unpredictable as your conscious mind—"

"No, I'm serious about it, Jim."

"I know, and I wish you weren't. In fact, I wish you'd stop thinking about it."

"I said I would."

"Promise?"

"All right."

The promise was as frail as a bubble; it broke before his car was out of the driveway.

Daisy got up and began to pace the room, her step heavy, her shoulders stooped, as if she were carrying the weight of the tombstone on her back.

2

*Perhaps, at this hour that is very late for me, I should not step
back into your life…*

Daisy didn't watch the car leave, so she had no way of knowing that
Jim had stopped off at Mrs. Fielding's cottage. The first suspicion
occurred to her when her mother, who was constantly and acutely
aware of time, appeared at the back door half an hour before she
was due. She had Prince, the collie, with her on a leash. When the
leash was removed, Prince bounced around the kitchen as if he'd
just been released after a year or two in leg-irons.

Since Mrs. Fielding lived alone, it was considered good policy
for her to keep Prince, a zealous and indefatigable barker, at her
cottage every night for protection. Because of this talent for barking, he enjoyed the reputation of being an excellent watchdog. The
fact was, Prince's talent was spread pretty thin; he barked with as
much enthusiasm at acorns falling on the roof as he would have
at intruders bursting in the door. Although Prince had never been
put to a proper test so far, the general feeling was that he would
come through when the appropriate time arrived, and protect his
people and property with ferocious loyalty.

Daisy greeted the dog affectionately, because she wanted to
and because he expected it. The two women saw each other too
frequently to make any fuss over good-mornings.

"You're early," Daisy said.

"Am I?"

"You know you are."

"Ah well," Mrs. Fielding said lightly, "it's time I stopped living by the clock. And it was such a lovely morning, and I heard on the radio that there's a storm coming, and I didn't want to waste the sun while it lasted—"

"Mother, stop that."

"Stop what, for goodness' sake?"

"Jim came over to see you, didn't he?"

"For a moment, yes."

"What did he tell you?"

"Oh, nothing much, actually."

"That's no answer," Daisy said. "I wish the two of you would stop treating me like an idiot child."

"Well, Jim made some remark about your needing a tonic, perhaps, for your nerves. Oh, not that I think your nerves are bad or anything, but a tonic certainly wouldn't do any harm, would it?"

"I don't know."

"I'll phone that nice new doctor at the clinic and ask him to prescribe something loaded with vitamins and minerals and whatever. Or perhaps protein would be better."

"I don't want any protein, vitamins, minerals, or anything else."

"We're just a mite irritable this morning, aren't we?" Mrs. Fielding said with a cool little smile. "Mind if I have some coffee?"

"Go ahead."

"Would you like some?"

"No."

"No, *thanks*, if you don't mind. Private problems don't constitute an excuse for bad manners." She poured some coffee from the electric percolator. "I take it there are private problems?"

"Jim told you everything, I suppose?"

"He mentioned something about a silly little dream you had which upset you. Poor Jim was very upset himself. Perhaps you shouldn't worry him with trivial things. He's terribly wrapped up in you, Daisy."

"Wrapped up." The words didn't conjure up the picture they were intended to. All Daisy could see was a double mummy, two people long dead, wrapped together in a winding sheet. Death again. No matter which direction her mind turned, death was around the corner or the next bend in the road, like a shadow that always walked in front of her. "It wasn't," Daisy said, "a silly little dream. It was very real and very important."

"It may seem so to you now while you're still upset. Wait till you calm down and think about it objectively."

"It's quite difficult," Daisy said dryly, "to be objective about one's own death."

"But you're not dead. You're here and alive and well, and, I thought, happy… You *are* happy, aren't you?"

"I don't know."

Prince, with the sensitivity of his breed to a troubled atmosphere, was standing in the doorway with his tail between his legs, watching the two women.

They were similar in appearance and perhaps had had, at one time, some similarity of temperament. But the circumstances of Mrs. Fielding's life had forced her to discipline herself to a high degree of practicality. Mr. Fielding, a man of great charm, had proved a fainthearted and spasmodic breadwinner, and Daisy's mother had been the main support of the family for many years. Mrs. Fielding seldom referred to her ex-husband, unless she was very angry, and she never heard from him at all. Daisy did, every now and then, always from a different address in a different city, but with the same message: *Daisy baby, I wonder if you could spare a bit of cash. I'm a little low at the moment, just temporarily, I'm expecting something big any day now…* Daisy, without informing her mother, answered all the letters.

26

"Daisy, listen. The maid will be here in ten minutes." Mrs. Fielding never called Stella by name because she didn't approve of her. "Now's our chance to have a little private talk, the kind we always used to have."

Daisy was aware that the private little talk would eventually become a rather exhaustive survey of her own faults: she was too emotional, weak-willed, selfish, too much like her father, in fact. Daisy's weaknesses invariably turned out to be duplications of her father's.

"We've always been so close," Mrs. Fielding said, "because there were just the two of us together for so many years."

"You talk as if I never had a father."

"Of course you had a father. But…"

There was no need to go on. Daisy knew the rest of it: Father wasn't around much, and he wasn't much when he was around.

Silently Daisy turned and started to go into the next room. Prince saw her coming, but he didn't budge from the doorway, and when she stepped over him, he let out a little snarl to indicate his disapproval of her mood and the way things were going in general. She reprimanded him, without conviction. She'd had the dog throughout the eight years of her marriage, and she sometimes thought Prince was more conscious of her real emotions than Jim or her mother or even herself. He followed her now into the living room, and when she sat down, he sat down, too, putting one paw in her lap, his brown eyes staring gravely into her face, his mouth open, ready to speak if it could: *Come on, old girl, cheer up. The world's not so bad. I'm in it.*

Even when the maid arrived at the back door, usually an occasion for loud and boisterous conduct, Prince didn't move.

. . .

27

Stella was a city girl. She didn't like working in the country. Though Daisy had explained frequently and patiently that it took only ten minutes to drive from the house to the nearest supermarket, Stella was not convinced. She knew the country when she saw it, and this was it, and she didn't like it one bit. All that nature around, it made her nervous. Wasps and hummingbirds coming at you, snails sneaking about, bees swarming in the eucalyptus trees, fleas breeding in the dry soil, every once in a while taking a sizable nip out of Stella's ankles or wrists.

Stella and her current husband occupied a second-floor apartment in the lower end of town where all she had to cope with was the odd housefly. In the city, things were civilized, not a wasp or snail or bird in sight, just people: shoppers and shopkeepers by day, drunks and prostitutes at night. Sometimes they were arrested right below Stella's front window, and occasionally there was a knife fight, very quick and quiet, among the Mexican nationals relaxing after a day of picking lemons or avocados. Stella enjoyed these excitements. They made her feel both alive (all those things happening) and virtuous (but not to her. No prostitute or drunk, she; just a couple of bucks on a horse, in the back room of the Sea Esta Café every morning before she came to work).

While the Harkers were still living in town, Stella was content enough with her job. They were nice people to work for, as people to work for went, never snippy or mean-spirited. But she couldn't stand the country. The fresh air made her cough, and the quietness depressed her—no cars passing, or hardly ever, no radios turned on full blast, no people chattering.

Before entering the house, Stella stepped on three ants and squashed a snail. It was the least she could do on behalf of civilization. *Those ants sure knew they was stepped on,* she thought, and pushed her two hundred pounds through the kitchen door. Since neither Mrs. Harker nor the old lady was around, Stella began her day's labors by making a fresh pot of coffee and eating five slices of bread and jam. One nice thing about the Harkers, they bought only the best victuals and plenty of.

"She's eating," Mrs. Fielding said in the living room. "Already. She hardly ever does anything else."

"The last one was no prize either."

"This one's impossible. You should be firmer with her, Daisy, show her who's boss."

"I'm not sure I know who's boss," Daisy said, looking faintly puzzled.

"Of course you do. *You* are."

"I don't feel as if I am. Or want to be."

"Well, you are, whether you want to be or not, and it's up to you to exercise your authority and stop being willy-nilly about it. If you want her to do something or not to do something, say so. The woman's not a mind reader, you know. She expects to be told things, to be ordered around."

"I don't think that would work with Stella."

"At least try. This habit of yours—and it is a habit, not a personality defect as I used to believe—this habit of letting everything slide because you won't take the trouble, because you can't be bothered, it's just like your—"

"Father. Yes. I know. You can stop right there."

"I wish I could. I wish I'd never had to begin in the first place. But when I see quite unnecessary mismanagement, I feel I must do something about it."

"Why? Stella's not so bad. She muddles through, and that's about all you can expect of anyone."

"I don't agree," Mrs. Fielding said grimly. "In fact, we don't seem to be agreeing on anything this morning. I don't understand what the trouble is. *I* feel quite the same as usual—or did, until this absurd business of a dream came up."

"It's not absurd."

"Isn't it? Well, I won't argue." Mrs. Fielding leaned forward stiffly and put her empty cup on the coffee table. Jim had made the table himself, of teakwood and ivory-colored ceramic tile. "I don't know why you won't talk to me freely anymore, Daisy."

"I'm growing up, perhaps that's the reason."

"Growing up? Or just growing away?"

"They go together."

"Yes, I suppose they do, but—"

"Maybe you don't want me to grow up."

"What nonsense. Of course I do."

"Sometimes I think you're not even sorry I can't have a child, because if I had a child, it would show I was no longer one myself." Daisy paused, biting her lower lip. "No, no, I don't really mean that. I'm sorry, it just came out. I don't mean it."

Mrs. Fielding had turned pale, and her hands were clenched in her lap. "I won't accept your apology. It was a stupid and cruel remark. But at least I realize now what the trouble is. You've started thinking about it again, perhaps even hoping."

"No," Daisy said. "Not hoping."

"When are you going to accept the inevitable, Daisy? I thought you'd become adjusted by this time. You've known about it for five whole years."

"Yes."

"The specialist in Los Angeles made it very clear."

"Yes." Daisy didn't remember how long ago it was, or the month or the week. She only remembered the day itself, beginning the first thing in the morning when she was so ill. Then, afterward, the phone call to a friend of hers who worked at a local medical clinic: "Eleanor? It's Daisy Harker. You'll never guess, never. I'm so happy I could burst. I think I'm pregnant. I'm almost sure I am. Isn't it wonderful? I've been sick as a dog all morning and yet so happy, if you know what I mean. Listen, I know there are all sorts of obstetricians in town, but I want you to recommend the very best in the whole country, the very, very best specialist..."

She remembered the trip down to Los Angeles, with her mother driving. She'd felt so ecstatic and alive, seeing everything in a fresh new light, watching, noticing things, as if she were preparing herself to point out all the wonders of the world to her child. Later the specialist spoke quite bluntly: "I'm sorry, Mrs. Harker. I detect no signs of pregnancy..."

This was all Daisy could bear to hear. She'd broken down then, and cried and carried on so much that the doctor made the rest of his report to Mrs. Fielding, and she had told Daisy: there were to be no children ever.

Mrs. Fielding had talked nearly all the way home while Daisy watched the dreary landscape (where were the green hills?) and the slate-gray sea (had it ever been blue?) and the barren dunes (barren, barren, barren). It wasn't the end of the world, Mrs. Fielding had said, count blessings, look at silver linings. But Mrs. Fielding herself was so disturbed she couldn't go on driving. She was forced to stop at a little café by the sea, and the two women had sat for a long time facing each other across a greasy, crumb-covered table. Mrs. Fielding kept right on talking, raising her voice against the crash of waves on pilings and the clatter of dishes from the kitchen.

Now, five years later, she was still using some of the same words. "Count your blessings, Daisy. You're secure and comfortable, you're in good health, surely you have the world's nicest husband."

31

"Yes," Daisy said. "Yes." She thought of the tombstone in her dream, and the date of her death, December 2, 1955. Four years ago, not five. And the trip to see the specialist must have taken place in the spring, not in December, because the hills had been green. There was no connection between the day of the trip and what Daisy now capitalized in her mind as The Day.

"Also," Mrs. Fielding continued, "you should be hearing from one of the adoption agencies any day now—you've been on the list for some time. Perhaps you should have applied sooner than last year, but it's too late to worry about that now. Look on the bright side. One of these days you'll have a baby, and you'll love it just as much as you would your own, and so will Jim. You don't realize sometimes how lucky you are simply to have Jim. When I think of what some women have to put up with in their marriages..."

Meaning herself, Daisy thought.

"...you are a lucky, lucky girl, Daisy."

"Yes."

"I think the main trouble with you is that you haven't enough to do. You've let so many of your activities slide lately. Why did you drop your course in Russian literature?"

"I couldn't keep the names straight."

"And the mosaic you were making..."

"I have no talent."

As if to demonstrate that there was at least some talent around the house, Stella burst into song while she washed the breakfast dishes.

Mrs. Fielding went over and closed the kitchen door, not too subtly. "It's time you started a new activity, one that will *absorb* you. Why don't you come with me to the Drama Club luncheon this noon? Someday you might even want to try out for one of our plays."

"I doubt that very—"

"There's absolutely nothing to acting. You just do what the director tells you. They're having a very interesting speaker at the luncheon. It would be a lot better for you to go out than to sit here brooding because you dreamed somebody killed you."

Daisy leaned forward suddenly in her chair, pushed the dog's paw off her lap, and got up. "What did you say?"

"Didn't you hear me?"

"Say it again."

"I see no reason to..." Mrs. Fielding paused, flushed with annoyance. "Well, all right. Anything to humor you. I simply stated that I thought it would be better for you to come with me to the luncheon than to sit here brooding because you had a bad dream."

"I don't think that's quite accurate."

"It's as close as I can remember."

"You said, 'because I dreamed somebody killed me.'" There was a brief silence. "Didn't you?"

"I may have." Mrs. Fielding's annoyance was turning into something deeper. "Why fuss about a little difference in words?"

Not a little difference, Daisy thought. *An enormous one.* "I died" had become "someone killed me."

She began to pace up and down the room again, followed by the reproachful eyes of the dog and the disapproving eyes of her mother. Twenty-two steps up, twenty-two steps down. After a while the dog started walking with her, heeling, as if they were out for a stroll together.

We were walking along the beach below the cemetery, Prince and I, and suddenly Prince disappeared up the cliff. I could hear him howling. I whistled for him, but he didn't come. I went up the path after him. He was sitting beside a tombstone. It had my name on it: Daisy Fielding Harker. Born November 13, 1930. Killed December 2, 1955...

33

3

But I cannot help it. My blood runs in your veins…

At noon Jim called and asked her to meet him downtown for lunch. They ate soup and salad at a café on State Street. The place was crowded and noisy, and Daisy was grateful that Jim had chosen it. There was no need to force conversation. With so many others talking, silence between any two particular people seemed to go unnoticed. Jim even had the illusion that they'd enjoyed a lively lunch, and when they parted in front of the café, he said, "You're feeling better, aren't you?"

"Yes."

"No more skirmishes with your unconscious?"

"Oh no."

"Good girl." He pressed her shoulder affectionately. "See you for dinner."

She watched him until he turned the corner to the parking lot. Then she began walking slowly down the street in the opposite direction, with no special destination in mind, only a strong desire to stay away from the house as long as she could.

A rising wind prodded her, and on the tips of the purple mountains storm clouds were gathering like great plumes of black smoke. For the first time that day she thought of something unconnected with herself: *Rain. It's going to rain.*

As the wind pushed the storm clouds toward the city, everyone on the street was caught up in the excitement of the coming rain. They walked faster, talked louder. Strangers spoke to strangers:

"How about that, look at those clouds…" "We're going to catch it this time…" "When I hung up the wash this morning, there wasn't a cloud in sight…" "Just in time for my cinerarias…"

"Rain," they said, and lifted their faces to the sky as if they were expecting not just rain but a shower of gold.

It had been a year without winter. The hot, sunny days, which usually ended in November, had stretched through Christmas and the New Year. It was now February, and the reservoirs were getting low, and large sections of the mountains had been closed to picnickers and campers because of the fire hazard. Cloud seeders were standing by, waiting for clouds, like actors ready with their roles waiting for a stage to appear.

The clouds came, their blacks and grays more beautiful than all the colors of the spectrum, and suddenly the sun vanished and the air turned cold.

I'll be caught in the rain, Daisy thought. *I should start for home.* But her feet kept right on going as if they had a mind of their own and would not be led by a timid girl afraid of getting a little wet.

Behind her, someone called her name: "Daisy Harker."

She stopped and turned, recognizing the voice immediately—Adam Burnett's. Burnett was a lawyer, an old friend of Jim's, who shared Jim's interest in cabinetmaking. Adam came over to the house quite frequently as a refugee from his family of eight, but Daisy didn't see much of him. The two men usually shut themselves up in Jim's hobby shop downstairs.

All morning Daisy had been thinking off and on of going to talk to Adam, and this sudden meeting confused her, as if she had conjured up his person out of her thoughts. She didn't even greet him. She said uncertainly, "How funny, running into you like this."

"Not so funny. My office is just two doors down the street, and the place where I eat lunch is directly across the road." He was a tall, heavily built man in his forties, with a brisk but pleasant professional manner. He noticed Daisy's confusion immediately but could think of no reason for it. "I'm pretty hard to miss, in this neck of the woods."

"I'd—forgotten where your office was."

"Oh? For a moment when I first spotted you, I thought you might be on your way to see me."

"No. No." *I didn't, I couldn't possibly have, come this way deliberately. Why, I didn't even remember his office was near here, or I can't remember remembering.* "I wasn't on my way to anywhere. I was just walking. It's such a lovely day."

"It's cold." He glanced briefly at the sky. "And about to be wet."

"I like rain."

"At this point, don't we all."

"I meant, I like to *walk* in the rain."

His smile was friendly but a little puzzled. "That's fine. Go right ahead. The exercise will do you good, and the rain probably won't hurt you."

She didn't move. "The reason I thought it was funny running into you like this was because—well, I was thinking about you this morning."

"Oh?"

"I was even thinking of—of making an appointment to see you."

"Why?"

"Something has sort of happened."

"How can anything sort of happen? It happens or it doesn't."

"I don't quite know how to explain." The first drops of rain had begun to fall. She didn't notice them. "Do you consider me a neurotic woman?"

"This is hardly the time or place to discuss a subject like that," he said dryly. "*You* may like walking in the rain. Some of us don't."

"Adam, listen."

"You'd better come up to my office." He consulted his wrist-watch. "I've got twenty-five minutes before I'm due at the courthouse."

"I don't want to."

"I think you want to."

"No, I feel like such a fool."

"So do I, standing around in the pouring rain. Come on, Daisy."

They took the elevator up to the third floor. Adam's receptionist and his secretary were both still out to lunch, and the suite was quiet and dark. Adam turned on the lamps in the reception room; then he went into his office, hung up his wet tweed jacket to dry on an old-fashioned brass clothes rack.

"Sit down, Daisy. You're looking great. How's Jim?"

"Fine."

"Has he been making any new furniture?"

"No. He's refinishing an old bird's-eye maple desk for the den."

"Where did he get hold of it?"

"The former owners of the house he bought left it behind as trash. I guess they didn't know what it was—it had so many layers of paint on it. Ten at least, Jim says."

She knew this was part of his technique, getting her started talking about safe, impersonal things first, and she half resented the fact that it was working. It was as if he'd applied a few drops of oil to the proper places and suddenly wheels began turning and she told him about the dream. The rain beat in torrents against the windows, but Daisy was walking on a sunny beach with her dog, Prince.

Adam leaned back in his chair and listened, his only outward reaction an occasional blink. Inwardly, he was surprised, not at the dream itself, but at the way she related it, coldly and without emotion, as if she were describing a simple factual chain of events, not a mere fantasy of her own mind.

She completed her account by telling him the dates on the tombstone. "November 13, 1930, and December 2, 1955. My birthday," she said, "and my death day."

The strange word annoyed him; he didn't understand why. "Is there such a word?"

"Yes."

He grunted and leaned forward, the chair squeaking under his weight. "I'm no psychiatrist. I don't interpret dreams."

"I'm not asking you to. No interpretation is necessary. It's all quite clear. On December 2, 1955, something happened to me that was so terrible it caused my death. I was psychically murdered."

Psychic murder, Adam thought. *Now I've heard everything. These damned silly idle women who sit around dreaming up trouble for themselves and everyone else...*

"Do you really believe that, Daisy?"

"Yes."

"All right. Suppose something catastrophic actually happened on that day. Why is it you don't remember what it was?"

"I'm trying to. That's the real reason I wanted to talk to you. I've got to remember. I've got to reconstruct the whole day."

"Well, I can't help you. And even if I could, I wouldn't. I see no point in people deliberately trying to recall an unpleasant occurrence."

"Unpleasant occurrence? That's a pretty mild expression for what happened."

"If you don't recall what happened," he said with a touch of irony, "how do you know it's a pretty mild expression?"

"I know."

"You know. Just like that, eh?"

38

"Yes."

"I wish all knowledge was as easy to come by."

Her gaze was cool and steady. "You don't take me very seriously, do you, Adam? That's too bad, because I'm actually quite a serious person. Jim and my mother treat me like a child, and I frequently respond like one because it's easier that way—it doesn't upset their image of me. My self-image is quite different. I consider myself fairly bright. I graduated from college when I was twenty-one... Well, we won't go into that. It's evident I'm not convincing you of anything." She rose suddenly and started toward the door. "Thanks for listening, anyway."

"What's your hurry? Wait a minute."

"Why?"

"Nothing's been settled, for one thing. For another, I'll admit your, ah, situation intrigues me. This business of reconstructing a whole day four years ago..."

"Well?"

"It's going to be very difficult."

"I'm aware of that."

"Suppose you're able to do it, what then, Daisy?"

"I will at least know what happened."

"What use would such knowledge be to you? It certainly won't make you any happier, will it? Or any wiser?"

"No."

"Why not let it drop, then? Forget the whole business. You have nothing to gain and perhaps a great deal to lose—have you considered that angle of it?"

"No. Not until now."

"Give it some thought, will you?" He got up and opened the door for her. "One more thing, Daisy. The chances are that nothing whatever happened to you on that particular day. Dreams are never that logical." He knew the word *never* was too strong in this connection, but he used it deliberately. She needed strong words to lean on or to test her own strength against.

"Well, I must be going," Daisy said. "I've taken up too much of your time. You'll send a bill, of course?"

"Of course not."

"I'd feel better about it if you did. I mean it."

"All right, then, I will."

"And thanks a lot for the advice, Adam."

"You know, a lot of my clients thank me for my advice and then go right home and do the exact opposite. Is that going to be the case with you, Daisy?"

"I don't think so," she said seriously. "I appreciate your letting me talk to you. I can't discuss things—problems, I mean—with Jim or Mother. They're too involved with me. They get upset when I step out of my role as the happy innocent."

"You should be able to talk freely to Jim. You have a good marriage."

"Any good marriage involves a certain amount of playacting."

His grunt indicated neither agreement nor disagreement: *I'll have to think about that before I decide. Playacting? Maybe.*

He walked her to the elevator, feeling pleased with himself for handling the situation well and with her for reacting so sensibly. He realized that although he'd known Daisy for a long time, he had never talked seriously to her before; he had been willing to accept her in her role of the happy innocent, the gay little girl, long after he'd discovered that she was not happy or innocent or gay.

The elevator arrived, and even though someone else was already buzzing for it, Adam held the door back with one hand. He had a sudden, uneasy feeling that he shouldn't let Daisy go, that nothing had been settled after all and the good solid advice he'd given her had blown away like smoke on a windy day.

"Daisy…"

"Someone's buzzing for the elevator."

"I just wanted to say that I wish you'd feel free to call me whenever you get upset."

"I'm not upset anymore."

"Sure?"

"Adam, someone wants the elevator. We can't just—"

"I'll take you down to the ground floor."

"That isn't nec—"

"I like the ride."

He stepped inside, the door closed, and the slow descent began. It wasn't slow enough, though. By the time Adam thought of anything more to say, they had reached the ground floor and Daisy was thanking him again, too politely and formally, as if she were thanking a host for a very dull party.

4

When I die, part of me will still be alive, in you, in your children, in your children's children...

It was 2:30 when Daisy arrived home. Stella met her at the front door looking so flushed and lively that Daisy thought for a moment she'd got into Jim's liquor cabinet.

"Some man's been trying to get hold of you," Stella said. "He's called three times in the last hour, kept telling me how urgent it was and when was I expecting you back and the like." It wasn't often that any excitement occurred out here in the sticks, and Stella was determined to stretch it out. "The first two times he wouldn't give no name, but the last time I just up and asked him, who is this calling please, I said. I could tell he didn't want to give it, but he did, and I got it written down right here on a magazine with a number for you to call."

Across the top of a magazine Stella had printed, "Stan Foster 67134 urgent." Daisy had never heard of any Stan Foster, and she thought either the caller or Stella had made an error: Stella may have misunderstood the name, or Mr. Foster might be wanting to get in touch with a different Mrs. Harker.

"You're sure of the name?" Daisy said.

"He spelled it out for me twice: S-t-a-n—"

"Yes. Thanks. I'll call after I change my clothes."

"How did you get so soaking wet? Is it raining even in the city?"

"Yes," Daisy said. "It's raining even in the city."

She was in the bedroom taking off her clothes when the phone started ringing again. A minute later Stella knocked on the door.

"It's that Mr. Foster on the line again. I told him you was home, is that all right?"

"Yes. I'll take the call in here." Throwing a bathrobe around her shoulders, she sat down on the bed and picked up the phone. "This is Mrs. Harker."

"Hello, Daisy baby."

Even if she hadn't recognized the voice, she would have known who it was. No one ever called her Daisy baby except her father.

"Daisy baby? You there?"

"Yes, Daddy." In that first moment of hearing his voice again, she felt neither pleasure nor pain, only a kind of surprise and relief that he was still alive. She hadn't received a letter from him for nearly a year, though she'd written several times, and the last time she'd spoken to him was three years ago, when he called from Chicago to wish her a happy birthday. He'd been very drunk, and it wasn't her birthday. "How are you feeling, Daddy?"

"Fine. Oh, I've got a touch of this and a touch of that, but in the main, fine."

"Are you in town?"

"Yes. Got here last night."

"Why didn't you call me?"

"I called you. Didn't she tell you?"

"Who?"

"Your mother. I asked for you, but you were out. She recognized my voice and hung up, just like that, wham."

Daisy remembered entering the house after taking Prince for a walk and finding her mother seated beside the telephone looking grim and granite-eyed. "A wrong number," Mrs. Fielding had said. "Some drunk." And the contrast of the voice, as soft and bland as

43

marshmallows coming out of that stone face, had reminded Daisy of something ugly which she couldn't fit into a time or place. "Very drunk," Mrs. Fielding had said. "He called me baby." Later Daisy had gone to bed thinking not of the drunk that had called her mother baby, but of a real adopted baby that might someday soon belong to her and Jim.

"Why didn't you phone me back, Daddy?"

"One call is all they allow you."

"They?"

He gave a sheepish little laugh that broke in the middle like an elastic stretched too far. "The fact is, I'm in a bit of a pickle. Nothing serious, but I need a couple of hundred dollars. I didn't want *you* to get involved, so I gave them a false name. I mean, you have a reputation to maintain in the community, so I figured there was no sense getting you mixed up in—Daisy, for God's sake, help me!"

"I always do, don't I?" she said quietly.

"You do. You're a good girl, Daisy, a good daddy-loving girl. I'll never forget how—"

"Where are you now?"

"Downtown."

"In a hotel?"

"No. I'm in somebody's office. His name's Pinata."

"Is he there, too?"

"Yes."

"Listening to all this?"

"He knows it all anyway," her father said with that sheepish little laugh again. "I had to tell him everything, who I was and who you were, or he wouldn't have sprung me. He's a bail bondsman."

"So you were in jail. What for?"

"Oh, gad, Daisy, do I have to go into it?"

"I'd like to hear about it, yes."

"Well, all right. I was on my way to see you, and suddenly I needed a drink, see? So I stopped in this bar downtown. Things were slack, and I asked the waitress to have a drink with me, just out of friendliness, you might say. Nita, her name was, a very fine-looking young woman who's had a hard life. To make a long story short, suddenly out of the blue her husband came in and started to get tough with her about not staying home to look after the kids. They exchanged a few words, and then he began pushing her around. Well, I couldn't just sit there and watch that kind of thing going on without doing anything about it."

"So you got into a fight?"

"That's about it."

"That *is* it, you mean."

"Yes. Someone called the cops, and the husband and I were hauled off to the pokey. Drunk and disorderly and disturbing the peace. Nothing serious. I gave the cops a false name, though, so no one would know I was your father in case the incident gets into the papers. I've already cast enough shame on you and your mother."

"Please," Daisy said, "don't try to make yourself out a hero because you gave a false name to protect Mother and me. In the first place, that's illegal when you have any sort of record, isn't it?"

"Is it?" He sounded very innocent. "Well, it's too late to worry about that now. Mr. Pinata isn't likely to tell on me. He's a gentleman."

Daisy could well imagine her father's definition of the word: a gentleman was somebody who'd just helped him out of a jam. Her own mental picture of Pinata showed him as a wizened, beady-eyed old man who smelled of jails and corruption.

"When I explained my situation to Mr. Pinata, he very kindly paid my fine. He's not in business for his health, though, so of

45

course I have to stay here in his office until I can raise the money to pay him. Two hundred dollars the fine was. I pleaded guilty to get the trial over with in a hurry. No sense in having to come up here from L.A. just to—"

"You're living in L.A.?"

"Yes. We—I moved there last week. I thought it would be nice to be closer to you, Daisy baby. Besides, the climate in Dallas didn't agree with me."

It was the first she'd heard that he'd been living in Dallas. Topeka, Kansas, had been his last address. Dallas, Topeka, Chicago, Toronto, Detroit, St. Louis, Montreal—they were all just names to Daisy, but she knew that her father had lived in all of these places, had walked along their streets, searching for something that was always a few hundred miles farther on.

"Daisy? You can get the money, can't you? I gave Pinata my solemn promise."

"I can get it."

"When? The fact is, I'm in kind of a hurry. I have to get back to L.A. tonight—someone's expecting me—and as you know, I can't leave Pinata's office until I pay up."

"I'll come down right away." Daisy could see him waiting in the office, Pinata's prisoner, not a free man at all. He had merely changed jails and jailers the way he changed towns and people, never realizing he would always be in bondage. "Where is the office?"

She could hear him consulting Pinata: "Just where is this place anyway?" And then Pinata's voice, surprisingly young and pleasant for an old man who'd spent his life hanging around jails: "107 East Opal Street, between the 800 and 900 blocks of State Street."

Her father repeated the directions, and Daisy said, "Yes, I know where it is. I'll be down in half an hour."

46

"Ah, Daisy baby, you're a good girl, a good daddy-loving girl."

"Yes," Daisy said wearily. "Yes."

Fielding put down the telephone and turned to Pinata, who was sitting at his desk writing a letter to his son, Johnny. The boy, who was ten, lived in New Orleans with his mother, and Pinata saw him only for a month out of every year, but he wrote to him regularly each week.

Pinata said, without looking up, "Is she coming?"

"Certainly she's coming. Right away. I told you she would, didn't I?"

"What people like you tell me I don't always believe."

"I could take exception to that remark but I won't, because I'm feeling good."

"You should be. You've gone through a pint of my bourbon."

"I called you a gentleman, didn't I? Didn't you hear me tell Daisy you were a gentleman?"

"So?"

"No gentleman ever begrudges a drink to a fellow gentleman in distress. That's one of the rules of civilized society."

"It is, eh?" Pinata finished his letter: *Be a good boy, Johnny, and don't forget to write. I enclose five dollars so you can buy your mother and your little sister a nice valentine. Best love from your loving Dad.*

He put the letter in an envelope and sealed it. He always had a sick, lost feeling when he wrote to this boy who was his only known relative; it made him mad at the world, or whatever part of the world happened to be available at the moment. This time it was Fielding.

Pinata pounded an airmail stamp on the envelope and said, "You're a bum, Foster."

"Fielding, if you please."

47

"Foster, Fielding, Smith, you're still a bum."

"I've had a lot of hard luck."

"For every ounce of hard luck you've had, I bet you've passed a pound of it along to other people. Mrs. Harker, for instance."

"That's a lie. I've never harmed a hair on Daisy's head. Why, I've never even asked her for money unless it was absolutely necessary. And it's not as if she can't afford it. She made a very good marriage—trust Mrs. Fielding to see to that. So what if I put the bite on her now and then? When you come right down to it—"

"Don't bother coming right down to it," Pinata said. "You bore me."

Fielding's lower lip began to pout as if it had been stung by the word. He hadn't minded so much being called a bum since there was some truth in the statement, but he'd never considered himself a bore. "If I'd known that was your opinion of me," he said with dignity, "I'd never have drunk your liquor."

"The hell you wouldn't."

"It was a very cheap brand anyway. Ordinarily I wouldn't demean myself by touching such stuff, but under the stress of the moment..."

Pinata threw back his head and laughed, and Fielding, who hadn't intended to be amusing, watched him with an aggrieved expression. But the laughter was contagious, and pretty soon Fielding joined in. The two of them stood in the dingy little rain-loud office, laughing: a middle-aged man in a torn shirt with dried blood on his face, and a young man wearing a crew cut and a neat dark business suit. He looked more as if he dealt in government bonds than in bail bonds.

Fielding said finally, wiping the moisture from his eyes with a soiled handkerchief, "Ah, how I dearly love a good laugh. It takes the kinks out of your mind, straightens out your thinking. There

I was, getting all fussed up over a few little words, a few silly little words. And you, what fussed you up so suddenly?"

Pinata glanced briefly at the letter on his desk. "Nothing."

"Moody, are you?"

"Moody, yes."

"Are you Spanish or Mexican?"

"I don't know. My parents didn't stick around long enough to tell me. Maybe I'm Chinese."

"Fancy that, not knowing who you are."

"I know who *I* am," Pinata said distinctly. "I just don't know who *they* were."

"Ah yes, I see your point. A good point, too. Now take me, I'm exactly the opposite. I know all about my grandparents and great-grandparents and uncles and cousins, the whole damn bunch of them. And it seems to me I got kind of lost in the shuffle. My ex-wife was always telling me I had no ego, in a reproachful way, as if an ego was something like a hat or pair of gloves which I'd carelessly lost or misplaced." Fielding paused, squinting up his eyes. "What happened to the girl's husband?"

"What girl?"

"The waitress, Nita."

"He's still in jail," Pinata said.

"I think she should have bailed him out, let bygones be bygones."

"Maybe she prefers him in."

"Say, Mr. Pinata, you wouldn't by any chance have another pint of bourbon around? That cheap stuff doesn't stay with you."

"You'd better get cleaned up first, before your daughter arrives."

"Daisy has seen me in worse—"

"I'm sure Daisy has. So why not surprise her? Where's your tie?"

Fielding put up one hand and felt his neck. "I guess I lost it someplace, maybe at the police station."

"Well, here's a spare one," Pinata said, pulling a blue-striped tie from one of his desk drawers. "A client of mine tried to hang himself with it. I had to take it away from him. Here."

"No. No, thank you."

"Why not?"

"I don't happen to like the idea of wearing a dead man's tie."

"Who said he's dead? As a matter of fact, he's selling used cars a couple of blocks up the street."

"In that case I suppose there's no harm in my borrowing it for a while."

"The bathroom's down the hall," Pinata said. "Here's the key."

When Fielding returned, five minutes later, he had washed the dried blood off his face and combed his hair. He was wearing the blue-striped tie, and his sports jacket was buttoned to hide the tear in his shirt. He looked quite sober and respectable for a man who was neither.

"Well, that's an improvement," Pinata said, wondering how soon it would be safe to let him have another drink. The old drinks were wearing off fast now, Pinata could tell by the jerky movements of Fielding's eyes and the nervous whine in his voice.

"What difference should it make to you, Pinata, how I look in front of my own daughter?"

"I wasn't thinking of you. I was thinking of her." *No, that's a lie. I was thinking of Johnny and how I never want him to see me in the same shape Daisy has seen, and will see, her father.*

It was mainly for the sake of the boy that Pinata kept himself in very good condition. He swam every day in the ocean in the summer, and in the winter he played handball at the Y and tennis at the municipal courts. He didn't smoke and seldom drank, and the women he took out were all very respectable, so that if, by some miraculous stroke of fate, he should ever meet Johnny accidentally on the street, the boy would have no reason to be ashamed of him or his choice of companion.

But it was difficult, living for a boy he only saw for a month out of each year, and the days were often hard to fill, like a jug with a hole in the bottom. His work, though, saved him from self-pity. Through it he came in contact with so many people in so many and various stages of despair that by comparison his own life seemed a good one. Pinata wanted to remarry and felt that he should. He was afraid, however, that if he did, his ex-wife might seize the occasion to go to court and try to have Johnny's yearly visits curtailed or stopped altogether; she begrudged the time and effort the visits cost her and the disruption they caused in the life of her new family.

Fielding was at the window, peering down into the street. "She should be here by this time. Half an hour, she said. Isn't it more than that already?"

"Sit down, and relax," Pinata said.

"I wish this damn rain would stop. It's making me nervous. It's enough of a strain on me having to face Daisy."

"How long is it since you've seen her?"

"Hell, I don't know. A long time anyway." He had begun to tremble, partly from the drinking he'd done, partly from dread of the emotional experience of seeing Daisy again. "How should I act when she gets here? And what the hell will I say to her?"

"You did all right on the telephone."

"That was different. I was desperate, I had to phone her. But listen, Pinata, there's no *real* reason why I should have to see her, is there? I mean, what's to be gained? You can give her a message for me. Tell her I'm O.K. and I'm working steady now, at the Harris Electrical Supply warehouse on Figueroa Street. Tell her—"

"I'll tell her nothing. You're going to do the talking, Fielding. Yourself personally."

"I won't. I can't. Be a sport for chrissake and let me out of here before she comes. I give you my word that Daisy will pay you the money I owe, my solemn word—"

"No."

"Why not, in God's name? Are you afraid you won't get your money?"

"No."

"Then let me go, let me out of here."

"Your daughter's expecting to see you," Pinata said. "So she's going to see you."

"She won't like what I came up here to tell her anyway. But I felt I ought to tell her. It was my duty. Then I got cold feet and went into that bar to warm them up a bit, and—"

"Tell her what?"

"That I'm married again," Fielding said. "It'll be a shock to her, hearing she's got a new stepmother. Maybe I'd better break the news to her more gradually, say in a letter. That's what I'll do. I'll write her a letter."

"No, you won't. You're staying right here, Fielding."

"How do you know Daisy wants to see me? Maybe she's dreading this as much as I am. Listen, you said before I was a bum. O.K., I'm a bum, I admit it. But I don't want to have to spell it out in front of my own daughter." He took two or three defiant steps toward the door. "I'm leaving. You can't stop me. You hear that? You can't stop me. You have no legal right to—"

"Oh, shut up." The time, Pinata felt, had come. He reached into one of the desk drawers, brought out another pint of bourbon, and unscrewed the top. "Here. Help yourself to some courage."

52

"You sound like a goddamn preacher," Fielding said. He grabbed for the bottle and held it to his mouth. Then, without warning, he made a sudden lunge for the door, holding the bottle against his chest.

Pinata didn't attempt to chase him. He was rather glad to see him go, in fact: the meeting between Daisy baby and her father wouldn't have been any fun to watch.

He went to the window and looked down. Fielding was running along the sidewalk in the pouring rain, still clutching his bottle. His step was quick and light for a big man, as if he'd had a lot of practice running in his life.

Daisy baby, Pinata thought, *you're in for a surprise.*

5

It is a thought that takes some of the ugliness out of these cruel years, some of the sting out of the tricks of time...

The lettering on the door at the end of the long, dark hallway spelled out STEVENS PINATA. BAIL BONDS. INVESTIGATIONS. WALK IN. The door was partly open, and Daisy could see a dark-haired, sharp-featured young man seated behind a desk, fooling with a typewriter ribbon. He jumped up when he became aware of her presence and gave her an anxious little smile. She didn't like the smile. It was as if she'd dropped in on him unexpectedly and caught him doing something he shouldn't.

He said, "Mrs. Harker?"

"Yes."

"I'm Steve Pinata. Please sit down. Let me take your coat. It's wet."

She made no move either to sit down or to unbutton her pink plaid raincoat. "Where's my father?"

"He left a few minutes ago," Pinata said. "He had an engagement in L.A. and couldn't wait."

"He—he couldn't wait even a few minutes after all these years?"

"It was a very important engagement. He asked me to be sure and tell you how sorry he was, and that he'll be getting in touch with you soon."

The lie came out easily. Practically anyone would have believed it, except Daisy. "He didn't want to see *me* at all, just the money, is that it?"

"It's not quite that simple, Mrs. Harker. He lost his nerve. He was ashamed of—"

"I'll write you out a check." She pulled a checkbook from her handbag with brusque impatience like a very efficient business-woman who had no time or taste for emotional exhibitions. "How much?"

"Two hundred and thirty. The fine was $200, ten is my straight fee, and the rest is my ten percent commission."

"I understand." She wrote out the check, bending over his desk, refusing the chair he had pushed up for her. "Is this correct?"

"Yes. Thank you." He put the check in his pocket. "I'm sorry things had to turn out like this, Mrs. Harker."

"Why should you be? I'm not. I'm as much of a coward as he is, perhaps more. I'm *glad* he ran out on me. I didn't want to see him any more than he wanted to see me. For once, he did the right thing. Why should you feel sorry, Mr. Pinata?"

"I thought you'd be disappointed."

"Disappointed? Oh no. Not at all. Not in the least." But she sat down suddenly and awkwardly, as if she'd lost her balance under the weight of something too heavy for her to handle.

Daisy baby, Pinata thought, *is going to cry.*

In his business Pinata had witnessed too many plain and fancy crying jobs not to know the preliminary signs, and they were all there, from the rapid blinking of her eyes to the clenching and unclenching of her hands. He waited for the inevitable, wishing he could prevent it, trying to think of something to say by way of encouragement, not sympathy; sympathy always pushed them over the line.

Two minutes passed, then three, and he began to realize that the inevitable wasn't going to happen after all. When she finally spoke, her question took him completely by surprise. It had nothing to do with long-lost fathers.

"What kind of things do you investigate, Mr. Pinata?"

"Not much of anything," he said frankly.

"Why not?"

"In a city this size there isn't much call for services like mine—people who need a detective usually hire one from L.A. Most of the work I do is for private attorneys around town."

"What are your qualifications?"

"What qualifications would I need to solve your problem?"

"I didn't say there was any problem. Or that it was mine."

"People don't ask me the kind of questions you've been asking without having something in mind."

She hesitated a moment, biting her under lip. "There is a problem. But it's only partly mine. Someone else is involved."

"Your father?"

"No. He has nothing to do with it."

"Husband? Friend? Mother-in-law?"

"I don't know yet."

"But you'd like to know?"

"I *have* to know."

She lapsed into another silence, her head cocked at an angle, as if she were listening to some debate going on inside herself. He didn't press her; he wasn't even very curious. She looked like the kind of woman whose darkest secret could be bleached out with a little chlorine.

"I have reason to believe," she said finally, "that on a certain day four years ago something very grave happened to me. I can't remember what it was. I want you to help me find out."

"Help you remember?"

"Yes."

"I'm sorry, that's not in my line of work," he said bluntly. "I might be able to help you find a lost necklace, even a missing person, but a lost day, no."

"You misunderstand, Mr. Pinata. I'm not asking you to pry into my unconscious like a psychiatrist. I simply want your assistance, your *physical* assistance. The rest would be up to me." She studied his face for any sign of interest or curiosity. He was staring, blank-faced, out of the window, as if he hadn't heard anything she'd said. "Have you ever tried to reconstruct a day, Mr. Pinata? Oh, not a special day like Christmas or an anniversary, just a plain ordinary day. Have you?"

"No."

"Suppose you were forced to. Say the police accused you of a crime and you had to prove exactly where you were and what you did—let's make it two years ago today. This is the ninth of February. Do you remember anything special about the ninth of February two years ago?"

He thought about it for a time, squinting up his eyes. "Well, no. Nothing specific. I know the general circumstances of my life at the time, where I was staying, and so on. I assume, if it was a weekday, that I got up and went to work as usual."

"The police wouldn't accept assumptions. They would ask for facts."

"I think I'll plead guilty," he said with a quick smile.

She didn't return the smile. "What would you do, Mr. Pinata? How would you go about finding the facts?"

"First, I'd check my records. Let's see, February the ninth two years ago, that would be a Saturday. Saturday night is usually a pretty busy time for me, since there are more arrests made. So I'd check the police files, too, in the hope of coming across a case I might remember."

57

"What if you had no files or records?"

The telephone rang. Pinata answered, talked in monosyllables, mostly negative, for a couple of minutes, and hung up. "Everyone has records of some kind."

"I haven't."

"No diary? Bank statement? Bills? Check stubs?"

"No. My husband takes care of things like that."

"What about this check you just gave me? Isn't it drawn on your own account?"

"Yes, but I don't write very many, and I certainly haven't kept track of the stubs from four years ago."

"Do you use an engagement book?"

"I throw away my engagement book at the end of each year," Daisy said. "I used to keep a diary a long time ago."

"How long?"

"I don't recall exactly. I just sort of lost interest in it—nothing seemed to happen to me that deserved writing down, no excitement or anything."

No excitement, Pinata thought. *So now she's scrounging around for some, looking for a lost day like a bored child during summer vacation looking for something to do, a game to play. Well, Daisy baby, I haven't got time for games. I won't play.* "I wish I could help you, Mrs. Harker, but as I told you, this is out of my line. You'd be wasting your money."

"I've wasted money before." She stared at him obstinately. "Anyway, you're not in the least concerned about my wasting my money, only about your wasting your time. You don't understand— I haven't made you realize how terribly important this is to me."

"Why is it important?"

She wanted to tell him about the dream, but she was afraid of his reaction. He might be amused like Jim, or impatient and

58

a little contemptuous like Adam, or annoyed like her mother. "I can't explain that right now."

"Why not?"

"You're already very skeptical and suspicious of me. If I told you the rest of it, well, you might consider me quite crazy."

Bored, Pinata thought. *Not crazy. Or maybe just a little.* "I think you'd better tell me the rest of it anyway, Mrs. Harker, so at least we'll understand each other. I've been asked to do some pretty funny things, but finding a lost day—that's a tall order."

"I didn't lose the day. It's not lost. It's still around someplace, here or there, wherever used days and old years go. They don't simply vanish into nothing. They're still available—hiding, yes, but not lost."

"I see," Pinata said, thinking that Daisy baby wasn't a little crazy after all; she was a whole lot crazy. He couldn't help being interested, however; he wasn't sure whether his interest was in Daisy's problem or Daisy herself, or whether the two could ever be separated. "If you don't remember this day, Mrs. Harker, why do you believe it was so important to you?"

It was almost the identical question Adam had asked. She hadn't been able to give a satisfactory answer then, and she couldn't now. "I know it was. Sometimes people know things in different ways. You know I'm sitting here because you can see and hear me. But there are other ways of knowing things than merely through the five senses. Some of them haven't been explained yet... I do wish you'd stop looking at me like that."

"Like what?"

"As if you expected me to announce that my name was Josephine Bonaparte or something. I'm quite sane, Mr. Pinata. *And* rational, if the two can possibly go together in this confused world."

"I thought they were the same thing."

"Oh, no," she said with a kind of prim politeness. "Sanity is a matter of culture and convention. If it's a crazy culture you live in, then you have to be irrational to want to conform. A completely rational person would recognize that the culture was crazy and refuse to conform. But by not conforming, he is the one who would be judged crazy by that particular society."

Pinata looked surprised and somewhat annoyed, as if a pet parrot, which he had taught to speak a few simple phrases, had suddenly started explaining the techniques of nuclear fission.

"That was a neat trick," he said at last.

"What was?"

"The way you changed the subject. When the box got a little hot for you, out you jumped. What are you trying to avoid telling me, Mrs. Harker?"

He's honest, Daisy thought. *He doesn't pretend to know things he doesn't know or to exaggerate what he does know. He isn't even very good at hiding his feelings. I think I can trust him.*

"I had a dream," Daisy said, and before he could tell her he didn't deal in dreams, she was telling him about the stroll on the beach with Prince and the tombstone with her name on it.

Pinata listened, without audible comment, to the end. Then he said, "Have you told anyone else about this dream, Mrs. Harker?"

"My mother, my husband Jim, and a friend of Jim's who's a lawyer, Adam Burnett."

"What was their reaction?"

She looked across the desk at him with a dry little smile. "My mother and Jim want me to take vitamins and forget the whole thing."

"And the lawyer, Mr. Burnett?"

"He understood more than the others how important it was to me to find out what happened. But he gave me a warning."

"Which was?"

"Whatever happened on that day to cause my—my death must have been very unpleasant, and I shouldn't try to dredge it up. I have nothing to gain and everything to lose."

"But you want to go ahead with it anyway?"

"It's no longer a question of wanting to. I have to. You see, we're about to adopt a baby."

"What's that got to do with it?"

"It won't be just my life and Jim's anymore. We'll be sharing it with a child. I must be sure that this child will be coming into the right home, a place of security and happiness."

"And at the moment you think yours isn't the right home?"

"I'm checking to be certain. Let's say you bought a house, Mr. Pinata, and you've been living in it for some time quite comfortably. Then something happens, say an important guest is arriving. You decide to check the place over, and you find certain serious structural defects. Would you consult a good contractor to see what he could do about the defects? Or would you just sit there with your eyes closed and pretend everything was fine?"

"That's a pretty desperate analogy," Pinata said. "All it amounts to is that you're determined to have your own way no matter what comes of it."

"I'm not a child demanding a stick of candy."

No, Pinata thought, *you're a grown woman demanding a stick of dynamite. You don't like your life or your house. You're afraid to share it with a child. So blow the whole thing sky high and watch the pretty pieces come falling down on your head.*

The phone rang again. This time it was Pinata's cleaning woman relaying the news that the roof was leaking in the kitchen and one of the bedrooms and reminding him that she'd warned him last year he was going to have to get a new roof put on.

"Do the best you can. I'll be home at five," Pinata said, and hung up, feeling depressed. New roofs cost money, and Johnny was having his teeth straightened. *I can't afford a new roof. But Daisy can. If she's determined to blow up her own roof, at least I can catch some of the lumber to build mine.*

"All right," he said, "I'll help you, Mrs. Harker. If I can, and against my better judgment."

She looked pleased, in a subdued way, as if she didn't want him to see how eager she actually was to begin this new game. "When do we start?"

"I'm tied up for a couple of days." It was a necessary lie: two days would give him a chance to do some checking up on Daisy, and Daisy a chance to change her mind. "Say Thursday afternoon."

"I was hoping right away…"

"No. Sorry. I have a case."

"Of jitters?"

"All right, of jitters."

"And you need time to investigate me, find out how many steps I am in front of the butterfly net? Well, I can't blame you, of course. If some woman came to me and told me the kind of story I've told you, I'd be suspicious, too. The only thing is, there's no need for secrecy. I'm perfectly willing to answer any questions you'd like to ask me: age, weight, education, background, religious preference—"

"No questions," he said, annoyed. "But it remains Thursday."

"Very well. Shall I come here to your office?"

"I'll meet you at three o'clock at the front door of the *Monitor-Press* building, if that suits you."

"Isn't that rather a—conspicuous place to meet?"

"I didn't know this was to be undercover stuff."

"It isn't really. But why advertise it?"

"Wait a minute, Mrs. Harker," Pinata said, leaning across the desk. "Let's get this straight. Do you intend to tell your husband and family that you've hired me?"

"I hadn't thought about it. I hadn't even thought about hiring you or anyone else until I noticed the sign on your door. It seemed like fate, in a way."

"Oh, Mrs. Harker," Pinata said very sadly.

"It did, it does. It's as if I were guided here."

"Misguided might be a better word."

Her gaze was cool and stubborn. "You've done everything possible to talk yourself out of a job. Why?"

"Because I think you're making a mistake. You can't just reconstruct one day, Mrs. Harker. It may turn out to be a whole life."

"Well?"

"You'll be kicking over quite a few stones. Maybe you won't like what you find underneath them." He stood up, as if he were the one who intended to leave. "Well, it's your funeral."

"Wrong tense," she said. "It *was* my funeral."

He went with her to the door and opened it. The long, dim hallway smelled of new rain and old wax.

"By the way," Daisy added casually, as if she hadn't been thinking about it at all, "did my father give you his Los Angeles address?"

"He gave the police an address when he was arrested. I copied it off the blotter." He had it written on the inside of a match folder, which he took out of his pocket and handed to Daisy. "1074 Delaney Avenue West. I wouldn't bother trying to reach him there, though, if I were you."

"Why not?"

"There is no Delaney Avenue in Los Angeles."

"Are you sure?"

"Yes."

"But what reason would he have to lie about it?"

"I don't read minds, palms, or tea leaves. Just street maps. There is no Delaney Avenue in L.A., east or west."

She was looking at him as if she believed he could have located the missing street if he'd only tried a little harder. "I'll take your word for it, of course."

"No need to. Any gas station in town will be happy to supply you with a map of Los Angeles so you can check for yourself. While you're at it, you might look up the Harris Electrical Supply ware-house on Figueroa Street. Fielding claims to be working there."

"Claims?"

"Well, there's no reason to believe he was telling the truth about that, either. I got the impression he's the kind of man who prefers to be left alone except when he needs help."

"You sound as though you don't like him."

"I like him fine," Pinata said with some truth. "But he could be hard to take in big doses."

"Is he—drinking very heavily?"

"He's drinking, I don't know how much. He told me some news about himself which he may or may not have intended me to pass on to you."

"What kind of news?"

"He's married again."

She stared in silence toward the end of the long, dim hall, as if she saw dark, half-familiar shapes moving in the shadows. "Mar-ried. Well, he's not an old man, I have no reason to be surprised. But I am. It doesn't seem real."

"I'm pretty sure he was telling the truth."

"Who is the woman?"

"He didn't say anything about her."

"Not even her name?"

"I presume," Pinata said dryly, "that her name is Mrs. Fielding."

"I meant—oh, it doesn't matter. I'm glad he's married again. I hope she's a good woman." She sounded not too glad, even less hopeful. "At least someone else is responsible for him now. Some stranger has lifted the load off my shoulders, and I'm grateful to her. I wish them both good luck. If you see him or hear from him, please tell him that for me, will you?"

"I don't expect to see or hear from him."

"My father does some rather unexpected things."

So do you, Daisy baby, Pinata thought. *Maybe you and Daddy have more in common than you'd like to admit.*

He walked her down the hall.

The rain had seeped under the front door of the building, and the welcome mat made a squishing sound when Daisy stepped out on it.

She told Jim that night all about her father's surprise appearance in town: the Sunday night phone call from the jail which Mrs. Fielding had deliberately kept secret, the second call the next afternoon from Pinata's office, the meeting which hadn't taken place because Fielding had run away. She gave Jim every detail except the one he would have been most interested in, the fact that she'd hired an investigator about whom she knew nothing more than his name.

"So your father got married again," Jim said, lighting his pipe. "Well, you can't quarrel with that, surely. It may be the best thing that ever happened to him. You should be very pleased."

"I am."

"It will be much better for him, having a life of his own."

"When has he ever had anything else?"

"Don't be bitter about it," Jim said, forcing patience into his voice. Daisy's combination of loyalty and resentment toward her father irritated him. He himself didn't think much or care much about Fielding, not even to the extent of begrudging him the money he cost. He considered, in fact, that the money was well spent if it kept Fielding at a distance. Los Angeles was a hundred miles away, not much of a distance. He hoped, for Daisy's sake, that Fielding would take a dislike to the city, the smog, the traffic, or living conditions, and head back to the East Coast or the Middle West. Jim knew, better than Daisy, how difficult it was to handle old family knots when they no longer held anything together and were too frayed to be retied.

The last time he'd seen his father-in-law was five years ago, when he'd gone to Chicago on a business trip. The two men met at the Town House, and the evening started well, with Fielding going out of his way to be charming and Jim out of his to be charmed. But by ten o'clock Fielding was drunk and blubbering about how Daisy baby had never had a real father: "You take good care of my little girl, you hear? Poor little Daisy baby. You take good care of her, you goddamn stuffed shirt." Later, Fielding was poured into a taxicab by a couple of waiters, and Jim put three twenty-dollar bills in the pocket of his understuffed shirt.

Well, I've taken good care of her, Jim thought now, *within my limits anyway. I haven't made a move without first thinking of her welfare. And sometimes the decisions have been almost impossibly difficult, like the business about Juanita. She never mentions Juanita. The corner of her mind where the girl lies has been sealed off like a tomb.*

His pipe had gone out. He relit it, and its hoarse wheezing brought back the memory of Fielding's voice: "You take good care of my little girl... you goddamn stuffed shirt."

6

This letter may never reach you, Daisy. If it doesn't, I will know why...

Two days later, on Wednesday afternoon, Jim Harker arrived home for dinner an hour earlier than usual. Daisy's car was missing from the garage, and the mail was still in the postbox. It meant that Daisy had been away since noon, when the mail arrived. The house seemed lifeless without her, in spite of the noise of Stella vacuuming the downstairs and singing bits of sad songs in a loud, cheerful voice.

He sorted the mail on the dining-room table, and was surprised to come across a bill from Adam Burnett for services rendered Mrs. James Harker, February 9, $2.50.

The bill was surprising in several ways: that Daisy had been to see Adam without telling him about it, that the fee was so small, less than minimal for a lawyer's, and that the timing was unusual. It had been sent directly after Daisy's visit instead of being postponed until the end of the month like ordinary bills for professional services. He concluded, after some thought, that sending the bill was Adam's way of informing him about Daisy's visit without actually breaking any code of ethics involving the confidences of a client.

It wasn't quite five o'clock, so he called Adam at his office. "Mr. Burnett, please. Jim Harker speaking."

"Just one second, Mr. Harker. Mr. Burnett's on his way out, but I think I can catch him. Hold on."

After a minute Adam said, "Hello, Jim."

"I received your bill today."

"Oh yes." Adam sounded embarrassed. "I wasn't going to send you any, but Daisy insisted."

"I didn't know until now that she'd been to see you."

"Oh?"

"What did she have in mind?"

"Come now, Jim, that's for Daisy to tell you, not me."

"You addressed the bill to me, so I presume you wanted me to know she'd consulted you."

"Well, yes. I thought it would be preferable if you were cognizant..."

"No lawyer talk, please," Jim said in a sharp, tense voice. "Did she come to you about—about a divorce?"

"Good Lord, no. What gave you such a crazy idea?"

"That's the usual reason women consult lawyers, isn't it?"

"As a matter of fact, no. Women make wills, sign contracts, fill out tax forms—"

"Stop beating around the bush."

"All right," Adam said cautiously. "I met Daisy by accident on the street early Monday afternoon. She seemed bewildered and anxious to talk. So we talked. I'd like to think that I gave her some good advice and that she took it."

"Was it concerning a dream she had about a certain day four years ago?"

"Yes."

"And she didn't mention a divorce?"

"Why, no. Where did you get this worm in your wig about a divorce? There was absolutely nothing in Daisy's attitude to indicate she was contemplating such a move. Besides, she couldn't get one in California. She has no grounds."

"You're forgetting, Adam."

68

"That was a long time ago," Adam said quickly. "What's the matter with you and Daisy anyway? A more lugubrious pair—"

"Nothing was the matter until she had this damned dream on Sunday night. Things have been going smoothly. We've been married eight years, and I honestly think this last year has been the best. Daisy has finally adjusted to the fact that she can't have children—maybe not adjusted, but at least reconciled—and she's looking forward eagerly to the one we're going to adopt. At least she had been, until this dream business cropped up. She hasn't mentioned our prospective child for three days now. You've had eight children, and you know how much preparation and talking and planning goes on ahead of time. I'm confused by her sudden lack of interest. Perhaps she doesn't want a child after all. If she doesn't, if she's changed her mind, God knows it wouldn't be fair for us to adopt one."

"Nonsense. Of course she wants a child." Adam spoke firmly, although he had no real convictions on the subject. Daisy, like most other women, had always puzzled him and always would. It seemed reasonable to suppose that she would want children, but she might have some deep, unspoken revulsion against adopting one. "The dream has confused her, Jim. Be patient. Play along with her."

"That might do more harm than good."

"I don't think so. In fact, I'm convinced this deathday business of hers will come to a dead end."

"How so?"

"There's no place else for it to go. She's attempting the impossible."

"Why are you so certain it's impossible?"

"Because I've been trying the same thing," Adam said. "The idea intrigued me, picking a day at random out of the past and reconstructing it. If it had been simply a matter of recalling a business appointment, I would have consulted my desk diary. But this was purely personal. Anyway, on Monday night, after the kids were in bed, Fran and I tried it. To make sure our choice of date was absolute chance, we picked it, blindfolded, from a set of calendars in the almanac. Now, Fran not only has a memory like an elephant, she also keeps a pretty complete record of the kids: baby books, report cards, artwork, and so on. But we didn't get to first base. I predict Daisy will have a similar experience. It's the kind of thing that sounds easy but isn't. After Daisy runs into a few blind alleys, she'll lose interest and give up. So let her run. Or better still, run with her."

"How?"

"Try remembering her day yourself, whatever day it was. I've forgotten."

"If you didn't get to first base, how do you expect me to?"

"I don't expect you to. Just play along. Step up to the plate and swing."

"I don't think Daisy would be fooled," Jim said dryly. "Perhaps it would be better if I distracted her attention, took her on a trip, something like that."

"A trip might be fine."

"I have to go up north this weekend anyway to look at a parcel of land in Marin County. I'll take Daisy along. She's always liked San Francisco."

He spoke to Daisy about it that night after dinner, describing the trip, lunch at Cambria Pines, a stopover at Carmel, dinner at Amelio's, a play at the Curran or the Alcazar, and afterwards a drink and floor show at the Hungry I. She looked at him as if he were proposing a trip to the moon in a rocket earned with Rice Krispies box tops.

Her refusal was sharp and direct, with no hint of her usual hesitance. "I can't go."

"Why not?"

"I have something important to attend to."

"Such as?"

"I'm doing—research."

"Research?" He repeated the word as if it tasted foreign to his tongue. "I tried to phone you this afternoon three or four times. You were out again. You've been out every afternoon this week."

"There have only been three afternoons in the week so far."

"Even so."

"Your meals are on time," Daisy said. "Your house is well kept."

Her slight but definite emphasis on the word *your* made it sound to Jim as though she were disclaiming any further share or interest in the house, as if she had, in some obscure sense, moved out. "It's *our* house, Daisy."

"Very well, our house. It's well kept, isn't it?"

"Of course."

"Then why should it bother you if I go out during the afternoon while you're at work?"

"It doesn't bother me. It concerns me. Not your going out, your attitude."

"What's the matter with my attitude?"

"A week ago you wouldn't have asked that, especially not in that particular tone, as if you were challenging me to knock a chip off your shoulder... Daisy, what's happening to us?"

"Nothing." She knew what was happening, though; what had, in fact, already happened. She had stepped out of her usual role, had changed lines and costumes, and now the director was agitated because he no longer knew what play he was directing. *Poor*

71

Jim, she thought, and reached over and took his hand. "Nothing," she said again.

They were sitting side by side on the davenport. The house was very quiet. The rain had stopped temporarily, Stella had gone home after surviving another day in the country, and Mrs. Fielding was at a concert with a friend. Prince, the collie, was sleeping in front of the fireplace, where he always slept in bad weather. Even though there was no fire in the grate, he liked the remembered warmth of other fires.

"Be fair, Daisy," Jim said, pressing her hand. "I'm not one of these heavy-handed husbands who wants his wife to have no interests outside of himself. Haven't I always encouraged your activities?"

"Yes."

"Well, then? What have you been doing, Daisy?"

"Walking around."

"In all this rain?"

"Yes."

"Walking around where?"

"The old neighborhood on Laurel Street."

"But why?"

"That was where we were living when I"—*when I died*—"when it happened."

His mouth looked as though she'd reached up and pinched it. "Did you imagine that what happened was still there, like a piece of furniture we forgot to bring along?"

"In a sense it's still there."

"Well, in that case, why didn't you walk up to the door and inquire? Why didn't you ask the occupants if they'd mind if you searched the attic for a lost day?"

"There was no one at home."

"Oh, for God's sake, you mean you actually *tried* to get in?"

"I rang the doorbell. No one answered."

"Thank heaven for small mercies. What would you have said if someone had answered?"

"Just that I used to live there once and would like to see the house again."

"Rather than have you make such an exhibition of yourself," he said coldly, "I'll buy the house back for you. Then you can spend all your afternoons there, you can search every nook and cranny of the damn place, examine every piece of junk you find."

She had withdrawn her hand from his. For a while the contact had been like a bridge between them, but the bridge had washed away in the bitter flood of his irony. "I'm not looking for—junk. I don't intend making an exhibition of myself either. I went back because I thought that if I found myself in the same situation as before, I might remember something valuable."

"Valuable? The golden moment of your death, perhaps? Isn't that just a little morbid? When did you fall in love with the idea of dying?"

She got up and crossed the room as if trying to get beyond the range of his sarcasm. The movement warned him that he was going too far, and he changed his tone.

"Are you so bored with your life, Daisy? Do you consider the past four years a living death? Is that what your dream means?"

"No."

"I think so."

"It's not your dream."

The dog had awakened and was moving his eyes back and forth, from Daisy to Jim and back to Daisy, like a spectator at a tennis match.

"I don't want to quarrel," Daisy said. "It upsets the dog."

"It upsets the—oh, for Pete's sake. All right, all right, we won't quarrel. Can't have the dog getting upset. It's O.K., though, if the rest of us are reduced to gibbering idiocy. We're just people, we don't deserve any better."

She was petting the dog's head in a soothing, reassuring way, her touch telling him that everything was fine, his eyes and ears were liars, not to be taken seriously.

I should play along with her, Jim thought. *That was Adam's advice. God knows, my own approach doesn't work.* "So you went back to Laurel Street," he said finally, "and walked around."

"Yes."

"Any results?"

"This quarrel with you," she said with bitterness. "That's all."

"You didn't remember anything?"

"Nothing that would pinpoint the actual day."

"I suppose you realize how unlikely it is that you'll ever succeed in pinpointing it?"

"Yes."

"But you intend to keep on trying?"

"Yes."

"Over my objections?"

"Yes, if you won't change your mind." She was quiet a moment, and her hand had paused on the dog's neck. "I remembered the winter. Perhaps that's a start. As soon as I saw the jasmine bushes on the south side of the house, I recalled that that was the year of the big frost when we lost all the jasmines. At least I thought we'd lost them, they looked so dead. But in the spring they all came to life again." *I didn't, though. The jasmines were tougher than I. There was no spring for me that year, no new leaves, no little buds.* "That's a start, isn't it, remembering the winter?"

"I guess so," he said heavily. "I guess that's a start."

74

"One day there was even snow on the mountain peaks. A lot of the high school kids ditched classes to go up and see it, and afterwards they drove down State Street with the snow piled high on their fenders. They looked very happy. It was the first time some of them had seen snow."

"Daisy."

"Snow in California never seems real to me somehow, not like back home in Denver, where it was a part of my life and often not a very pleasant part. I wanted to go up and see the snow that day, just like the high school kids, to make sure it was the real stuff, not something blown out of a machine from Hollywood... The year of the frost, you must remember it, Jim. I ordered a cord of wood for the fireplace, but I didn't realize what a lot of wood a cord was, and when it came, we didn't have any place to store it except outside in the rain."

She seemed anxious to go on talking, as if she felt she was on her way to convincing him of the importance of her project and the necessity for carrying on with it. Jim didn't try again to interrupt her. He felt with relief that Adam had been right: the whole thing was impossible. All Daisy had been able to remember so far was a little snow on the mountain peaks and some high school kids riding down State Street and a few dead jasmine bushes.

7

Your mother has vowed to keep us apart at any cost because she is ashamed of me...

The next morning, between the time Jim left and Stella arrived, Daisy phoned Pinata at his office. She didn't expect him to be there so early, but he answered the phone on the second ring, his voice alert and wary, as if early calls were the kind to watch out for.

"Yes."

"This is Daisy Harker, Mr. Pinata."

"Oh. Good morning, Mrs. Harker." He sounded suddenly a little too cordial. She didn't have to wait long to find out why. "If you want to cancel our agreement, that's fine with me. There'll be no charge. I'll mail you the retainer you gave me."

"Your extrasensory perception isn't working very well this morning," she said coldly. "I'm calling merely to suggest that I meet you at your office this afternoon instead of at the *Monitor-Press* building."

"Why?"

She told him the truth without embarrassment. "Because you're young and good-looking, and I wouldn't want people to get the wrong impression if they saw us together."

"I gather you haven't informed your family that you've hired me?"

"No."

"Why not?"

76

"I tried to, but I couldn't face another argument with Jim. He's right, according to his lights, and I'm right, according to mine. What's the point of arguing?"

"He's bound to find out," Pinata said. "Word gets around pretty fast in this town."

"I know, but by that time perhaps everything will be settled, you will have solved—"

"Mrs. Harker, I can't solve a thing pussyfooting around back alleys trying to avoid your family and friends. In fact, we're going to need their cooperation. This day you're fixated on, it wasn't just your day. It belonged to a lot of other people, too—650,000,000 Chinese, to name a few of them."

"I fail to see what 650,000,000 Chinese have to do with it."

"No. Well, forget it." His sigh was quite audible. *Intentionally audible*, she thought, annoyed. "I'll be in front of the *Monitor-Press* building at three o'clock, Mrs. Harker."

"Isn't it usually the employer who gives the orders?"

"Most employers know their business and are in a position to give orders. I don't think that applies to you in this particular instance, no insult intended. So, unless you've come up with some new ideas, I suggest we go about it my way. Have you any new ideas?"

"No."

"Then I'll see you this afternoon."

"Why there, at that specific place?"

"Because we're going to need some official help," Pinata said. "The *Monitor* knows a great deal more about what happened on December 2, 1955, than you or I do at the moment."

"They surely don't keep copies of newspapers from that far back."

"Not in the sense that they're offering them for sale, no. But every edition they've printed is available on microfilm. Let's hope something interesting will turn up."

They were both exactly on time, Pinata because punctuality was a habit with him, Daisy because the occasion was very important to her. All day, ever since her phone call to Pinata, she'd been impatient and excited, as if she half expected the *Monitor* to open its pages and reveal some vital truth to her. Perhaps a very special event had taken place in the world on December 2, 1955, and once the event was recalled to her, she would remember her reactions to it; it would become the peg on which she could hang the rest of the day, hat and coat and dress and sweater and, finally, the woman who fitted into them.

The carillon in the courthouse tower was ringing out the hour of three when Pinata approached the front door of the *Monitor* building. Daisy was already there, looking inconspicuous and a little dowdy in a loosely cut gray cotton suit. He wondered whether she had dressed that way deliberately to avoid calling attention to herself, or whether this was one of the latest styles. He'd lost touch with the latest styles since Monica had left him.

He said, "I hope I didn't keep you waiting."

"No. I just arrived."

"The library's on the third floor. We can take the elevator. Or would you rather walk?"

"I like to walk."

"Yes, I know."

She seemed a little surprised. "How could you know that?"

"I saw you yesterday afternoon."

"Where?"

"On Laurel Street. You were walking in the rain. I figured that anyone who walks in the rain must be very fond of walking."

"The walking was incidental. I had a purpose in visiting Laurel Street."

"I know. You used to live there. From the time of your marriage in June 1950 until October of last year, to be exact."

Her surprise this time was mixed with annoyance. "Have you been investigating me?"

"Just a few black and white statistics. Not in living color." He squinted up at the afternoon sun and rubbed his eyes. "I imagine the place on Laurel Street has many pleasant memories for you."

"Certainly."

"Then why try to destroy them?"

She regarded him with a kind of weary patience, as if he were a backward child who must be told the same thing over and over.

"I'm giving you," Pinata said, "another chance to change your mind."

"And I'm refusing it."

"All right. Let's go inside."

They went through the swinging doors and headed for the staircase, walking some distance apart like two strangers accidentally going in the same direction. The apartness was of Daisy's choosing, not Pinata's. It reminded him of what she'd said over the phone about not wanting people to see them together because he was young and good-looking. The compliment, if it was one, had embarrassed him. He didn't like any reference, good or bad, made to his physical appearance, because he felt such things were, or should be, irrelevant.

In his early years Pinata had been extremely conscious of the fact that he didn't know his own racial origin and couldn't identify with any particular racial group. Now, in his maturity, this lack of group identification had the effect of making him tolerant of every race. He was able to think of men as his brothers because some of them might very well be his brothers, for all he knew. The name Pinata, which enabled him to mix freely with the Spanish Americans and the Mexicans who made up a large part of the city, was not his. It had been given to him by the Mother Superior of the orphanage in Los Angeles where he'd been abandoned.

He still visited the orphanage occasionally. The Mother Superior was very old now, and her eyesight and hearing were failing, but her tongue was as lively as a girl's when Pinata came to see her. More than any of the other hundreds of her children, he was hers, because she'd found him, in the chapel on Christmas Eve, and because she'd named him, Jesus Pinata. As the Mother Superior grew older, her mind, no longer nimble or inquisitive, chose to follow certain well-worn roads. Her favorite road led back to a Christmas Eve thirty-two years ago.

"There you were, in front of the altar, a wee mite of a bundle barely five pounds, and squalling so hard I thought your little lungs would break. Sister Mary Martha came in then, looking as white as a sheet, as if she'd never seen a brand-new baby before. She picked you up in her arms and called you the Lord Jesus, and immediately you stopped crying, like any lost soul recognizing his name called out in the wilderness. So we called you Jesus.

"Of course, it's a very difficult name to live up to," she would add with a sigh. "Ah, how well I remember as you got older, all the fighting you had to do every time one of the other children laughed at your name. All those bruises and black eyes and chipped teeth, dear me, it became quite a problem. You hardly looked human half the time. Jesus is a lovely name, but I felt something had to be done. So I asked Father Stevens for his advice, and he came over and talked to you. He asked you what name you would like to have, and you said Stevens. A very fine choice, too. Father Stevens was a great man."

At this point she always stopped to blow her nose, explaining that she had a touch of sinusitis because of the smog. "You could have changed the Pinata part as well. After all, it was just a name we picked because the children were playing the piñata game that Christmas Eve. We took a vote on it. Sister Mary Martha was the only one who objected to the name. 'Suppose he is a Smith or a Brown or an Anderson,' she said. I reminded her that very few whites lived in our neighborhood, and since you were to be brought up among us, you would do better as a Pinata than as a Brown or Anderson. I was right, too. You've developed into a fine young man we're all proud of. If the good Father were only here to see you… Dear me, I think this smog gets worse each year. If it were the will of the Lord, I wouldn't complain, but I fear it's just sheer human perversity."

Perversity. The word reminded him of Daisy. She was racing up the steps ahead of him as if she were in training for a track meet. He caught up with her on the third floor. "What's your hurry? The place stays open until 5:30."

"I like to move fast."

"So do I, when someone's chasing me."

The library was at the end of a long, elaborately tiled corridor. It was rumored that no two tiles in the entire building were alike. So far no one had gone to the trouble of checking this, but the rumor was repeated to tourists, who relayed it via postcard and letter to their friends and relatives in the East and Middle West.

In the small room marked library, a girl in horn-rimmed glasses was seated behind a desk pasting clippings into a scrap-book. She ignored Daisy and fixed her bright, inquisitive eyes on Pinata. "Is there anything I can do for you?"

Pinata said, "You're new around here, aren't you?"

"Yes. The other girl had to quit. Allergic to paste, broke out all over her hands and arms. A real mess."

"Sorry to hear it."

"She's trying to get workman's compensation, but I'm not sure it applies to allergies. Can I help you with anything?"

"I'd like to see the microfilm of one of your back copies."

"Year and month?"

"December '55."

"One roll of film covers half a month. Which half are you interested in, the first or last?"

"The first."

She unlocked one drawer of a metal filing cabinet and brought out a roll of microfilm, which she fitted into the projection machine. Then she turned on the light in the machine and showed Pinata the hand crank. "You just keep turning this until you come to the day you want. It starts at December the first and goes through to the fifteenth."

"Yes. Thanks."

"Pull up a chair if you want." The girl for the first time looked directly at Daisy. "Or two chairs."

Pinata arranged a chair for Daisy. He remained standing, with one hand on the crank. Although the girl in charge had returned to her desk and was presumably intent on her work, Pinata lowered his voice. "Can you see properly?"

"Not too well."

"Close your eyes for a minute while I turn to the right day, or you might get dizzy."

She closed her eyes until he said crisply, "Well, here's your day, Mrs. Harker."

Her eyes remained closed, as if the lids had become calcified and too stiff and heavy to move.

"Aren't you going to look at it?"

"Yes. Of course."

She opened her eyes and blinked a couple of times, refocusing. The headlines meant nothing to her: CIO AND AFL MERGED AFTER TWENTY-YEAR SPLIT. BODY OF UNIDENTIFIED MAN FOUND NEAR RAILROAD JUNGLE. FEDERAL SCHOOL AID PLAN BACKED. YOUTH CONFESSES DOZEN BURGLARIES. BAD WEATHER MAY CLOSE AIRPORT. SEVEN HUNDRED TO PARTICIPATE IN CHRISTMAS PARADE TONIGHT. CRASH INJURES PIANIST WALTER GIESEKING, KILLS WIFE. MORE SNOW PREDICTED FOR MOUNTAIN AREAS.

Snow on the mountains, she thought, *the kids driving down State Street, the dead jasmines.* "Could you read the fine print to me, please?"

"Which fine print?"

"About the snow on the mountains."

"All right. 'Early risers were given a rare treat this morning in the form of a blanket of snow on the mountains. Forest rangers at La Cumbre peak reported a depth of seven inches in some places, and more is predicted during the night. Some senior classes of both public and private schools were dismissed for the morning so that students could drive up and experience, many of them for the first time, real snow. Damage to citrus crops—'"

"I remember that," she said, "the students with the snow piled on the fenders of their cars."

"So do I."

"Very clearly?"

"Yes. They made quite a parade out of it."

"Why should both of us remember a little thing like that?"

"Because it was very unusual, I suppose," Pinata said.

"So unusual that it could only have happened once that year?"

"Perhaps. I can't be sure of it, though."

"Wait." She turned to him, flushed with excitement. "It must have happened only once. Don't you see? The students wouldn't have been dismissed from class a second time. They'd already been given their chance to see the snow. The school authorities surely wouldn't keep repeating the dismissal if it snowed a second or third or fourth time."

Her logic surprised and convinced him. "I agree. But why is it so important to you?"

"Because it's the first *real* thing I remember about the day, the only thing that separates it from a lot of other days. If I saw those students parading in their cars, it means I must have gone downtown, perhaps to have lunch with Jim. And yet I can't remember Jim being with me, or my mother either. I think—I'm almost sure—I was alone."

"When you saw the kids, where were you? Walking along the street?"

"No. I think I was inside some place, looking out through a window."

"A restaurant? A store? Where did you usually shop in those days?"

"For groceries at the Fairway, for clothes at Dewolfe's."

"Neither of those is on State Street. How about a restaurant? Do you have a favorite place to eat lunch?"

"The Copper Kettle. It's a cafeteria in the 1100 block."

"Let's assume for a minute," Pinata said, "that you were having lunch at the Copper Kettle, alone. Did you often go downtown and have lunch alone?"

"Sometimes, on the days I worked."

"You had a job?"

"I was a volunteer for a while at the Neighborhood Clinic. It's a family counseling service. I worked there every Wednesday and Friday afternoon."

"December 2 was a Friday. Did you go to work that afternoon?"

"I don't remember. I don't even know if I was still working at that time. I quit because I wasn't very good with chil—with people."

"You were going to say 'with children,' weren't you?"

"Does it matter?"

"It might."

She shook her head. "My job wasn't important anyway. I'm not a trained social worker. I acted mainly as a baby-sitter for the children of the mothers and fathers who came in for counseling, some of them voluntarily, some by order of the courts or the Probation Department."

"You didn't like the job?"

"Oh, but I did. I was crazy about it. I just wasn't competent enough. I couldn't handle the children. I felt too sorry for them. I was too—personal. Children, especially children of families who reach the point of going to the Clinic, need a firmer and more objective approach. The fact is," she added with a grim little smile, "if I hadn't quit, they'd probably have fired me."

"What gave you that idea?"

"Nothing specific. But I got the impression that I was more of a hindrance than a help around the place, so I simply failed to show up the next time."

"The next time after what?"

"After—after I got the impression that I was a hindrance."

"But something must have given you that impression at a definite time or you wouldn't have used the phrase 'the next time.'"

"I don't follow you."

He thought, *You follow me, Daisy baby. You just don't like the bumps in the road I'm taking. Well, it's not my road; it's yours. If there are potholes in it, don't blame me.*

"I don't follow you," she repeated.

"All right, let's skip it."

She looked relieved, as if he'd pointed out to her a nice, easy detour. "I don't see how a little detail like that could be important when I'm not even sure I was working at the Clinic at the time."

"We can make sure. They keep records, and I shouldn't have any trouble getting the information you want. Charles Alston, the director, is an old friend of mine. We've had a lot of clients in common—on their way up they land in his lap; on their way down they land in mine."

"Will you have to use my name?"

"Of course. How else—"

"Can't you think of any other way?"

"Look, Mrs. Harker. If you worked at the Clinic, you must know that their file room isn't open to the public. If I want information, I ask Mr. Alston, and he decides whether I get it or not. How am I going to find out if you were working on a certain Friday or not if I don't mention your name?"

"Well, I wish you didn't have to." She pleated a corner of her gray jacket, smoothed it out carefully, and began all over again. "Jim said I mustn't make an—an exhibition of myself. He's very conscious of public opinion. He's had to be," she added, raising her head in a sudden defensive gesture, "to get where he is."

"And where is that?"

"The end of the rainbow, I guess you'd call it. Years ago, when he had nothing at all, Jim made plans for himself: how he would live, the type of house he would build, how much money he'd make, yes, even the kind of wife he would choose—he had everything on the drawing board when he was still in his teens."

"And it's all worked out?"

"Most of it," she said. *One thing hasn't, and never will. Jim wanted two boys and two girls.*

"What, if I may ask, was on your drawing board, Mrs. Harker?"

86

"I'm not a planner." She fixed her eyes on the projector again. "Shall we continue with the newspaper?"

"All right."

He turned the crank, and the headlines of the next page rolled into view. Gunman John Kendrick, one of the FBI's most wanted men, was captured in Chicago. California had nine traffic deaths on Safe Driving Day. The Abbott murder trial was still going on in San Francisco. A woman celebrated her 110th birthday in Dublin. High tides were demolishing several houses at Redondo Beach. In Sacramento the future of the State Junior College was discussed by educators, and in Georgia 2,000 students rioted over the racial ban in the Bowl game.

"Any bells ringing?" Pinata said.

"No."

"Well, let's try the local news. The American Penwomen gave a Christmas party and the Trinity Guild a bazaar. The Bert Petersons celebrated their thirtieth anniversary. The harbor dredging contract was O.K.'d. A Peeping Tom was apprehended on Colina Street. A four-year-old boy was bitten by a cocker spaniel and the dog ordered confined for fourteen days. A woman called Juanita Garcia, age twenty-three, was given probation on charges of neglecting her five children by locking them in her apartment while she visited several west-side taverns. The city council referred to the water commission a petition concerning—"

He stopped. Daisy had turned away from the projector with a noise that sounded like a sigh of boredom. She didn't look bored, though. She looked angry. Her jaw was set tight, and blotches of color appeared on her cheeks as if she'd been slapped, silently, invisibly, hard. Her reaction puzzled Pinata: did she have a grudge against the city council or the water commission? Was she afraid of biting dogs, Peeping Toms, thirtieth anniversaries?

He said, "Don't you want to go on with this, Mrs. Harker?"

The slight movement of her head was neither negative nor affirmative. "It seems hopeless. I mean, what difference does it make to me whether a woman called Juanita Garcia got probation or not? I don't know any Juanita Garcia." She spoke the words with unnecessary force, as if Pinata had accused her of having had a part in Mrs. Garcia's case. "How would I know a woman like that?"

"Through your work at the Clinic, perhaps. According to the newspaper account, one of the conditions of Mrs. Garcia's two-year probation was that she get some psychiatric help. Since she had five children and was expecting a sixth, and her husband was an Army private stationed in Germany, it seems unlikely she could afford a private psychiatrist. That leaves the Clinic."

"No doubt your reasoning is sound. But it has no connection with me. I have never met Mrs. Garcia, at the Clinic or anywhere else. As I told you before, my work there was concerned entirely with the children of patients, not the patients themselves."

"Then perhaps you knew Mrs. Garcia's children. She had five."

"Why do you keep harping like this on the name Garcia?"

"Because I got the impression it meant something to you."

"I've denied that, haven't I?"

"Several times, yes."

"Then why are you accusing me of lying to you?"

"Not to me, exactly," Pinata said. "But there's the possibility that you may be lying to yourself without realizing it. Think about it, Mrs. Harker. You overreacted to the name…"

"Perhaps I overreacted. Or perhaps you overinterpreted."

"That could be."

"It was. It is."

She got up and walked over to the window. The movement was so obviously one of protest and escape that Pinata felt as if she'd told him to shut up and leave her alone. He had no intention of doing either.

"It will be easy enough to check up on Mrs. Garcia," he said. "The police will have a file on her, as well as the Probation Department and probably Charles Alston at the Clinic."

She turned and gave him a weary look. "I wish I could convince you that I never in my life heard of the woman. But it's a free country; you can check everyone in the city directory if you like."

"I may have to. You've given me very little to go on. The only facts I have are that on December 2, 1955, there was snow on the mountains, and you ate lunch at a cafeteria downtown. How did you get downtown, by the way?"

"I must have driven. I had my own car."

"What kind?"

"An Oldsmobile convertible."

"Did you usually drive with the top up or down?"

"Down. But I can't see how all this is important."

"When we don't know what's important, anything can be. You can't tell what particular detail will jog your memory. For instance, that Friday was a cold day. Maybe you can remember putting the top up. Or you might have had trouble starting your car."

She looked honestly bewildered. "I *seem* to remember that I did. But that may be only because you suggested it. You say things in such a positive way. Like about the Garcia woman—you're so sure I know her or knew her." She sat down again and began repleating the corner of her jacket. "If I did know her, why have I forgotten? I'd have no reason to forget a friend or a casual acquaintance, and I'm not forceful enough to make enemies. Yet you seem so positive."

"Seeming and being are two different things," Pinata said with a faint smile. "No, I'm not positive, Mrs. Harker. I saw a straw and grasped it."

"But you're holding on?"

"Only until I find something more substantial to hold on to."

"I wish I could help. I'm trying. I'm really *trying*."

"Well, don't get tense about it. Perhaps we should stop for today. Have you had enough?"

"I guess so."

"You'd better go home. Back to Rainbow's End."

She stood up stiffly. "I regret telling you that about my husband. It seems to amuse you."

"On the contrary. It depresses me. I had a few plans on the drawing board myself." *Just one of them worked out*, Pinata thought. *His name is Johnny. And the only reason I'm trying to track down your precious day, Daisy baby, is because Johnny's having his teeth straightened, not because you got your head stuck in the pot of gold at the end of the rainbow.*

He turned the roll of microfilm back to the beginning and switched off the light in the projector.

The girl in the horn-rimmed spectacles came hurrying over, looking alarmed as if she expected him to wreck the machine or at least run off with the film. "Let me handle that," she said. "These things are quite valuable, you know. History being made right before our eyes, you might say. Did you find what you wanted?"

Pinata glanced at Daisy. "Did you?"

"Yes," Daisy said. "Yes, thank you very much."

Pinata opened the door for her, and she began walking slowly and silently down the corridor, her head bent as if she were studying the tiles on the floor.

"No two are alike," he said.

"Pardon?"

"The tiles. There are no two alike in the whole building."

"Oh."

"Someday when this current project of yours is finished and you need something new to amuse yourself with, you could come down here and check."

He said it to get a rise out of her, preferring her hostility to her sudden, unexpected withdrawal, but she gave no indication that she'd heard him or even that he was there at all. Whatever corridor she was walking along, it wasn't this one and it wasn't with him. As far as she was concerned, he had already gone back to his office or was still up in the library looking at microfilm. He felt canceled, erased.

When they reached the front of the building, the carillon in the courthouse tower across the street was chiming four o'clock. The sound brought her to attention.

"I must hurry," she said.

"Why?"

"The cemetery closes in an hour."

He looked at her irritably. "Are you going to take some flowers to yourself?"

"All week," she said, ignoring his question, "ever since Monday, I've been trying to gather up enough courage to go there. Then last night I had the same dream again, of the sea and the cliff and Prince and the tombstone with my name on it. I can't endure it any longer. I must satisfy myself that it's not there, it doesn't exist."

"How will you go about it, just wander around reading off names?"

"That won't be necessary. I'm quite familiar with the place. I've visited it often with Jim and my mother—Jim's parents are buried there, and one of my mother's cousins. I know exactly what to look for, and where, because in all my dreams the tombstone is the same, a rough-hewn unpolished gray cross, about five feet high, and it's always in the same place, by the edge of the cliff,

91

underneath the Moreton Bay fig tree. There's only one tree of that kind in the area. It's a famous sailor's landmark."

Pinata didn't know what a Moreton Bay fig tree looked like, and he had never been a sailor or visited the cemetery, but he was willing to take her word. She seemed sure of her facts. He thought, *So she's familiar with the place, she's been there often. The dream didn't just come out of nowhere. The locale is real, perhaps even the tombstone is real.*

"You'd better let me come along," he said.

"Why? I'm not afraid anymore."

"Oh, let's just say I'm curious." He touched her sleeve very delicately, as if he were directing a highly trained but nervous mare who would go to pieces under too much pressure. "My car's over on Piedra Street."

8

Right from the beginning, she has been ashamed, not only of me but of herself, too…

The iron gates looked as though they had been made for giants to swing on. Bougainvillea concealed the twelve-foot steel fence, its fluttery crimson flowers looking innocent of the curved spikes lurking beneath the leaves, sharper than any barbed wire. Between the street and the fence, rows of silver dollar trees shook their money like demented gamblers.

The gray stone gatehouse resembled a miniature prison, with its barred windows and padlocked iron door. Both the door and the lock were rusted, as if the gatekeeper had long since vanished into another part of the cemetery. Century plants, huge enough to be approaching the end of their designated time, lined both sides of the road to the chapel, alternating with orange and blue birds of paradise that looked ready to sing or to fly away.

In contrast to the gatehouse, the chapel was decorated with vividly colored Mexican tiles, and organ music was pouring out of its open doors, loud and lively. Only one person was visible, the organist. He seemed to be playing to and for himself; perhaps a funeral had just taken place, and he had stayed on to practice or to drown out a persistent choir of ghosts.

There was a threat of darkness in the air, and a threat of fog. Daisy buttoned her jacket to the throat and put on her white gloves. They were pretty gloves, of nylon net and linen, but they looked to her now like the kind that were passed out to pallbearers.

She would have taken them off immediately and stuffed them back in her purse if she hadn't been afraid Pinata would observe the gesture and put his own interpretation on it. His interpretations were too quick and sure and, at least in one case, wrong. She thought, *I know no person called Juanita, only an old song we sang at home when I was a child. Nita, Juanita, ask thy soul if we should part…*

She began to hum it unconsciously, and Pinata, listening, recognized the tune and wondered why it disturbed him. There was something about the words. *Nita, Juanita, ask thy soul if we should part…* Nita, that was it. Nita was the name of the waitress in the Velada Café, the one Fielding had "rescued" from her husband. It could be, and probably was, a coincidence. And even if it wasn't a coincidence, and Nita Donelli and Juanita Garcia were the same woman, it meant nothing more than that she had divorced Garcia and married Donelli. She was the kind of woman who would ordinarily seek employment in places like the Velada, and Fielding was the kind of man who frequented them. It seemed perfectly natural that their paths should cross. As for the fight with the woman's husband, that certainly hadn't been planned by Fielding. He'd told the police when he was arrested that she was a stranger to him, a lady in distress, and he'd gone to her assistance out of his respect for womanhood. It was the type of thing Fielding, at the euphoric level of the bottle, would say and do.

They had come to a fork in the road at the top of the mesa which formed the main part of the cemetery. Pinata stopped the car and looked over at Daisy. "Have you heard from your father?"

"No. We turn right here. We're going to the west end."

"The waitress your father got into a fight over was named Nita. Possibly Juanita."

"I know that. My father told me when he phoned about the bail money. He also told me she was a stranger to him, a good-looking young woman who'd led a hard life—those were his words. Don't you believe him?"

"Yes. Yes, I do."

"Well, then?"

Pinata shrugged. "Nothing. I just thought I'd mention it."

"What a fool he is." The contempt in her voice was softened by pity and sorrow. "What a fool. Will he *never* learn that you can't walk into a squalid little café and pick up waitresses without inviting disaster? He could have been seriously injured, even killed."

"He's pretty tough."

"Tough? My father?" She shook her head. "No, I wish he were. He's like a marshmallow."

"Speaking from my own experience, some marshmallows can be very tough. Depends on their age."

She changed the subject by pointing out of the window. "The fig tree is over there by the cliff. You can see the top of it from here. It's a very unusual specimen, the largest of its kind in this hemisphere, Jim says. He's taken dozens of pictures of it."

Pinata started the car, keeping down to the posted limit of ten miles an hour although he felt like speeding through the place and out again, and to hell with Daisy baby and her fig tree. The rolling lawns, the green and growing things, made too disquieting a contrast to the dead buried beneath them. A cemetery shouldn't be like a park, he thought, but like a desert: all tans and grays, rock and sand, and cacti which looked alive briefly only once a year, at the time of the resurrection.

Most of the visitors had gone for the day. A young woman dressed in black was arranging a bouquet of gladioli above a bronze nameplate, while her two children, T-shirted and blue-jeaned, played hide-and-seek among the crypts and tombstones. A hundred yards farther on, four workmen in overalls were starting to fill in a freshly dug grave. The green cloth, intended to simulate grass, had been pulled away from the excavated mound of earth, and the workmen were stabbing at it listlessly with their shovels. An old man with white hair sat on a nearby bench and looked down at the falling earth, stupefied by grief.

"I'm glad you came along," Daisy said suddenly. "I would have been frightened by myself or depressed."

"Why? You've been here before."

"It never affected me much. Whenever I came with Jim and my mother, it was more like taking part in a pageant, a ritual that meant nothing to me. How could it? I never even met Jim's parents or my mother's cousin. People can't seem dead to you unless they were once alive. It wasn't real, the flowers, the tears, the prayers."

"Whose tears?"

"Mother cries easily."

"Over a cousin so remote or so long dead that you hadn't even met her?"

Daisy leaned forward in the seat with a sigh of impatience or anxiety. "They were brought up together as children in Denver. Besides, the tears weren't really for her, I guess. They were for—oh, life in general. *Lacrimae rerum.*"

"Were you specifically invited to go on these excursions with your husband and mother?"

"Why? What's that got to do with anything?"

"I just wondered."

"I was invited. Jim thought it proper for me to go along, and Mother used me to lean on. It isn't often she does. I suppose I—I rather enjoyed the feeling of being strong enough for anyone else to lean on, especially my mother."

"Where are Jim's parents buried?"

"The west end."

"Anywhere near where we're headed?"

"No."

"You said your husband has taken many pictures of the fig tree?"

"Yes."

"Were you with him on some of those occasions?"

"Yes."

They were approaching the cliff, and the sound of breakers was like the roar of a great wind through a distant forest, rising and falling. As the roar increased, the fig tree came into full view: a huge green umbrella, twice as wide as it was tall. The glossy, leathery leaves showed cinnamon color on the undersides, as if they, too, like the lock and the iron door of the gatehouse, were rusting away in the sea air. The trunk and larger branches resembled gray marble shapes of subhuman figures entwined in static love. There were no graves directly under the tree because part of the vast root system grew above ground. The monuments began at the periphery—all shapes and sizes, angels, rectangles, crosses, columns, polished and unpolished, gray and white and black and pink—but only one of them exactly matched the description of the tombstone in Daisy's dream.

Pinata saw it as soon as he got out of the car: a rough-hewn gray stone cross about five feet high.

Daisy saw it, too. She said, with a look of terrible surprise, "It's there. It's—real."

He felt less surprise than she did. Everything in the dream was turning out to be real. He glanced toward the edge of the cliff as if he almost expected the dog Prince to come running up from the beach and start to howl.

Daisy had stepped out of the car and was leaning against the hood of the engine for support or warmth.

97

"I can't see any name on it at this distance," Pinata said. "Let's go over and examine it."

"I'm afraid."

"There's nothing to be afraid of, Mrs. Harker. What's obviously happened is that you've seen this particular stone in this particular location on one of your visits here. For some reason it impressed and interested you, you remembered it, and it cropped up in your dreams."

"Why should it have impressed me?"

"For one thing, it's a handsome and expensive piece of work. Or it might have reminded you of the old rugged cross in the hymn. But instead of standing here theorizing, why don't we go over and check the facts?"

"Facts?"

"Surely the important fact," Pinata said dryly, "is whose name is on it."

For a moment he thought she was going to turn and run for the exit gates. Instead, she straightened up, with a shake of her head, and stepped over the small lantana hedge onto the graveled path that wound around the periphery of the fig tree. She began walking toward the gray cross very quickly, as though she were putting her trust in momentum to keep her going if fear should try to stop her.

She had almost reached her destination when she stumbled and fell forward on her knees. He caught up with her and helped her to her feet. There were grass stains on the front of her skirt, and prickly little pellets of burr clover.

"It's not mine," she said in a whisper. "Thank God it's not mine."

A small rectangular area in the center of the cross had been cut and polished to hold the inscription:

CARLOS THEODORE CAMILLA
1907–1955

Pinata was sure from her reaction that the name meant nothing to her beyond the fact that it was not her own. She was looking relieved and a little embarrassed, like a child who's had the lights turned on and recognized the bogeyman for what it was, a discarded coat, a blowing curtain. Even with the lights on, there was one small bogeyman left that she apparently hadn't noticed yet—the year of Camilla's death. Perhaps from where she stood she couldn't discern the numbers; he suspected from her actions in the newspaper library that she was nearsighted and either didn't know it or didn't want to admit it.

He stepped directly in front of the tombstone to hide the inscription in case she came any closer. It made him feel uneasy, standing on this stranger's coffin, right where his face would be, or had been. Carlos Camilla. What kind of face had he once had? Dark, certainly. It was a Mexican name. Few Mexicans were buried in this cemetery, both because it was too expensive and because the ground was not consecrated by their church. Fewer still had such elaborate monuments.

"I feel guilty," Daisy said, "at being so glad that it's his and not mine. But I can't help it."

"No need to feel guilty."

"It must have happened just as you said it did. I saw the tombstone, and for some reason it stuck in my memory—perhaps it was the name on it. *Camilla*, it's a very pretty name. What does it mean, a camellia?"

"No, it means a stretcher, a little bed."

"Oh. It doesn't sound so pretty when you know what it means."

"That's true of a lot of things."

Fog had started to drift in from the sea. It moved in aimless wisps across the lawns and hung like tatters of chiffon among the leather leaves of the fig tree. Pinata wondered how quietly Camilla was resting, with the roots of the vast tree growing inexorably toward his little bed.

"They'll be closing the gates soon," he said. "We'd better leave."

"All right."

She turned toward the car. He waited for her to take a few steps before he moved away from the tombstone, feeling a little ashamed of himself for the deception. He didn't know it wasn't a deception until they were back inside the car and Daisy said suddenly, "Camilla died in 1955."

"So did a lot of other people."

"I'd like to find out the exact date, just out of curiosity. They must keep records of some kind on the premises—there's an office marked 'Superintendent' just behind the chapel, and a caretaker's cottage over on the east side."

"I was hoping you intended to drop this whole business."

"Why should I? Nothing's really changed, if you think about it."

He thought about it. Nothing had really changed, least of all Daisy baby's mind.

The superintendent's office was closed for the day, but there were lights burning in the caretaker's cottage. Through the living-room window Pinata could see a stout elderly man in suspenders watching a TV program: two cowboys were shooting freely at each other from behind two rocks. Both the cowboys and the rocks appeared exactly the same as the ones Pinata remembered from his boyhood.

He pressed the buzzer, and the old man got hurriedly to his feet and zigzagged across the living room as if he were dodging bullets. He turned off the TV set, with a furtive glance toward the window, and came running to open the door.

"I hardly never watch the stuff," he said, wheezing apology.

"My son-in-law Harold don't approve, says it's bad for my heart, all them shootings."

"Are you the caretaker?"

"No, that's my son-in-law Harold. He's at the dentist, got himself an absence on the gum."

"Maybe you could give me some information?"

"Can't do no more than try. My name's Finchley. Come in and close the door. That fog clogs up my tubes, can't hardly breathe certain nights." He squinted out at the car. "Don't the lady care to come in out of the fog?"

"No."

"She must have good serviceable tubes." The old man closed the door. The small, neat living room was stifling hot and smelled of chocolate. "You looking for a particular gra—resting-place? Harold says never to say grave, customers don't like it, but all the time I keep forgetting. Now right here I got a map of the whole location, tells you who's buried where. That what you want?"

"Not exactly. I know where the man's buried, but I'd like some more information about the date and circumstances."

"Where's he buried?"

Pinata indicated the spot on the map while Finchley wheezed and grunted his disapproval. "That's a bad place, what with the spring tides eating away at the cliff and that big old tree getting bigger every day and 'tracting tourists that stomp on the grass. People buy there because of the view, but what's a view good for if you can't see it? Me, when I die, I want to lie safe and snug, not with no big old tree and them high tides coming after me hellbent for leather... What's his name?"

"Carlos Camilla."

"I'd have to go to the file to look that up, and I ain't so sure I can find the key."

101

"You could try."

"I ain't so sure I oughta. It's near closing time, and I got to put supper on the stove. Absence or no absence, Harold likes to eat and eat good, same as me. All them dead people out there, they don't bother me none. When it comes quitting time, I close the door on them, never think of them again till next morning. They don't bother my sleep or my victuals none." But he belched suddenly, in a genteel way, as if he had, unawares, swallowed a few indigestible fibers of fear. "Anyhow, maybe Harold wouldn't like me messing with his file. That file's mighty important to him; it's exactly the same as the one the Super has in his office. You can tell from that how much the Super thinks of Harold."

Pinata was beginning to suspect that Finchley was stalling not because of his inability to find the key or any inhibitions about using it, but because he couldn't spell.

"You find the key," he said, "and I'll help you look up the name."

The old man looked relieved at having the burden of decision lifted from his shoulders. "Now that's fair enough, ain't it?"

"It won't take me a minute. Then you can turn on the TV again and catch the end of the program."

"I don't mind admitting I ain't sure which was the good guy and which was the bad guy. Now what's that name again?"

"Camilla."

"K-a—"

"C-a-m-i-l-l-a."

"You write it down, just like it shows on the cards, eh?"

Pinata wrote it down, and the old man took the paper and sped out of the room as if he'd been handed the baton in a relay race to the frontier where the bad guys were shooting it out with the good guys.

He returned in less than a minute, put the file drawer on the table, turned on the TV set, and retired from the world.

Pinata bent over the file. The card bearing the name Carlos Theodore Camilla bore little else: a technical description of his burial plot and the name of the funeral director, Roy Fondero. Next of kin, none. Address, none. Born April 3, 1907. Died December 2, 1955. *Sui mano.*

Coincidence, he thought. The date of Camilla's suicide must be just a crazy coincidence. After all, the chances were one in 365. Things a lot more coincidental than that happen every day.

But he didn't believe it, and he knew Daisy wouldn't either if he told her. The question was whether to tell her, and if he decided not to, the problem was how to lie successfully. She wasn't easily deceived. Her ears were quick to catch false notes, and her eyes were a good deal sharper than he'd thought.

A new and disturbing idea had begun to gnaw at a corner of his brain: suppose Daisy already knew how and when Camilla had died, suppose she had invented the whole business of the dreams as a means of getting him interested in Camilla without revealing her own connection with him. It seemed highly improbable, however. Her reaction to the name had been one of simple relief that it was not her own; she'd shown no signs of emotional involvement or confusion or guilt beyond the spoken artificial guilt over her gladness that the tombstone was Camilla's instead of hers. Besides, he could think of no valid reason why Daisy would choose such a devious way of accomplishing her purpose. *No,* he thought, *Daisy is a victim, not a manipulator of circumstances.* She didn't plan, couldn't possibly have planned the sequence of events that led to his meeting her in the first place: the arrest of her father, the bail, her visit to his office. If any planning had been done, it was on Fielding's part, but this was equally unlikely.

Fielding seemed incapable of planning anything farther than the next minute and the next bottle.

All right, he thought irritably. *So nobody planned anything. Daisy had a dream, that's all. Daisy had a dream.*

He said, "Thanks very much, Mr. Finchley."

"Eh?"

"Thank you for letting me see the file."

"Oh my, look at him take that bullet right in the belly. I knew all along it was the bad guy in the black hat. You can always tell by the horse's eyes. A horse looks mean and shifty, and you can bet he's got a mean and shifty critter on his back. Well, he got his, yes sir, he got his." Finchley wrenched his eyes from the screen. "Program's changing, must be five o'clock. You better get a move on before Harold comes home and locks the gates. He won't be in so good a humor with that absence on his gum and all. Harold's fair," he added with a grunt, "but he ain't merciful. Not since his wife died. That's what women are put in this world for, mercy, ain't that right?"

"I guess so."

"Someday, you live long enough and you'll know so."

"Good night, Mr. Finchley."

"You get out of them gates before Harold comes."

Daisy had turned on the radio and the heater in the car, but she didn't look as though she were feeling any warmth or hearing any music. She said, "Please, let's hurry and get out of here."

"You could have come inside the house."

"I didn't want to interfere with your work. What did you find out?"

"Not much."

"Well, aren't you going to tell me?"

"I suppose I'll have to."

He told her, and she listened in silence while the car rolled noisily down the graveled hill past the chapel. It was dark. The organist was gone, leaving no echoes of music. The birds of paradise were voiceless. The money on the silver dollar trees was spent; the bougainvillea wept in the fog.

Harold, holding his swollen jaw, watched the car leave and closed the iron gates. The day was over; it was good to be home.

9

Even when she talked of love, her voice had bitterness in it, as if the relationship between us was the result of a physical defect she couldn't help, a weakness of the body which her mind despised...

The lights of the city were going on, in strings and clusters along the sea and highway, thinning out as they rose up the foothills until, at the very top, they looked like individual stars that had fallen on the mountains, still burning. Pinata knew that none of the lights belonged to him. His house was dark; there was no one in it, no Johnny, no Monica, not even Mrs. Dubrinski, who left at five o'clock to take care of her own family. He felt as excluded from life as Camilla in his grave under the great tree, as empty as Camilla's mind, as deaf as his ears to the sound of the sea, as blind as his eyes to the spindrift.

"What's a view good for," the old man had said, "if you can't see it?"

Well, the view's there, Pinata thought. *I'm looking at it, but I'm not part of it. None of those lights have been lit for me, and if anyone's waiting for me, it's some drunk in the city jail anxious to get out and buy another bottle.*

Beside him, Daisy was sitting mute and motionless, as if she were thinking of nothing at all or of so many things so quickly that they had crashed the sound barrier into silence. Glancing at her, he wanted suddenly to do something shocking, arresting, to force her to pay attention to him. But a second later the idea seemed so absurd that he went cold with anger at himself: *Christ, what's the matter with me? I must be losing my marbles. Johnny, I must think of Johnny. Or Camilla. That's safe, think of Camilla, the stranger in Daisy's grave.*

This stranger had died, and Daisy had dreamed the tombstone was her own—that much of it was explicable. The rest wasn't, unless Daisy had extrasensory perception, which seemed highly improbable, or a singular ability to deceive herself as well as other people. The latter was more likely, but he didn't believe it. As he became better acquainted with her, he was struck by her essential naïveté and innocence, as if she had somehow walked through life without touching anything or being touched, like a child wandering through a store where all the merchandise was out of reach and not for sale, and dummy clerks stood behind plate glass and sold nothing. Had Daisy baby been too well disciplined to protest, too docile to demand? And was she demanding now, through her dreams, for the plate glass to be removed and the dummy clerks put into action?

"The stranger," she said at last. "How did he die?"

"Suicide. His file card was marked *sui mano*, 'by his own hand.' I presume someone thought putting it in Latin would take the curse off it."

"So he killed himself. That makes it even worse."

"Why?"

"Perhaps I had some connection with his death. Perhaps I was responsible for it."

"That's pretty far-fetched," Pinata said quietly. "You've had a shock, Mrs. Harker. The best thing you can do now is to stop worrying and go home and have a rest." *Or take a pill, or a drink, or throw fits, or whatever else women like you do under the circumstances. Monica used to cry, but I don't think you will, Daisy baby. You'll brood, and God only knows what you'll hatch.* "Camilla was a stranger to you, wasn't he?"

107

"Yes."

"Then how is it possible that you were connected in any way with his death?"

"Possible? We're not dealing in 'possibles' anymore, Mr. Pinata. It isn't possible that I should have known the day he died. But it happened. It's a fact, not something whipped up by an over-imaginative or hysterical woman, which is probably how you've been regarding me up until now. My knowing the date of Camilla's death, that's changed things between us, hasn't it?"

"Yes." He would have liked to tell her that things between them had changed a great deal more than she thought, changed enough to send her running for cover back to Rainbow's End, Jim and Mamma. She would run, of course. But how soon and how fast? He glanced at his hands gripping the steering wheel. In the dim lights of the dashboard they looked very brown. *She would run very soon*, he thought, *and very fast. Even if she weren't married*. The fact dug painfully into his mind as though in her flight she wore the spiked shoes of a sprinter.

She was talking about Camilla again, the dead man who was more important to her than he ever would be, in all his youth and energy. Alive, present, eager, he was no match for the dead stranger lying under the fig tree at the edge of the cliff. Pinata thought, *I am, here beside her, in time and space, but Camilla is part of her dreams.* He was beginning to hate the name. *Damn you, Camilla, stretcher, little bed...*

"I have this very strong feeling," she said, "of involvement, even of guilt."

"Guilt feelings are often transferred to quite unrelated things or people. Yours may have nothing to do with Camilla."

"I think they have, though." She sounded perversely obstinate, as if she wanted to believe the worst about herself. "It's an odd coincidence that both the names are Mexican, first the girl's, Juanita Garcia, and now Camilla's. I hardly know, in fact I don't know, any Mexicans at all except casually through my work at the Clinic. It's not that I'm prejudiced like my mother; I simply never get to meet any."

"Your never getting to meet any means your prejudice or lack of it hasn't been tested. Perhaps your mother's has, and at least she's playing it straight by admitting it."

"And I'm not playing things straight?"

"I didn't say that."

"The implication was clear. Perhaps you think I found out the date of Camilla's death before this afternoon? Or that I knew the man himself?"

"Both have occurred to me."

"It's easier, of course, to distrust me than to believe the impossible. Camilla is a stranger to me," she repeated. "What motive would I have in lying to you?"

"I don't know." He had tried, and failed, to think of a reason why she should lie to him. He meant nothing to her; she was not interested in his approval or disapproval; she was not trying to influence, entice, convince, or impress him. He was no more to her than a wall you bounce balls off. Why bother lying to a wall?

"It's too bad," she said, "that you met my father before you met me. You were prepared to be suspicious of me before you even saw me, speaking of prejudice. My father and I aren't in the least alike, although Mother likes to tell me we are when she's angry. She even claims I look like him. Do I?"

"There's no physical resemblance."

"There's no resemblance in any other way either, not even in the good things. And there are a lot of good things about him, but I guess they didn't show up the day you met him."

109

"Some of them did. I never judge anyone by his parents, anyway. I can't afford to."

She turned and looked at him as if she expected him to elaborate on the subject. He said nothing more. The less she knew about him, the better. Walls weren't supposed to have family histories; walls were for protection, privacy, decoration, for hiding behind, jumping over, playing games. *Bounce some more balls at me, Daisy baby.*

"Camilla," she said. "You'll find out more about him, of course."

"Such as?"

"How he died, and why, and if he had any family or friends."

"And then what?"

"Then we'll know."

"Suppose it turns out to be the kind of knowledge that won't do anybody any good?"

"We've got to take that chance," she said. "We couldn't possibly stop now. It's unthinkable."

"I find it quite thinkable."

"You're bluffing, Mr. Pinata. You don't want to quit now any more than I do. You're much too curious."

She was half right. He didn't want to quit now, but a surplus of curiosity wasn't the reason.

"It's 5:15," she said. "If you drive faster, we can get back to the *Monitor* before they close the library. Since Camilla committed suicide, there's sure to be a report of it, as well as his obituary."

"Aren't you expected at home about this time?"

"Yes."

"Then I think you'd better go there and leave the Camilla business to me."

"Will you call me as soon as you find out anything?"

"Wouldn't that be a little foolish under the circumstances?" Pinata said. "You'd have some fancy explaining to do to your

110

husband and your mother. Unless, of course, you've decided to come clean with them."

"I'll call you at your office tomorrow morning at the same time as this morning."

"Still playing secrets, eh?"

"I'm playing," she said distinctly, "exactly the way I've been taught to play. Your system of all cards face up on the table wouldn't work in my house, Mr. Pinata."

It didn't work in mine either, he thought. *Monica got herself a new partner.*

When he returned to the third floor of the *Monitor-Press* building, the girl in charge of the library was about to lock up for the day.

She jangled her keys at him unplayfully. "We're closing."

"You're ahead of yourself by four minutes."

"I can use four minutes."

"So can I. Let me see that microfilm again, will you?"

"This is just another example," she said bitterly, "of what it's like working on a newspaper. Everything's got to be done at the last minute. There's just one crisis after another."

She kept on grumbling as she took the microfilm out of the file and put it in the projection machine. But it was a mild kind of grumbling, not directed at Pinata or even the newspaper. It was a general indictment of life for not being planned and predictable. "I like things to be *orderly*," she said, switching on the light. "And they never are."

Camilla had made the front page of the December 3rd edition. The story was headlined suicide leaves bizarre farewell note and accompanied by a sketch of the head of a gaunt-faced man with deep-set eyes and high cheekbones. Although age lines scarred the man's face, long dark hair curling over the tips of his ears gave

111

him an incongruous look of innocence. According to the caption, the sketch had been made by *Monitor-Press* artist Gorham Smith, who'd been among the first at the scene. Smith's byline was also on the story:

The body of the suicide victim found yesterday near the railroad jungle by a police patrolman has been identified as that of Carlos Theodore Camilla, believed to be a transient. No wallet or personal papers were found on the body, but further search of his clothing revealed an envelope containing a penciled note and the sum of $2,000 in large bills. Local authorities were surprised by the amount of money and by the nature of the note, which read as follows: "This ought to pay my way into heaven, you stinking rats. Carlos Theodore Camilla. Born, too soon, 1907. Died, too late, 1955."

The note was printed on Hotel Parker stationery, but the management of the hotel has no record of Camilla staying there. A check of other hotels and motor lodges in the area failed to uncover the suicide victim's place of residence. Police theorize that he was a transient who hitchhiked or rode the roads into the city after committing a holdup in some other part of the state. This would explain how Camilla, who appeared destitute and in an advanced stage of malnutrition, was carrying so much money. Inquiries have been sent to police headquarters and sheriffs' offices throughout the state in an effort to find the source of the $2,000. Burial services will be postponed until it is established that the money is not the proceeds of a robbery but belongs legally to the dead man. Meanwhile, Camilla's body is under the care of Roy Fondero, funeral director.

According to Sheriff-Coroner Robert Lerner, Camilla died of a self-inflicted knife wound late Thursday night or early Friday morning. The type of knife was identified by authorities as a *navaja*, often carried by Mexicans and Indians of the Southwest. The initials C.C.

112

were carved on the handle. A dozen cigarette butts found at the scene of the tragedy indicate that Camilla spent considerable time debating whether to go through with the act or not. An empty wine bottle was also found nearby, but a blood test indicated that Camilla had not been drinking.

The residents of so-called Jungleland, the collection of shacks between the railway tracks and Highway 101, denied knowing anything about the dead man. Camilla's fingerprints are being sent to Washington to determine whether he had a criminal record or is registered with immigration authorities. An effort is being made to locate the dead man's place of residence, family, and friends. If no one claims the body and if the money is found to be legally his, Camilla will be buried in a local cemetery. The Coroner's inquest, scheduled for tomorrow morning, is expected to be brief.

It was brief. As reported in the December 5th edition, Camilla was found to have died of a knife wound, self-inflicted while in a state of despondency. Witnesses were few: the police patrolman who discovered him, a doctor who described the fatal wound, and a pathologist who stated that Camilla had been suffering from prolonged malnutrition and a number of serious physical disorders. The time of death was fixed at approximately 1:00 a.m. on December 2.

Probably, Pinata thought, *Daisy had read all this in the newspaper at the time it happened.* The pathos of the case must have struck her—a sick, starving man, fearful ("This ought to pay my way into heaven"), rebellious ("You stinking rats"), despairing ("Born too soon. Died too late"), had sent his final message to the world and committed his final act.

Pinata wondered whether the stinking rats referred to specific people, or whether the phrase, like the grumbling of the girl in charge of the library, was an indictment of life itself.

113

The girl was jangling her keys again. Pinata switched off the projector, thanked her, and left.

He drove back to his office, thinking of the money Camilla had left in the envelope. Obviously the police hadn't been able to prove it had come from a robbery, or Camilla wouldn't be lying now under his stone cross. The big question was why a destitute transient would want to spend $2,000 on his own funeral instead of on the food and clothing he needed. Cases of people dying of malnutrition with a fortune hidden in a mattress or under some floorboards were not common, but they happened every now and then. Had Camilla been one of these, a psychotic miser? It seemed improbable. The money in the envelope had been in large bills. The collection of misers was usually a hodgepodge of dimes, nickels, dollars, hoarded throughout the years. Furthermore, misers didn't travel. They stayed in one place, often in one room, to protect their hoard. Camilla had traveled, but from where and for what reason? Had he picked this town because it was a pretty place to die in? Or did he come here to see someone, find someone? If so, was it Daisy? But the only connection Daisy had with Camilla was in a dream, four years later.

His office was cold and dark, and although he turned on the gas heater and all the lights, the place still seemed cheerless and without warmth, as if Camilla's ghost was trapped inside the walls, emanating an eternal chill.

Camilla had come back, quietly, insidiously, through a dream. He had changed his mind—the sea was too noisy, the roots of the big tree too threatening, the little bed too dark and narrow—he was demanding reentry into the world, and he had chosen Daisy to help him. The destitute transient, whose body no one had claimed, was staking out a claim for himself in Daisy's mind.

I'm getting as screwy as she is, he thought. *I've got to keep this on a straightforward, factual basis. Daisy saw the report in the newspaper. It was painful to her, and she repressed it. For almost four years it was forgotten. Then some incident or emotion triggered her memory, and Camilla popped up in a dream, a pathetic creature whom she identified, for unknown reasons, with herself.*

That's all it amounted to. No mysticism was involved; it was merely a case of the complexities of memory.

"It's quite simple," he said aloud, and the sound of his own voice was comforting in the chilly room. It had been a long time since he'd actually listened to himself speak, and his voice seemed oddly pleasant and deep, like that of a wise old man. He wished he could think of some wise old remarks to match it, but none occurred to him. His mind seemed to have shrunk so that there was no room in it for anything except Daisy and the dead stranger of her dreams.

A drop of sweat slid down behind his left ear into his collar. He got up and opened the window and looked down at the busy street. Few whites ventured out on Opal Street after dark. This was his part of the city, his and Camilla's, and it had nothing to do with Daisy's part. Grease Alley, some of the cops called it, and when he was feeling calm and secure, he didn't blame them. Many of the knives used in brawls were greased. Maybe Camilla's had been, too.

"Welcome back to Grease Alley, Camilla," he said aloud, but his voice didn't sound like a wise old man's anymore. It was young and bitter and furious. It was the voice of the child in the orphanage, fighting for his name, Jesus.

"All those bruises and black eyes and chipped teeth," the Mother Superior had said. "You hardly looked human, half the time."

He closed the window and stared at his reflection in the dusty glass. There were no chipped teeth or bruises or black eyes visible, but he hardly looked human.

"Of course, it's a very difficult name to live up to…"

THE CITY

10

But there was love, Daisy. You are proof there was love…

Through all of Fielding's travels only one object had remained with him constantly, a grimy, pockmarked, rawhide suitcase. It was so old now that the clasps no longer fastened, and it was held together by a dog's chain leash which he'd bought in a dime store in Kansas City. The few mementos of his life that Fielding had chosen to keep were packed inside this suitcase, and when he was feeling nostalgic or guilty or merely lonesome, he liked to bring them out and examine them, like a bankrupt shopkeeper taking stock of whatever he had left.

These mementos, although few in number, had such a strong content of emotion that the memories they evoked seemed to become more vivid with the passing of the years. The plastic cane from the circus at Madison Square Garden took him back to the big top so completely that he could recall every clown and juggler, every bulging-thighed aerialist and tired old elephant.

The suitcase contained, in addition to the cane:

A green derby from a St. Patrick's Day party in Newark. (Oh, what a beautiful binge that had been!)

Two pieces of petrified wood from Arizona.

A silver locket. (Poor Agnes.)

A ukulele, which Fielding couldn't play but liked to hold expertly in his hands while he hummed "Harvest Moon" or "Springtime in the Rockies."

A little box made of sweet grass and porcupine quills by an Indian in northern Ontario.

A beribboned cluster of small gilded pine cones that had been attached to a Christmas present from Daisy: a wristwatch, later hocked in Chicago.

Several newspaper clippings about exotic ports on the other side of the world.

A package of letters, most of them from Daisy; the money orders which had been enclosed were long since cashed.

A pen which didn't write, made of gold which wasn't real.

Two train schedules.

A splinter of wood—allegedly from the battleship *West Virginia* after it was bombed at Pearl Harbor—which he'd got from a sailor in Brooklyn in exchange for a bottle of muscatel.

There were also about a dozen pictures: Daisy holding her high school diploma; Daisy and Jim on their honeymoon; a framed photograph of two identical middle-aged matrons who ran a boardinghouse in Dallas and had inscribed across the picture "To Stan Fielding, hoping he won't forget 'the Heavenly Twins'"; an enlarged snapshot of a coal miner from Pennsylvania, who looked exactly like Abraham Lincoln and whose chief sorrow in life was that Lincoln was dead and no advantage could be taken of the resemblance. ("Think of it, Stan, all the fun we could have had, me being Abraham Lincoln, and you being my Secretary of State, and everybody bowing and scraping in front of us and buying us drinks. Oh, it just makes me sick thinking of all them free drinks we missed!")

Another picture, mounted on cardboard, showed Ada and Fielding himself and a ranch hand he'd worked with near Albuquerque, a handsome dark-eyed young man called Curly. On spring days, when dust storms obscured the range and made work impossible, the three of them used to play pinochle together. Ada had been a good sport in those early times, full of fun and life, ready for anything. Having a child had changed her. It was a year of drought. During the months of Ada's pregnancy more tears had come from her eyes than rain from the skies.

He brought the suitcase out now and began unpacking its contents on the big round table under the green-shaded ceiling light.

Muriel came in from the kitchen, the only other room in the apartment. She was a short, stout middle-aged woman with a hard mouth and eyes soft and round and pale green, like little mint patties with a licorice drop in the middle. She snorted at the sight of the open suitcase. "What do you want to go dragging out that old thing again for?"

"Memories, my dear. Memories."

"Well, I've got a few memories myself, but I don't go spreading them out in the middle of a table every couple of weeks." She leaned over his shoulder to get a closer look at the picture taken at the ranch. "You look like you were a real lively bunch."

"We were, thirty years ago."

"Oh go on, you haven't changed so much."

"Not as much as Curly anyway," he said grimly. "I looked him up last time I went through Albuquerque, and I hardly recognized him. He was an old man already, and his hands were so crippled by arthritis he couldn't even play pinochle anymore, let alone work cattle. We talked about old times for a while, and he said he'd drop in on me next time he came to Chicago. But we both knew he'd never make it."

"Well, don't *dwell* on it," Muriel said brusquely. "That's the trouble with your poking around in the past like this—you get to dwelling on things. You mark my words, Stan Fielding. That old suitcase of yours is your worst enemy in this world. And if you were smart, you'd take it right down to the pier and chuck it in the briny with a farewell and amen."

"I don't claim to be smart. I'm thirsty, though. Bring me out a beer like a good wife, will you? It's a hot day."

"You're not going to make it any cooler by lapping up beer," she said. But she went out to the kitchen anyway, because she liked his reference to her being a good wife. They'd only been married for a month, and while she wasn't passionately in love with him, he had many qualities she admired. He was kinder, in or out of his cups, than any man she'd ever known; he had a sense of humor and good manners and a fine head of hair and all his teeth. Above all, though, she appreciated his gift of gab. No matter what anyone said, really educated people with brains, Stan could always top them. Muriel was proud to be the wife of a man who had an answer for everything even though it might be, and often was, wrong. Being wrong, in a classy way, was to Muriel every bit as good as being right.

His easy manner of conversation had encouraged Muriel and emboldened her. From the taciturn and rather timid woman he'd met in Dallas she had developed into quite a loud and lively talker. She knew she had nothing to fear from him no matter what she said. He took all spoken words, including his own, with a grain of salt and a shrug. To written words his attitude was different. He believed absolutely everything he read, even flat contradictions, and when he received a letter, he treated it as if it were a message from a king, delivered via diplomatic pouch and much too special to be opened immediately. He always spent at least five minutes turning it over, examining it, holding it up to the light, before he finally slit the envelope.

When Muriel returned with his beer, she found him hunched over one of the letters, looking tense and anxious, as if this were the first time he'd read it instead of the fiftieth.

Most of the letters from Daisy he had read aloud to her, and she couldn't understand his excitement over such dull stuff: The weather was warm. Or cold. The roses were out. Or in. Went to the dentist, the park, the beach, the museum, the movies... Probably a nice girl, this Daisy of his, Muriel thought, but not very interesting.

"Stan."

"Eh?"

"Here's your beer."

"Thanks," he said, but he didn't reach for it immediately, as he usually did, and she knew this letter must be one of the bad ones he didn't read aloud or talk about.

"Stan, you won't get the blues, will you? I hate when you get the blues. It's lonesome for me. Bottoms up, eh?"

"In a minute."

"Hey, I know. Why don't you show me the picture of the guy that looked like Abraham Lincoln? He must have been a real card, that one. Tell me about him, Stan, about how you would have been Secretary of State, wearing a top hat and a cutaway—"

"You've heard it before."

"Tell me again. I'd like a good laugh. It's so hot in here I'd like a good laugh."

"So would I."

"What's stopping us, then? We've got a lot to laugh about."

"Sure. I know."

"Don't get the blues, Stan."

"Don't worry." He put the letter back in the envelope, wishing that he hadn't reread it. It had been written a long time ago, and there was nothing he could do now to change things. There was nothing he could have done then either. What bothered him was that he hadn't tried, hadn't phoned her, written to her, gone to see her.

"Come on, Stan. Bottoms up and mud in your eye, eh?"

"Sure." He drank the beer. It had a musky odor, as if it had been chilled and warmed too many times. He wondered if he had the same odor for the same reason. "You're a good woman, Muriel."

"Oh, can that now," she said with an embarrassed and pleased little laugh. "You're not so bad yourself."

"No? Don't bet on it."

"I think you're swell. I did right from that first night I saw you."

"Then you're dead wrong. Stone cold dead wrong."

"Oh, Stan, don't."

"There comes a time when every man must evaluate his own life."

"Why pick a time like this, a nice sunny Saturday morning when we could hop on a bus and go out to the zoo? Why don't we do that, eh, go out to the zoo?"

"No," he said heavily. "Let the monkeys come and look at me if they want a good laugh."

The fear in her eyes was turning into bitterness, and her mouth looked as though it had been tightened by a pair of pliers. "So you got the blues, you got them after all."

He didn't seem to hear. "I let her down. I always let her down. Even last Monday I walked out on her. I shouldn't have walked out on her like that without an apology or an explanation. I'm a coward, a bum. That's what Pinata called me, a bum."

"You told me that before. You told me all about it. Now why don't you forget it? If you ask me, he had his nerve. He may be a bigger bum than you are for all you know."

"So now you're calling me a bum, too."

"No, honest, I didn't mean it like the way it sounded. I only—"

"You should have meant it. It's true."

She reached down suddenly and pounded her fist on the table. "Why don't you keep that damned suitcase locked up the way it ought to be?"

He looked at her with a kind of sorrowful affection. "You really shouldn't scream like that, Muriel."

"And why not? I've got things to scream about, why shouldn't I scream?"

"Because it doesn't become a lady. 'The Devil hath not, in all his quiver's choice, an arrow for the heart like a sweet voice.' Remember that."

"You've got an answer for everything, haven't you, even if you got to pinch it from the Bible."

"Lord Byron, not the Bible."

"Stan, put the suitcase away, will you?" She picked up the chain leash from the floor and held it out to him. "Let's lock everything up and put the suitcase under the bed again and pretend you never opened it, how about that? I'll help you."

"No. I can do it myself."

"Do it, then. *Do* it."

"All right." He began replacing everything in the battered suitcase, the photographs and letters and clippings, the petrified wood and circus cane and box made of porcupine quills. "I'm fifty-three," he said abruptly.

"Well, I know. I must say you don't look it, though. You've got a fine head of hair. I bet there's many a man not forty yet who envies—"

"Fifty-three. And this is all I have to show for all those years. Not much, is it?"

"As much as most."

"No, Muriel, don't try to be kind. I've had too much kindness given to me in my life, too many allowances and excuses made for me. I don't deserve a good girl like Daisy. And then to think I walked out on her, didn't even stay to say hello or to see how she looked after all these years. She used to be such a pretty little girl with those big innocent blue eyes and a smile so shy and sweet—"

"I know," Muriel said shortly. "You told me. Now, have you got everything back in here? I'll close it up for you."

"Any decent father stays with his children even if he doesn't get along very well with his wife. Children, they're our only hope of immortality."

"Well, I'm fixed then. I've got two hopes of immortality chasing cows back in Texas."

"When my time comes, I won't completely die, because part of me will keep on living in Daisy." He wiped a little moisture from his eyes because it was so sad thinking of his own death, far sadder than thinking of anyone else's.

"If you're such a bum," Muriel said, "how come you want part of you to stay alive in Daisy?"

"Ah, you wouldn't understand, Muriel. You're not a man."

"Well, I'm glad you've noticed it. How about you notice it a little more often?"

Fielding winced. Muriel was a well-meaning woman, but her earthiness could be embarrassing, even destructive at times. When he was on a delicate train of thought, such as this one, it was a great shock to find himself suddenly derailed by the sound waves of Muriel's powerful voice.

To cushion the shock, he opened another bottle of beer while Muriel pushed the suitcase back under the bed.

"There," she said with satisfaction, and made a gesture of wiping her hands, like a doctor who has just stitched up an especially bad wound. "Out of sight, out of mind."

"Things are not that simple."

"They're not as complicated as you make out, Stan Fielding. If they were, we might as well all go jump in the ocean. Say, how about that? Why don't we go down to the beach and sit in the sand and watch the people? That always gives you a laugh, Stan, watching people."

"Not today. I don't feel like it."

"You just going to stay here and brood?"

"A little brooding may be exactly what I need. Maybe I haven't brooded enough in my lifetime. Whenever I became depressed, I simply packed up and moved on. I ran away, just as I ran away from Daisy. I shouldn't have done that, Muriel. I shouldn't have done it."

"Stop crying over spilled milk," she said harshly. "Every drunk I've ever known, that's their trouble. Bawling over things they done and then having to get tanked up to forget they done them and then going ahead and doing them all over again."

"Well," he said, blinking, "you're quite a psychologist, Muriel. That's an interesting theory."

"Nobody needs a fancy degree to figure it, just eyes and ears like I've got. And like you've got, too, if you'd use them." She came over to him, rather shyly, and put her hands on his shoulders. "Come on, Stan. Let's go to the beach and watch the people. How about trying to find that place where everybody's building up their muscles? We could take a bus."

"No, Muriel. I'm sorry. I have other things to do."

"Like what?"

"I'm going back to San Félice to see Daisy."

She didn't speak for a minute. She just backed away from him and sat down on the bed, looking bewildered. "What do you want to do that for, Stan?"

"I have my reasons."

"Why don't you take me along? I could see you didn't get into any trouble like you did last time over that waitress."

When he returned to Los Angeles on Monday night, he'd told her all about his encounter with Nita and Nita's husband in the bar. To diminish the importance of the incident, in his own mind and hers, he'd made quite a funny story of it, and they'd both had a good laugh. But Muriel's laughter hadn't been too genuine: suppose the girl's husband had been bigger and meaner? Suppose, and it often happened this way, that the girl Nita had suddenly decided to take her husband's side against Stan? Suppose no one had called the police? Suppose... "Stan," she said, "take me along to look out for you."

"No."

"Oh, I wouldn't ask you to introduce me to Daisy, if that's what you're thinking. I wouldn't dream of asking such a thing, her being so high class and everything. I could keep out of sight, Stan. I just want to be there to look out for you, see?"

"We haven't the money for bus fare."

"I could borrow some. The old lady in the apartment across the hall—I know she's got some hidden away. And she likes me, Stan; she says I look exactly like her younger sister that got put away last year. I don't think she'd mind lending me a little money on account of the resemblance, just enough for bus fare. How about it, Stan?"

"No. Stay away from the old lady. She's poison."

"All right, then, maybe we could hitchhike?"

He gathered from her hesitance and tone that she had never done any hitchhiking, and the thought of it scared her almost as much as the thought of his going to San Félice without her and getting into trouble. "No, Muriel, hitchhiking isn't for ladies."

She looked at him suspiciously. "You just don't want me along, that's it. You're afraid I might interfere if you decided to pick up some cheap waitress in a—"

"I didn't pick up anyone." Fielding's tone was all the sharper and more positive because he was lying. He'd gone deliberately into the café with the idea of finding the girl, but no one suspected this (except Muriel, who suspected everything), least of all the girl herself. Nothing had worked out as he planned, because the husband had walked in before he had a chance to ask her any questions or even to find out for sure if it was the right girl. "I was trying to protect a young woman who was being assaulted."

"How come you can protect everyone but yourself? The whole damn world you can protect, except Stan Fielding, who needs it worse than—"

"Now, Muriel, don't go on." He went over to the bed and sat down beside her. "Put your head on my shoulder, that's my girl. Now listen. I have a certain matter to take care of in San Félice. I won't be away long, no later than tomorrow night if things go well."

"What things? And why shouldn't they?"

"Daisy and Jim might be away for the weekend or something like that. In that case I won't be back until Monday night. But don't worry about me. In spite of your low opinion of my powers of self-protection, I can take care of myself."

"Sure you can. When you're sober."

"I intend to stay sober." No matter how many hundreds of times he had said this in his life, he still managed to put so much conviction into it that he believed himself. "This time, not one drink. Unless, of course, it would look conspicuous if I refused, and then I would take one—I repeat, one—and nurse it along."

She pressed her head hard against his shoulder as if she were trying to imprint on him by sheer force an image of herself which would go along with him on the trip, as her substitute, to protect him while he was protecting everyone else.

"Stan."

"Yes, my love."

"Don't get tanked up."

"I said I wouldn't, didn't I? No drinks, except maybe one to avoid looking conspicuous."

"Like for instance?"

"Suppose Daisy invites me to the house and opens a bottle of champagne to celebrate."

"Celebrate what?" With her head against his shoulder she couldn't see the sudden grimness of his face. "What's there to celebrate, Stan?"

"Nothing," he said. "Nothing."

"Then why should she open the bottle of champagne?"

"She won't."

"Then why did you say—"

"Please be quiet, Muriel."

"But—"

"There'll be no celebration, no champagne. I was just dreaming for a minute, see? People dream, even people like me, who should know better."

"There's no harm in a little dreaming now and then," Muriel said softly, stroking the back of his neck. "Say, you need a haircut, Stan. Could we spare the money for a haircut?"

"No."

"Well, wait right there while I go get my sewing scissors. Out on the ranch I always cut my kids' hair, there being nobody else to do it." She stood up, smoothing her dress down over her hips. "There was never any complaints either, once I got a little practiced."

"No, Muriel. Please—"

"It'll only take a minute. You want to look presentable, don't you, if you're going to that fancy house of hers? Remember that letter she wrote telling you her change of address? She described

130

the whole house. It sounded just like a palace. You wouldn't want to go to a place like that needing a haircut, would you?"

"I don't care."

"You're always saying you don't care when you do." Muriel went out to the kitchen and returned with the sewing scissors. She said as she began trimming his hair, "You might meet up with your ex, think of that."

"Why should I?"

"There's nothing worse than meeting up with your ex when you're not looking your best. Hold your chin down a little."

"I don't intend to see my former wife."

"You might see her by accident on the street."

"Then I'd look the other way and cross the street."

She had been waiting and wanting to hear this. She exhaled suddenly and noisily, as if she'd been holding her breath until she was reassured. "You'd *really* look the other way?"

"Yes."

"Tell me about her, Stan. Is she pretty?"

"I'd prefer not to discuss it."

"You never ever talk about her—move your head a bit to the right—the way other men talk about their exes. What harm would it do if you told me a little about her, like is she pretty?"

"What good would it do?"

"Then at least I'd know. Chin down."

Chin down, he stared at his belt buckle. "And would you *like* to know she's pretty?"

"Well, no. I mean, it would be nicer if she wasn't."

"She's not," Fielding said. "Does that satisfy you?"

"No."

"All right, she's ugly as sin. Fat, pimply, cross-eyed, bow-legged, pigeon-toed—"

"Now you're kidding me, Stan."

"I'd be kidding you even more," he said soberly, "if I told you she looked pretty to me."

"She must have once, or you wouldn't have married her."

"I was seventeen. All the girls looked good in those days." It wasn't true. He couldn't even remember any of the other girls, only Ada, delicate and pink and fluffy like a cloud at sunset. He had intended, in his youth and strength, to spend the rest of his life looking after her; instead, she had spent hers doing it for him. He didn't know, even now, at what point or for what reason their roles had been reversed.

"Some of them still look good to you." Muriel put down the sewing scissors. "You know what I bet? I bet that waitress of yours is nothing but a chippy."

"She's a married woman with six children."

"A husband and six kids don't make you an angel."

"Stop worrying, will you, Muriel? I'm not going up to San Félice to get involved with a waitress or my ex-wife. I'm going up solely to see Daisy."

"You had a chance to see her last Monday," Muriel said anxiously. "Why don't you just phone her long distance or write her a letter? Then you could go and see her some other time, when you're sure she's at home."

"I want to see her now, today."

"Why so all of a sudden?"

"I have reasons."

"Does it have something to do with Daisy's old letters you were reading?"

"Not a thing." He hadn't told her about the new letter, the one that had been sent special delivery to the warehouse where he worked and which was now hidden in his wallet, folded and

132

refolded to the size of a postage stamp. This last letter wasn't like the others he kept in the suitcase. It contained no money, no news, no polite inquiries about his health or statements about her own: *Dear Father: I would be very much obliged if you'd let me know at once whether the name Carlos Theodore Camilla means anything to you. Please call collect, Robles 24663. Love, Daisy.* Fielding would have liked to pretend that the brief, brusque, almost unfriendly note had never reached him, but he realized he couldn't. He'd signed for it at the warehouse, and there would be a record of the signature at the post office. How had she got hold of the name and address of the warehouse? From Pinata, obviously, although Fielding couldn't remember telling Pinata about his job—he'd been feeling bad that day, fuzzy around the edges, not sure where one thing ended and another began. Or maybe Pinata had found out in some other way; he was a detective as well as a bail bondsman. A detective...

God Almighty, he thought suddenly. *Maybe she's hired him. But why? And what did it have to do with Camilla?*

"You look awful flushed, Stan, like maybe you've got a fever coming on."

"Stop making a pest of yourself, will you? I have to get ready."

While he washed and shaved in the bathroom they shared with the old lady across the hall, Muriel laid out fresh underwear for him and a clean shirt and the new blue-striped tie Pinata had lent him earlier in the week. He had told Muriel he bought the tie after seeing it in a store window, and she had believed him because it seemed too slight a thing to lie about. She hadn't known him long enough yet to realize that this secrecy about very trivial matters was as much a part of his nature as his devastating frankness about some of the important and serious ones. There had been no real need, for instance, for him to have recounted the details of the

133

episode involving Nita and her husband and the jail and Pinata. Yet he had told her all about it, leaving out only the small detail of the tie he'd borrowed from Pinata.

When he returned from the bathroom and saw that this tie was the one she'd picked out for him to wear, he put it back in the bureau drawer.

"I like that one," Muriel protested. "It goes with your eyes."

"It's a little too gaudy. When you're hitchhiking, it pays to look as conservative as possible, like a gentleman whose Cadillac has just had a flat tire and he can't find a telephone."

"Like that, eh?"

"Yes."

"What are you going to use for a Cadillac?"

"My imagination, love. When I'm standing out there on the freeway, I'm going to imagine that Cadillac so hard that other people will see it."

"Why don't you start right now so's I can see it, too?"

"I *have* started." He went over to the window and pulled back the grimy pink net curtain. "There. What do you see?"

"Cars. About a million cars."

"One of them's my Cadillac." Letting the curtain drop into place, he drew himself up to his full height and adjusted an imaginary monocle to his eye. "I beg your pardon, madam, but I wonder if you would be so kind as to direct me to the nearest petrol parlor?"

She began to laugh, a girlish, giggly sound. "Oh Stan, honestly. You're a scream. You ought to be an actor."

"I hesitate to contradict you, madam, but I *am* an actor. Permit me to introduce myself. My name—ah, but I quite forgot I am traveling incognito. I must not identify myself for fear of the terrifying adulation of my millions of fanatic admirers."

"Gee, you could fool anybody, Stan. You talk just like a gentle-man."

He stared down at her, suddenly sober. "Thanks."

"Why, I could see that Cadillac as plain as could be for a minute there. Red and black, with real leather upholstery and your initials on the door." She touched his arm. It had gone stiff as a board. "Stan?"

"Yeah."

"What the heck, we wouldn't know what to do with a Cadillac if we had one. We'd have to pay the license and insurance and gas and oil, and then we'd have to find a place to park it—well, it just wouldn't be worth the trouble, as far as I'm concerned, and I'm not just shooting the breeze either. I mean it."

"Sure. Sure you do, Muriel." He was touched by her loyalty, but at the same time it nagged at him; it reminded him that he didn't deserve it and that he would have to try harder to deserve it in the future. *The future,* he thought. When he was younger, the future always seemed to him like a bright and beribboned box full of gifts. Now it loomed in front of him, dark gray and impenetrable, like a leaden wall.

He picked out a tie from the bureau drawer, dark gray to match the wall.

"Stan? Take me with you?"

"No, Muriel. I'm sorry."

"Will you be back in time to go to your job Monday night?"

"I'll be back." He'd had the job, as night watchman for an electrical appliance warehouse on Figueroa Street, for only a week. The work was dull and lonely, but he made it more interest-ing for himself by imagining the place was going to be robbed any night now and visualizing how he would foil the robbers, with a flying tackle or a rabbit punch from behind, or a short, powerful left hook, or simply by outwitting them in a very clever way which he hadn't figured out yet. Having outthought, or out-fought, the robbers, he would go on to receive his reward from the president of the appliance firm. The rewards varied from money or some shares in the company to a large bronze plaque inscribed with his name and a description of his deed of valor: "To Stanley Elliott Fielding, Who, Above and Beyond the Call of Duty, Did Resist the Onslaught of Seven Masked and Desperate Criminals…"

It was all fantasy, and he knew it. But it helped to pass the time and ease the tension he felt whenever he was alone.

Muriel helped him on with his jacket. "There. You look real nice, Stan. Nobody'd ever take you for a night watchman."

"Thank you."

"Where will you stay when you get there, Stan?"

"I haven't decided."

"I should know how to get in touch with you in case something comes up about your job. I suppose I could call Daisy's house if it was real important."

"No, don't," he said quickly. "I may not even be going to Daisy's house."

"But you said before you—"

"Listen. Remember the young man I told you about who paid my fine? Steve Pinata. His office is on East Opal Street. If anything urgent should come up, leave a message for me with Pinata."

She went with him to the door, clinging to his arm. "Remember what you promised, Stan, about laying off the liquor and behaving yourself in general."

"Of course."

"I wish I was going along."

"Next time."

He kissed her good-bye before he opened the door because of Miss Wittenburg, the old lady who lived across the hall. Miss Wittenburg kept the door of her apartment wide open all day and sat just inside it, with her spectacles on and a newspaper across her knee. Sometimes she read the paper in silence; at other times she became quite voluble, addressing her comments to her younger sister, who'd been gone for a year.

"There they are now, Rosemary," Miss Wittenburg said in her strong New England accent. "He appears to be groomed for the street. Good riddance, I say. I'm glad you agree. Did you notice the deplorable condition in which he left the bathroom again? All that wetness. Wet, wet, wet everywhere... I am surprised at you, Rosemary, making such a vulgar remark. Father would turn over in his grave to hear such a thing fall from your lips."

"Go inside and lock the door," Fielding said to Muriel. "And keep it locked."

"All right."

"And don't worry about me. I'll be home tomorrow night, or Monday at the latest."

"Whispering," said Miss Wittenburg, "is a mark of poor breeding."

"Stan, please take care of yourself, won't you?"

"I will. I promise."

"Do you love me?"

"You know I do, Muriel."

"Whispering," Miss Wittenburg repeated, "is not only a mark of poor breeding, but I have it on very good authority that it is going to be declared illegal in all states west of the Mississippi. The penalties, I understand, will be very severe."

Fielding raised his voice. "Good-bye, Rosemary. Good-bye, Miss Wittenburg."

"Pay no attention, Rosemary. What effrontery the man has, addressing you by your first name. Next thing he'll be trying to—oh, it makes me shudder even to think of it." She, too, raised her voice. "Good manners compel me to respond to your greeting, Mr. Whisper, but I do so with grave misgivings. Good-bye."

"Oh Lord," Fielding said, and began to laugh. Muriel laughed with him, while Miss Wittenburg described to Rosemary certain legislation which was about to go into effect in seventeen states prohibiting laughter, mockery, and fornication.

"Keep your door locked, Muriel."

"She's just a harmless old lady."

"There's no such thing as a harmless old lady."

"Wait. Stan, you forgot your toothbrush."

"I'll pick one up in San Félice. Good-bye, love."

"Good-bye, Stan. And good luck."

After he'd gone, Muriel locked herself in the apartment and, standing by the window, cried quietly and efficiently for five minutes. Then, red-eyed but calm, she dragged out from under the bed Fielding's battered rawhide suitcase.

11

Memories are crowding in on me so hard and fast that I can barely breathe…

The Neighborhood Clinic was housed in an old adobe building off State Street near the middle of town. A great many of Pinata's clients had been in and out of its vast oak doors, and over the years Pinata had come to know the director, Charles Alston, quite well. Alston was neither a doctor nor a trained social worker. He was a retired insurance executive, a widower, who devoted most of his time and energy to the solution of other people's problems. To keep the clinic operating, he persuaded doctors and laymen to donate their services, fought city and county officials for funds, plagued the local newspaper for free publicity, addressed women's clubs and political rallies and church groups, and bearded the Lions in their den and the Rotarians and Knights of Columbus in theirs.

Whenever and wherever there was any group to be enlightened, Alston could be found doing the enlightening, shooting statistics at his audience with the speed of a machine gun. This rapid delivery was essential: it kept his listeners from examining the facts and figures too closely, an effect that Alston found highly desirable, since he frequently made up his own statistics. He had no qualms about doing this, believing that it was a legitimate part of his war on ignorance. "Did you know," he would cry out, pointing the finger of doom, "that one in seven of you good, unsuspecting, innocent people out there will spend some time in a mental institution?" If the audience appeared listless and unimpressionable, he changed this figure to one in five or even one in three. "Prevention is the answer. Prevention. We at the Clinic may not be able to solve everyone's problems. What we hope to do is to keep them small enough to be manageable."

At noon on Saturday, Alston put the closed sign on the oak doors and locked up for the weekend. It had been a strenuous but successful week. The Democratic League and the Veterans of Foreign Wars had contributed toward the new children's wing, the Plasterers and Cement Finishers Local 341 had volunteered their services, and the *Monitor-Press* was planning a series of articles on the Clinic and offering a prize for the best essay entitled "An Ounce of Prevention."

Alston had just shoved the steel bolt into place when someone began pounding on the door. This frequently happened when the Clinic was closed for the night or the weekend. It was one of Alston's dreams that someday he might have enough personnel and money to keep it open at all times, like a hospital, or at least on Sundays. Sunday was a bad day for the frightened.

"We're closed," Alston shouted through the door. "If you're desperately in need of help, call Dr. Mercado, 5-3698. Have you got that?"

Pinata didn't say anything. He just waited, knowing that Alston would open the door because he couldn't turn anyone away.

"Dr. Mercado, 5-3698, if you need help. Oh, what the hell," Alston said, and pushed open the door. "If you need—oh, it's you, Steve."

"Hello, Charley. Sorry to bother you like this."

"Looking for one of your clients?"

"I'd like some information."

140

"I charge by the hour," Alston said. "Or shall I say that I accept donations for the new children's wing? A check will do, providing it's good. Come in."

Pinata followed him into his office, a small, high-ceilinged room painted a garish pink. The pink had been Alston's idea; it was a cheerful color for people who saw too many of the blues and grays and blacks of life.

"Sit down," Alston said. "How's business?"

"If I told you it was good, you'd put the bite on me."

"The bite's on you. This is after hours. I get time and a half."

In spite of the lightness of his tone, Pinata knew he was quite serious. "All right, that suits me. Say ten dollars?"

"Fifteen would look prettier on the books."

"On yours, sure, but not mine."

"Very well, I won't argue. I would, however, like to point out that one person in every five will—"

"I heard that last week at the Kiwanis."

Alston's face brightened. "That was a rousing good meeting, eh? I hate to scare the lads like that, but if fear is what makes them bring out their wallets, fear is what I have to provide."

"Today," Pinata said, "I'm just scared ten dollars' worth."

"Maybe I'll do better next time. Believe me, I'll try."

"I believe you."

"All right, so what's your problem?"

"Juanita Garcia."

"Good Lord," Alston said with a heavy sigh. "Is she back in town?"

"I have reason to think so."

"You know her, eh?"

"Not personally."

"Well, consider yourself lucky. We don't use the word *incorrigible* around here, but I never got closer to using it than when we were trying to cope with Juanita. Now, there's a case where an ounce of prevention might have been worth a few pounds of cure. If she'd been brought to us when she first showed signs of disturbance as a child—well, we might have done some good and we might not. With Juanita it's difficult to say. When we finally saw her, by order of the Juvenile Court, she was sixteen, already divorced from one man and about eight months pregnant by another. Because of her condition, we had to handle her with kid gloves. I think that's where she got the idea."

"What idea?"

Alston shook his head in a mixture of sorrow and grudging admiration. "She worked out a simple but absolutely stunning device for hog-tying the whole bunch of us: the courts, the Probation Department, our staff. Whenever she got in trouble, she outwitted us all with classic simplicity."

"How?"

"By becoming pregnant. A delinquent girl is one thing; an expectant mother is quite different." Alston stirred in his chair and sighed again. "To tell you the truth, none of us knows for sure if Juanita actually figured out this device in a conscious way. One of our psychologists believes that she used pregnancy as a means of making herself feel important. I'm not positive about that, though. The girl—woman, rather, she must be twenty-six or twenty-seven by this time—isn't stupid by any means. She did quite well on several of her tests, especially those that required use of imagination rather than knowledge of facts. She could study an ordinary little drawing and describe it with such vivid imagination that you'd think she was looking at something by Van Gogh. The term *psychopathic personality* is no longer in vogue, but it certainly would have applied to Juanita."

"What does she look like?"

"Fairly pretty in a flashing-eyed, toothy sort of way. About her figure I couldn't say. I never saw her between pregnancies. The tragic part of it," Alston added, "is that she didn't really care about the kids. When they were small babies, she liked to cuddle them and play with them as if they were dolls, but as soon as they grew up a little, she lost interest. Three or four years ago she was arrested on a child-neglect charge, but once again she was in the throes of reproduction and got off on probation. After the birth of that particular child—her sixth, I think it was—she broke probation and left town. Nobody tried very hard to find her, I'm afraid. I wouldn't be surprised if my own staff chipped in to pay her traveling expenses. Juanita herself was enough of a problem. But multiply her by six—oh Lord, I hate to think about it. So now she's back in town."

"I believe so."

"Doing what? Or need I ask?"

"Working as a waitress in a bar," Pinata said. "If it's the same girl."

"Is she married?"

"Yes."

"Are the kids with her?"

"Some of them are, anyway. She got into a fight with her husband a few days ago. He claimed she was neglecting them."

"If you don't even know the girl," Alston said, "where did you pick up all your information?"

"A friend of mine happened to be in the bar when the fight started."

"And this is how you became interested in the prolific Juanita, through a friend of yours who happened to witness a fight?"

"You might say that."

"I might say it but it wouldn't be the truth, is that it?" Alston peered over the top of his spectacles. "Is the girl in trouble again?"

"Not that I know of."

"Then why exactly are you here?"

Pinata hesitated. He didn't want to tell the whole story, even to Alston, who'd heard some whoppers in his day. "I'd like you to check your files and tell me if Juanita Garcia came here on a certain date."

"What date?"

"Friday, December 2, 1955."

"That's a funny request," Alston said. "Care to give me a reason for it?"

"No."

"I assume you have a good reason."

"I'm not sure how good it is. I have one, though. It concerns a—client of mine. I'd like to keep her name out of it, but I can't, since I need some information about her, too. Her name's Mrs. James Harker."

"Harker, Harker, let me think a min—Daisy Harker?"

"Yes."

"What's a woman like Daisy Harker doing getting mixed up with a bail bondsman?"

"It's a long, implausible story," Pinata said with a smile. "And since it's Saturday afternoon and I'm paying you time and a half, I'd rather go into it on some other occasion."

"What do you want to know about Mrs. Harker?"

"The same thing: if she was working at the Clinic on that particular day. Also when, and why, she stopped coming here."

"The why part I can't tell you, because I don't know. It mystified me at the time and still does. She made some excuse about her mother being ill and needing attention, but I happen to know Mrs. Fielding from my connection with the Women's Club. The old girl's as healthy as a horse. Quite an attractive woman, if she could remember to keep her velvet gloves on… No, it wasn't Mrs. Fielding's illness, I'm sure of that. As for the work itself, I believe Mrs. Harker enjoyed it."

"Was she good at it?" Pinata asked.

"Excellent. Sweet-natured, understanding, dependable. Oh, she had a tendency to get overexcited at times and lose her head a bit in an emergency, but nothing serious. And the kids all loved her. She had a way, as childless women sometimes have, of making the kids feel very important and special, not just something that happened from an accidental meeting of a sperm and ovum. A fine young woman, Mrs. Harker. We were sorry to lose her. Have you known her long?"

"No."

"Next time you see her, give her my kind regards, will you? And tell her we'd like to have her back whenever she can come."

"I'll do that."

"In fact, if I could find out the circumstances that made her quit, I might be able to change them."

"The circumstances are entirely Daisy's, not the Clinic's."

"Well, I just thought I'd check," Alston said. "We have occasional disagreements and disgruntlements among the members of our staff just like any other business. It's surprising we don't have more when you consider that psychology is not an exact science and there are consequently differences of opinion on diagnosis and procedure. Procedure especially," he added with a frown. "Just what does one *do* with a girl like Juanita, for instance? Sterilize her? Keep her locked up? Enforce psychiatric treatment? We did our best, but the reason it didn't work was that Juanita herself wouldn't admit there was anything the matter with her. Like most incorrigibles, she'd managed to convince herself (and tried, of course, to convince us) that women were all the same

145

and that what made her different was the fact that she was honest and above board about her activities. Honest and above board, the favorite words of the self-deceiver. Take my advice, Steve. Whenever anyone insists too vigorously on his honesty, you run and check the till. And don't be too surprised if you find some-body's fingers in it."

"I don't believe in generalizations," Pinata said. "Especially that one."

"Why not?"

"Because it includes me. I make frequent claims to honesty. In fact, I'm making one now."

"Well, well. This puts me in the embarrassing position of either taking back the generalization or going to check the till. This is a serious decision. Let me meditate a moment." Alston leaned back in his chair and closed his eyes. "Very well. I take back the gen-eralization. I'm afraid it's easy to become a bit cynical in this job. So many promises made and broken, so many hopes dashed—it leaves you with a tendency to believe in the psychology of oppo-sites, that is, when a person comes in and tells me he is affable, honest, and simple, I tend to tag him as a complex and irritable cheat. This is an occupational hazard I must avoid. Thanks for pointing it out, Steve."

"I didn't point out anything," Pinata said, embarrassed. "I was merely defending myself."

"I insist upon thanking you."

"All right, all right, you're welcome. At time and a half I don't want to argue with you."

"Oh yes, time and a half. I must get on with the job. I address the Newcomers Club at two, a good, malleable group usually. I have considerable hopes for our treasury." He took a ring of keys from his desk drawer. "Please wait here. I can't ask you into the

146

file room. Not that our records are top secret, but many people like to believe they are. Want something to read while I'm gone?"

"No thanks. I'll just think."

"Got a lot to think about?"

"Enough."

"Daisy Harker," Alston said casually, "is a very pretty and, I believe, an unhappy young woman. That's a bad combination."

"What's it got to do with me?"

"Not a thing, I hope."

"Save your hopes for the treasury," Pinata said. "My relationship with Mrs. Harker is strictly professional. She hired me to get some information about a certain day in her life."

"And Juanita was part of this day?"

"Possibly." Possibly Camilla was, too, though so far there was no indication of it. When Daisy called his office the previous morning, as scheduled, and learned the details of Camilla's death, she was surprised, pained, curious—a perfectly normal reaction, which dispelled his last trace of doubt about her sincerity. She had, she said, asked both Jim and her mother if they'd ever known a man named Camilla, and she was waiting to hear from her father, to whom she'd sent a special delivery letter.

Alston was staring at him with a mixture of amusement and suspicion. "You're not very communicative today, Steve."

"I like to think of myself as the strong, silent type."

"You do, eh? Well, just watch out for that Lancelot syndrome you're carrying around. Rescuing ladies in distress can be dangerous, especially if the ladies happen to be married. Harker has the reputation of being a very good guy. And a smart one. Think it over, Steve. I'll be back in a few minutes."

Pinata thought it over. Lancelot syndrome, hell. I'm not interested in saving Daisies in distress. Daisy, what a silly name for a grown woman. I'll bet that was Fielding's idea. Mrs. Fielding would have picked something a little more high-toned or exotic, Céleste, Stephanie, Gwendolyn.

He got up and began pacing the room. Thinking about names depressed him because his own were only borrowed, from a parish priest and a child's Christmas game. During the past three years especially, since Monica had taken Johnny away, Pinata had wondered a great deal about his parents, trying, not too successfully, to follow the advice the Mother Superior had given him many times: "There's no room in this world for self-pity, Stevens. You're a strong man because you had no one to lean on, and that's a good thing sometimes, to live without leaning. Think of all the fixations you might have developed, and dear me, there are a lot of them around these days. The essential thing for a boy is to have a good man to pattern himself after. And you had that in Father Stevens... Your mother? What else could she have been but a young woman who found herself bearing too heavy a cross? You must not blame her for being unable to carry it. Perhaps she was just a schoolgirl..."

Or a Juanita, Pinata thought grimly. *But why should it matter now after more than thirty years? I could never trace her anyway; there wasn't a single clue. And even if I found her, what about him? It's possible she wouldn't even know which of the men in her life was my father. Or care.*

Alston returned, carrying several cards picked out of a file. "Well, you have something, Steve. I'm not sure what. December 2, '55, was the last day Mrs. Harker worked here. She was on duty from 1:00 to 5:30, in charge of the children's playroom. That's where the younger children are kept while their parents or relatives are being counseled. No actual therapy is done there, but it was part of Mrs. Harker's job to observe any behavior problems, such as excessive destructiveness or shyness, and report them in writing to the professional members of the staff. The way a three-year-old plays with a doll often gives us more of a clue to the cause of family trouble than several hours of talking on the part of the parents. So you can see Mrs. Harker's work was important. She took it seriously, too. I just checked one of her reports. It was full of details that some of our other volunteers would have failed to notice or at least to record."

"The report you checked, was it one from that particular day?"

"Yes."

"Did anything unusual or disturbing happen?"

"A lot of unusual and disturbing things happen here every day," Alston said cheerfully. "You can count on that."

"I meant, as far as Mrs. Harker was concerned. Did she have some trouble with any of the children, for instance?"

"Nothing on the record indicates it. Mrs. Harker might have had some trouble with a relative of one of the children or even a staff member, but such an incident wouldn't be included in her written report. And I very much doubt that one occurred. Mrs. Harker got along well with everybody. If I had to make a personal criticism of her, that would be it. She was overeager to please people; it led me to think that she didn't set a very high value on herself. These constant smilers usually don't."

"Constant smiler?" Pinata said. "Overeager to please? Could we possibly be talking about the same woman? Maybe there are two Daisy Harkers."

"Why? Has she changed?"

"She shows no signs of being eager to please, believe me."

"Now, that's highly interesting. I always knew she was putting up a front. It's probably a good sign that she's stopped. These little Daddy's-girl wiles can look pretty nonsensical in a grown woman.

Perhaps she's maturing, and that's about all any of us can hope for. Maturity," he added, "is not a destination like Hong Kong, London, Paris, or heaven. It's a continuing process, rather like a road along which one travels. There's no Maturitytown, U.S.A. Say, I wonder if I could put that across to the Soroptimists at their banquet tonight... No, no, I don't think I'll try. It wouldn't be much of a fund-raiser. I'd better stick with my statistics. People, alas, are more impressed by statistics than they are by ideas."

"Especially yours?"

"Mine can be very impressive," Alston said with a grin. "But to get back to our subject, I'll admit I'm becoming curious about the connection between Juanita and Mrs. Harker."

"I'm not sure there is one."

"Then I guess this is just a coincidence." Alston tapped the cards he'd picked from the file. "Friday, December 2, was the last time Mrs. Harker appeared here. It was also the last time any of us heard from Juanita."

"Heard from?"

"She was scheduled to come in Friday morning to talk to Mrs. Huxley, one of our social workers. It wasn't to be a therapy session, merely a discussion of finances and what could be done with Juanita's children, who'd been released from Juvenile Hall into the custody of Juanita's mother, Mrs. Rosario. None of us considered this an ideal arrangement. Mrs. Rosario is a clean-living, respectable woman, but she's a bit of a nut on religion, and Mrs. Huxley was going to try to talk Juanita into allowing the children to be placed in foster homes for a time.

"At any rate Juanita called Mrs. Huxley early Friday morning and said she couldn't keep her appointment, because she wasn't feeling well. This was natural enough, since she was just a couple of jumps ahead of the obstetrician. Mrs. Huxley explained to her that the business about the children was urgent, and another appointment was made for late that afternoon. Juanita was quite docile about it, even amiable. That alone should have warned us. She didn't show up, of course. Thinking the baby might have arrived on the scene a bit prematurely, I called Mrs. Rosario next day. She was in a furious state. Juanita had left town, taking the children with her, and Mrs. Rosario blamed me."

"Why you?" Pinata asked.

"Because," Alston said, grimacing, "I have *mal ojo*, the evil eye."

"I hadn't noticed."

"In case you think belief in *mal ojo* has disappeared, let me hasten to correct you. Like many older members of her race, Mrs. Rosario is still living in the distant past, medically speaking: hospitals are places to die in, psychiatry is against the Church, illness is caused not by germs but by *mal ojo*. If you accused her of believing these things, she would probably deny it. Nevertheless, Juanita's first child was born in the kitchen of an elderly midwife, and when Juanita was sent to us for psychiatric help, Mrs. Rosario proved to be as big a stumbling block as the girl herself. Very few medical doctors, and not enough psychiatrists, have attempted to bridge this cultural gap. They tend to dismiss people like Mrs. Rosario as obstinate, backward, perverse, whereas she is simply reacting according to her cultural pattern. That pattern hasn't changed as much as we'd like to think it has. It will take more than time to change it. It will take effort, intent, training. But that's lecture number twenty-seven and not much of a fund-raiser either... I hope, by the way, that you're not taking any of my remarks about your race personally."

"Why should I?" Pinata said with a shrug. "I'm not even sure it is my race."

"But you think so?"

"Yes, I think so."

"You know, I've often wondered about that. You don't quite fit the—"

"Mrs. Rosario is a more interesting subject than I am."

"Very well. As I said, she was extremely angry when I called her. She'd gone to a special mass the previous night to pray for various lost souls, including, I hope, Juanita's. I've often wondered—haven't you?—how the parish priests handle people like Mrs. Rosario who believe with equal fervor in the Virgin Mary and the evil eye. Must be quite a problem. Anyway, on returning home, she discovered that Juanita had left, bag and baggage and five children. I'm not aware of any reason why Mrs. Rosario should have lied about it, but it did strike me at the time that it was a very convenient story. It saved her from having to answer questions from the police and the Probation Department. If she was at church when Juanita left, then obviously she couldn't be expected to know anything. She's a complex woman, Mrs. Rosario. She distrusts and disapproves of Juanita; she seems, in fact, to hate her; but she has a fierce maternal instinct.

"Well, there you have it." Alston leaned back in his chair and studied the pink ceiling. "The end of Juanita. Or what I fondly hoped was the end. After a year or so we closed her file. The last entry on it is in November 1956: Garcia, when he was released from the Army, brought suit for divorce, charging desertion. Which of the children belonged to him, I have no idea. Perhaps none. In any case he didn't ask for custody. Nor was any alimony or child support demanded of him, since Juanita didn't show up for the hearing. The chances are she knew about it, though. Most Mexican families here in the Southwest, in spite of dissension among themselves, have a way of retaining their tribal loyalties and ties when confronted with trouble from the whites. And the law is always 'white' to them. There's no doubt in my mind that Juanita remained in touch in some way with relatives who kept her posted on what was going on and when it was safe for her to come back here. I take it you're sure she *is* back?"

"Reasonably," Pinata said.

"Married again?"

"Yes, to an Italian called Donelli. I gather he's not a bad guy, but Juanita has given him a rough time, and he's carrying a chip on his shoulder."

"How do you know all that?"

"I saw him in court after he got into the fight in the bar. My client was involved in the fight. Donelli couldn't scrape up enough money to pay his fine, so he's still in jail. It could be that's exactly where Juanita wants him."

"What bar is she working at?"

"The Velada, on lower State."

Alston nodded. "That's where she's worked before, off and on. It's owned by a friend of her mother's, a Mrs. Brewster. Both Mrs. Brewster and the Velada are known to every health and welfare agency in the county, though the place has never actually been closed. It looks as if you're on the right track, Steve. If you find out the girl is really Juanita, let me know immediately, will you? I feel a certain responsibility towards her. If she's in trouble, I want to help her."

"How will I get in touch with you?"

"I'll be home about the middle of the afternoon. Call me there. Meanwhile, I'll keep hoping a mistake has been made and the real Juanita is happily and securely ensconced on an island in the middle of the Pacific."

Alston got up and closed and locked the window as an indication that as far as he was concerned, the interview was ended.

"Just one more minute," Pinata said.

"Hurry it up, will you? I don't want to keep the Newcomers Club waiting."

"If they knew how much you were going to touch them for, I don't think they'd mind waiting."

"Oh yes. Speaking of money…"

"Here." Pinata gave him a ten-dollar bill. "Have you ever heard of a man called Carlos Camilla?"

"Offhand, I'd say no. That's an unusual name. I think I'd remember if I'd ever heard it before. What about him?"

"He killed himself four years ago. Roy Fondero was in charge of the funeral."

"I know Fondero," Alston said. "He's an old friend of mine. A good man, level-headed and straight as a die, no pun intended."

"Will you do me a favor?"

"I might."

"Call him up and tell him I'd like to ask some questions about the Camilla case."

"That's easy enough." Alston reached for the phone and dialed. "Mr. Fondero, please… When will he be back? This is Charles Alston speaking… Thanks. I'll call him back later this afternoon." He hung up. "Fondero's out on business. I'll try and set up an appointment for you. What time would you prefer?"

"As soon as possible."

"I'll see if I can arrange it for today, then."

"Thanks very much, Charley. Now, just one more question, and I'll leave. Did Mrs. Harker know Juanita?"

"Everyone at the Clinic did, by sight if not by name. But why ask me? Why not ask Mrs. Harker?" Alston leaned across the desk, his eyes narrowed. "Is there anything the matter with her?"

"I don't think so."

"I heard on the grapevine she and Harker are planning to adopt a child. Would this mysterious visit of yours have anything to do with that?"

"In a remote way," Pinata said. "I wish I could tell you more, Charley, but certain things are confidential. All I can do is assure you that the matter is, to everyone else but Mrs. Harker, quite trivial. There are no lives at stake, no money, no great issue."

He was wrong: all three were at stake. But he hadn't the imagination or the desire to see it.

12

*I wish they were good memories, that like other men I could sit
back in the security of my family and review the past kindly. But
I cannot…*

Fielding's first hitch got him as far as Ventura, and his second,
with a jukebox repairman, landed him in San Félice at the corner
of State Street and Highway 101. From there it was only a short
walk up to the Velada Café, sandwiched between a pawnshop
(we buy and sell anything) and a hotel for transients (rooms
without bath, $2.00), modestly called the Ritz. Fielding regis-
tered at the hotel and was given a room on the second floor. He
had stayed in a hundred rooms like it in his life, but he liked
this one better than most, partly because he was feeling excited
and partly because he could see through the dirty window the
shimmer of sun on the ocean and some fishing boats lying at
anchor beyond the wharf. They looked so tranquil and at ease
that Fielding had a brief notion of going down and applying
for a job as deckhand. Then he remembered that he'd even got
seasick on the Staten Island ferry. And there was Muriel now,
too. He was a married man with responsibilities; he couldn't
go dashing off on a boat with Muriel expecting him home…
I should have gone to sea when I was younger, he thought. *I might
have been a captain by this time. Captain Fielding, it sounds very
right and proper.*

"Heave to," Fielding said aloud, and as a substitute for going
to sea, he rinsed his face in the washbasin. Then he combed his

hair (the jukebox repairman had been driving a convertible with the top down) and went downstairs to the Velada Café.

There was no cocktail hour at the Velada. Anytime you had the money was the time for drinking, and business was often as brisk in midmorning as it was at night. Brisker, sometimes, since the smell of stale grease that permeated the place increased the agonies of a hangover and encouraged the customers to dull their senses as quickly as possible. The manager of the Ritz Hotel and the operator of the pawnshop frequently complained about this smell to the Department of Health, the police, the State Board of Equalization, but Mrs. Brewster, who owned the Velada, fought back tooth, nail, and tongue. She was a scrawny little miser of a woman who wore an oversize denim apron which she used for everything—wiping counters, swatting flies, mopping her face, handling hot pans, blowing her nose, shooing away newsboys who came in to sell papers, collecting her meager tips, drying her hands. This apron had become the expression of her whole personality. When she took it off at night before going home, she felt lost, as if some vital part of her had been amputated.

Fielding noticed the smell and the dirty apron, but they didn't bother him. He'd smelled worse and seen dirtier. He sat down at a booth near the front window. The waitress, Nita, wasn't in sight, and no one seemed interested in taking his order. A Mexican busboy, who looked about fifteen, was sweeping up cigarette butts from the floor. He worked very intently, as if he were new at the job or expected to find something more in the morning's debris than just cigarette butts.

"Where's the waitress?" Fielding said.

The boy raised his head. He had huge dark eyes, like prunes swelling in hot water. "Which one?"

"Nita."

"Fixing her face, I guess. She likes to fix her face."

"What's your name, son?"

"Chico."

"Tell the old lady behind the counter I want a ham on rye and a bottle of beer."

"I can't do that, sir. The girls get mad; they think I'm trying to con them out of their tips."

"How old are you, Chico?"

"Twenty-one."

"Come off it, kid."

The boy's face turned dark red. "I'm twenty-one," he said, and returned to his sweeping.

Five minutes passed. The other waitress, who was attending to the back booths, glanced casually in Fielding's direction a couple of times, but she didn't approach him, and neither did Mrs. Brewster, who was wiping off the grill with her apron.

Juanita finally appeared wearing fresh lipstick and powder. She had outlined her eyes so heavily with black pencil that she looked like a coal miner who'd been working in the pits for years. She acknowledged his presence with a little flick of her rump, like a mare twitching her tail out of recognition or interest.

She said, unsmiling, "So you're back again."

"Surprised?"

"Why should I be surprised? Nothing surprises me. What'll you have?"

"Ham on rye, bottle of Western beer."

She shouted the order at Mrs. Brewster, who gave no response at all, not even a flutter of her apron. Fielding wondered whether she'd recognized him as the man involved in the fight and was trying to freeze him out to avoid further trouble.

"The service in this place is lousy," he said.

"So's the food. Why come here?"

"Oh, I just wanted to see how everybody was doing after the fracas last Monday."

"I'm doing fine. Joe's still in the cooler. He got thirty days."

"I'm sorry to hear that."

Juanita put one hand on her hip in a half-pensive, half-aggressive manner. "Say, your being always sorry for people is going to get you in some real trouble one of these days. Like your being sorry for me, and pretty soon you're trading punches with Joe."

"I was a little drunk."

"Well, I just thought I'd warn you, you oughta let people feel sorry for themselves. Most of them are pretty damn good at it, me included. Wait a minute, I'll light a match under the old girl. She's having one of her spooky days."

"There's no hurry. Why don't you sit down for a while?"

"What for?" Juanita asked suspiciously.

"Rest your feet."

"So now you're feeling sorry for my *feet?* Say, you're a real spooky guy, you know that?"

"I've been told once or twice."

"Well, it's no skin off my elbows." She sat down, with considerably more squirming than was necessary. "Got a cigarette?"

"No."

"Well, I'll smoke my own, then. I figure there's no sense smoking my own if I can bum one."

"Smart girl."

"Me, smart? Nobody else thinks so. You should hear my old lady on the subject. She throws fits telling me how dumb I am. I don't have to stand it much longer, though. I'm just living with her for the time being while Joe's in the cooler, so I'll have someone to look after the kids. When Joe gets out, maybe we'll take off again. I've always hated this town; it's treated me rotten. But don't go feeling sorry for me. What they can dish out, I can take."

"They?" Fielding said. "Who are they?"

"Nobody. Just them. The town."

"Where have you been living?"

"L.A."

"Why'd you come back here?"

"Joe lost his job. It wasn't his fault or anything. The boss's nephew just got old enough to work, and Joe was thrown out on his can to make room for him. So I thought, why not come back here for a while? Maybe things are different, maybe the town's changed, I thought. Hell, *this* town *change?* I must of been crazy. The only thing'll change this place is the Russians, and me personally I couldn't care less if they started dropping bombs like confetti and everybody fell dead in their tracks." She lit a cigarette and blew the smoke across the table directly into his face, as if she were challenging him to disagree with her. "What do you think of that, eh?"

"I haven't thought about it yet."

"Joe has. Joe says when I talk like that, I oughta have my mouth washed out with soap. And I says, listen, Dago, you try it and you get a hand full of teeth." She smiled, not out of amusement, but as if she wanted to show she had the teeth to carry out the threat. "Joe's a real flag-waver. Hell, I bet while they were locking him in his cell, he was waving the flag. Some dagos are like that. Even with the cops sitting on their faces, they open their yaps and sing 'God Bless America.'"

Fielding started to laugh but immediately checked himself when he realized Juanita wasn't attempting to be funny; she was merely presenting her own personal picture of the world, a place where people sat on your face and you retaliated in the only logical way, which wasn't by singing "God Bless America."

Behind the counter Mrs. Brewster had come to life and was putting the finishing touches on the ham sandwich, a slice of pickle and five potato chips. Juanita went over to pick up the order, and Fielding could hear the two women talking.

"Since when am I paying you to sit with the customers?"

"He's a friend of mine."

"Since when, five minutes ago?"

"Being nice to customers," Juanita said smoothly, "is good for business. You'll make more money. You like money, don't you?"

Mrs. Brewster let out a sudden little giggle, as if she'd been tickled in some vulnerable place. Then she smothered the giggle with a corner of her apron, slammed the ham sandwich on a tray, and opened a bottle of beer.

Juanita returned with the order and sat down opposite Fielding again. The exchange of words with Mrs. Brewster had improved her spirits. "Didn't I tell you she was a real spook? But I can handle her. All I do is say 'money,' and she giggles like that every time. I always get along with spooks," she added with a touch of pride. "Maybe I ought to of been a nurse or a doctor. How's the sandwich?"

"It's not bad."

"You must be awful hungry. Me, I've got a cast-iron stomach, but you couldn't pay me to eat in this joint."

"It's lucky for you the old girl hasn't taken up lip-reading." Fielding finished half the sandwich, pushed the plate away, and reached for the beer. "So your mother looks after the children while you work, eh?"

"Sure."

"You look too young to have children."

"That's a laugh," she said, but she looked pleased. "I got six of them."

"Go on, you're pulling my leg."

"No, that's the honest-to-God fact. I got six."

"Why, you're hardly more than a child yourself."

"I started young," Juanita said with considerable truth. "I never liked school much, so I quit and got married."

"Six. Well, I'll be damned."

She was obviously enjoying his incredulity. She reached down and patted her stomach. "Of course I kept my figure. A lot of girls don't; they let themselves go. I never did."

"I'll say you didn't. Six. God, I can't believe it." He kept shaking his head as if he really couldn't believe it, although he'd known since Monday, the day of the fight, that she had six children. "How many boys?"

"The oldest and the youngest are boys; the middle ones are girls."

"I bet they're cute."

"They're O.K." But a note of boredom was evident in her voice, as if the children themselves were not very interesting, only the fact that she'd had them was important. "I guess there's worse around."

"Have you any pictures of them?"

"What for?"

"A lot of people carry pictures of their family."

"Who would I show them to? Who'd want to look at pictures of my kids?"

"I would, for one."

"Why?"

The idea that a stranger might be legitimately interested in her children was incredible to her. Her eyes narrowed in suspicion, and he thought for a minute that he'd lost her confidence. But he said easily, "Say, what's got into you anyway? Your kids have two heads or something?"

"No, they haven't got two heads, Mr. Foster."

"How did you know my name?" This time his surprise was genuine, and she reacted to it as she'd reacted to his feigned disbelief that she'd had six children, with a look of mischievous pleasure. Apparently this was what Juanita liked best, to surprise people. "Where'd you find out who I was?"

"I can read. It was in the paper, about the fight. Joe never had his name in the paper before, so I clipped it out to save for him. Joe Donelli and Stan Foster, it said, was involved in a fight over a woman in a local café."

"Well," Fielding said, smiling. "Now you know my name, and I know yours. Juanita Garcia, meet Stan Foster."

She half rose from the bench, then suddenly dropped back with a noisy expulsion of her breath.

"Garcia? Why did you say Garcia? That's not my name."

"It used to be, didn't it?"

"It used to be a lot of different things. Now it's Donelli, nothing else, see? And it's Nita, not Juanita. Nita Donelli, that's my name, understand?"

Fielding nodded. "Of course."

"Where'd you get a hold of that Juanita business anyway?"

"I thought the two names were the same. There's this old song, see, about a girl called Nita, Juanita."

"There is, eh?"

"Yes, and I naturally assumed—"

"Hey, Chico." She motioned to the busboy, and he came over to the booth, pushing his broom ahead of him. "You ever hear tell of a song called 'Nita, Juanita'?"

"Nope."

Juanita turned back to Fielding, her full mouth pressed tight against her teeth, so that it seemed half its size. "Sing it for me. Let's hear how it sounds."

"Here? Now?"

"Sure, here now. Why not?"

"I don't remember all the words. Anyway, I can't sing. I have a voice like—"

"Try."

She was very quiet in her insistence. No one in the café was paying any attention to the scene except Mrs. Brewster, who was watching them with her bright, beady little eyes.

"Maybe there's no such song, eh?" Juanita said.

"Sure there is. It goes back a long way. You're too young to remember."

"So remind me."

Fielding was sweating from the heat, from the beer, and from something he didn't want to identify as fear. "Say, what's the matter with you anyway?"

"I like music, is all. Old songs. I like old songs."

Mrs. Brewster came out from behind the counter making little sweeps of her apron as if she were brushing away invisible cobwebs. Juanita saw her coming and turned her face stubbornly toward the wall.

"What's up?" Mrs. Brewster asked Fielding.

"Nothing, I just—that is, she just wanted me to sing a song."

"What's wrong with a bit of music?"

"It wouldn't be music. I can't sing."

"She's a little crazy," Mrs. Brewster said. "But I can handle her." She put a scrawny hand firmly on Juanita's right shoulder. "Snap out of it. You hear, girl?"

"Leave me alone," Juanita said.

"You don't snap out of it, I call your mother and tell her you're having trouble with your *cabeza* again. Also, I write to Joe. I tell him, Dear Joe, that wife of yours, you better come and get her locked up. O.K., you snap out of it now?"

"All I wanted was to hear a song."

"What song?"

"'Nita, Juanita.' He says it's a song. I never heard of it, I think he's lying. I think he's a spy from the police or the Probation Department."

"He's not lying."

"I think he is."

"I can spot a cop a mile away." Mrs. Brewster said. "Also, I know that song. I used to sing it when I was a girl. I had a pretty voice once, before I breathed in all this foul air. Now you believe me?"

"No."

"O.K., we sing it together for you, him and me. How about that, mister? We make a little music to cheer Nita up?"

Fielding cleared his throat. "I can't—"

"I begin. You follow."

"But—"

"Now. One, two, three, here we go:

> *'Soft o'er the fountain,*
> *Lingering falls the southern moon;*
> *Far o'er the mountain,*
> *Breaks the day too soon.*
> *In thy dark eyes' splendor*
> *Where the warm light loves to dwell,*
> *Weary looks yet tender,*
> *Speak their fond farewell.'"*

Juanita's face was still turned to the wall. Mrs. Brewster said, "You're not listening."

"I am so."

"Isn't it pretty, all that sadness? Now comes the chorus with your very own name in it."

Fielding joined, softly and a little off key, in the chorus:

>*"'Nita, Juanita,*
>*Ask thy soul if we should part.*
>*Nita, Juanita,*
>*Lean thou on my heart.'"*

During the chorus Juanita slowly turned her head to watch the two songsters, and her mouth began to move slightly, as if she were silently singing along with them. She looked like a child again in that moment, a little girl wanting desperately to be part of a song she never knew, a harmony she never heard.

When the chorus was over, Mrs. Brewster blew her nose on her apron, thinking of her pretty voice that had vanished in the foul air.

"I like the part with my name in it the best," Juanita said.

Mrs. Brewster patted her shoulder. "Naturally. That's the best part."

"*'Lean thou on my heart.'* Imagine anyone saying that to me. I'd drop dead."

"Things like that don't get said in real life. You feeling better now, girl?"

"I'm all right. I was all right before, too. I just wanted to hear the song to make sure he wasn't lying."

"She's a little crazy," Mrs. Brewster said to Fielding. "But she handles easy if you know how."

"I didn't really think you were lying," Juanita said when Mrs. Brewster had gone. "I have to check things, that's all. I always check things. It's funny the way spooks like her think everybody else is crazy."

Fielding nodded. "It *is* funny. I've noticed it myself."

"You didn't believe her for a minute, did you?"

"Not for a minute."

"I could tell you didn't. You have a very kind expression. I bet you like dogs."

"Dogs are fine."

His fear had gone now, leaving in his throat a little knot of pity which he couldn't swallow or cough up. It wasn't often that Fielding experienced pity for anyone but himself, and he didn't like the feeling. It seemed to immobilize him. He wanted to get up and run away and forget about this strange, sad girl, forget about the whole bunch of them—Daisy, Jim, Ada, Camilla. Camilla was dead. Jim and Daisy had their own lives, and Ada had hers... *What the hell am I doing here? It's dangerous. I may stir up a storm and get caught in the middle of it. I'd better go while the going's good.*

The girl was staring at him gravely. "What kind of dogs do you like best?"

"Sleeping ones."

"I had a fox terrier once, but it chewed up one of my old lady's crucifixes, and she made me take it to the pound."

"That's too bad."

"I get off work in fifteen minutes. Maybe we could take in a movie this afternoon."

It was the last thing in the world he wanted to do, but he didn't hesitate. "That would be very nice."

"I have to go home first and change clothes. I only live about three blocks away. You could wait here for me."

"Why don't I come along? It's a good day for a walk."

She looked suddenly tense again. "Who said I was going to walk?"

"I assumed—well, since you only live three blocks away..."

"I thought maybe you meant I wasn't the kind of girl that'd have a car."

"I didn't mean that at all."

167

"That's good, because it's not true. I've got a car. I just don't bring it to work. I don't like leaving it parked in the hot sun for all those niggers to lean against and scratch up the finish."

He wondered whether the car, and "all those niggers" who leaned against it, existed outside Juanita's mind. He hoped they were real and not symbols of the dark and ugly things that had happened to her, in or out of the hot sun.

"I take real good care of the finish."

"I'm sure you do."

"Here's your check. Eighty-five cents."

He gave her a dollar, and she went behind the counter to get his change.

"How you feeling now, girl?" Mrs. Brewster said softly.

"Fine."

"When you get off work, you go home to your mother, lie down, take a little rest. You do that, eh?"

"I'm going to the movies."

"With *him*?"

Both the women turned and looked at Fielding. He wasn't sure what was expected of him, so he smiled in a tentative way. Neither of them smiled back.

"He's all right," Juanita said. "He's old enough to be my father."

"Sure, *we* know that, but does *he*?"

"We're only going to the movies."

"He looks like a lush," Mrs. Brewster said, "all those broken veins on his nose and cheekbones, and see the way he shakes."

"He only had one beer."

"And suppose one of Joe's friends sees you with this man?"

"Joe doesn't know anybody in town."

Mrs. Brewster began fanning herself with her apron. "It's too hot to argue. Just you be careful, girl. Your mother and me, we're old friends; we don't want you to start running wild again. You're a respectable married woman with a husband and kids, remember that."

Juanita had heard it all a hundred times; she could have recited it forward and backward and in Spanish. She listened without interest, watching the clock on the wall, leaning her weight first on one foot, then another.

"You hear me, girl?"

"Yeah."

"Pay it some mind, then."

"Oh sure," Juanita said, and gave Fielding an amused little glance: *Listen to this spook, will you?* "Can I go now?"

"It's not two yet."

"Can't I go early just this once?"

"All right, just this once. But it's no way to conduct a business, I ought to have my head examined for soft spots."

Juanita went over to the booth where Fielding was sitting. "Here's your change."

"Keep it."

"Thanks. I can go now; the spook says it's O.K. Shall I say 'money' and make her giggle again, just for fun?"

"No."

"Don't you want to hear it?"

"No."

For some reason she couldn't figure out, Juanita didn't want to hear it again either. She walked very quickly to the door without glancing back to see whether Mrs. Brewster was watching or Fielding was following.

Outside. This was what Juanita liked best, to be out and free, to be moving fast, going from one place to another, not being anywhere in particular or with anyone in particular, which was the same thing, because people were like places, like houses, they tied you down and made you live in them. She wanted to be a train, a huge, beautiful, shiny train, which never had to stop for fuel or to let people off or on. It just kept on going, blowing its big whistle, frightening everyone off the tracks.

These were the high points of her life, the times between places. She was a train. *Awhoooeeeee…*

13

I am alone, surrounded by strangers in a strange place…

It was 2:30 when Pinata reached the neighborhood of the Velada Café. Before he got out of the car, he took off his tie and sports coat, rolled up the sleeves of his shirt, and unbuttoned it at the neck. He planned on using the direct approach, asking for the girl and letting it be assumed he was one of her admirers.

But he hadn't figured on Mrs. Brewster's sharp, suspicious eyes. He was barely inside the door when she spotted him and said to Chico the busboy out of the corner of her mouth, "Cop. You in trouble?"

"No, Mrs. Brewster."

"Don't lie to me."

"I'm not lying. I'm—"

"If he asks your age, you're twenty-one, see?"

"He won't believe it. I know him. I mean, he knows me from the Y; he taught me handball."

"O.K., hide in the back room till he leaves."

Chico made a dash for the back room, riding his broom like a witch frightened by a bigger witch.

Pinata sat down at the counter. Mrs. Brewster approached him, holding her apron in front of her like a shield, and said very politely, "Can I get you something, sir?"

"What's your lunch special?"

"We're not serving lunch. It's after hours."

"How about a bowl of soup?"

"We're fresh out of soup."

"Coffee?"

"It's stale."

"I see."

"I could make you some fresh, but it'd take a long time. I move slow."

"Chico moves pretty fast," Pinata said. "Of course, he's young."

Mrs. Brewster's eyes glittered. "Not so young. Twenty-one."

"My guess would be sixteen."

"Twenty-one. He's got a birth certificate says twenty-one, all printed up proper."

"He must have his own printer."

"Chico looks young," Mrs. Brewster said stubbornly, "because his whiskers are slow to come through the skin."

Pinata was well aware by this time that his plans for a direct approach were useless, that it would be impossible to get information from a woman who'd refused to serve him lunch or coffee. He said, "Look, I'm not a policeman. It's not my concern if you're employing underage help. Chico just happens to be a friend of mine. I'd like to talk to him for a minute."

"What for?"

"To see how he's getting along."

"He's getting along good. He minds his own business, which is how everybody should do."

Pinata looked toward the rear of the café and saw Chico's eyes peering out at him through the little square of glass in one of the swinging doors. Pinata smiled, and the boy grinned back in a friendly way.

Seeing the grin, Mrs. Brewster hesitated, wiping her hands uneasily on her apron. "Chico's not in trouble?"

"No."

"And you met him at the Y, eh?"

"That's right."

Mrs. Brewster's snort indicated her low opinion of the Y, but she motioned to Chico with her apron, and he came sidling out of the door dragging his broom behind him. He was still wearing his grin, but it seemed in close-up to be less friendly than anxious.

"Hello, Chico."

"Hello, Mr. Pinata."

"I haven't seen you for a long time."

"No, well, I been busy, one thing and another like."

Three men in coveralls came in and sat at the far end of the counter. Mrs. Brewster went over to take their orders, giving Chico a little frown of warning as she passed.

"How's your schoolwork coming along?" Pinata said.

Chico stared up at an interesting spot on the ceiling. "Not so good."

"You're getting passing grades, I hope."

"That grade bit's all in the past. I quit school at Christmastime."

"Why?"

"I had to get a steady job to keep my car running. That after-school errand stuff wasn't enough. You can't take the chicks out in a machine that don't run good."

"That's a foolish reason for quitting school."

The boy shrugged. "You asked. I answered. Maybe in your day the chicks was different, maybe they liked to do things like walk in the park, see? Now when you ask a chick out, she wants to go to a drive-in movie like, and you can't go to a drive-in without you got a car."

"Unless you have a car."

"That's what I mean. Without you got a car, you don't rate, you're the most nothing."

In the past few years Pinata had heard this same story fifty times, often from brighter and more educable boys than Chico. Each time it depressed him a little further. He said, "You're pretty young to be working in a place like this, aren't you, Chico?"

"There ain't no harm in it," the boy said nervously. "Honest to God, Mr. Pinata. It's not like I go around lapping up what's left in the glasses. Croaky does that—he's the dishwasher. It's part of his salary like."

"What about the other people who work here? The waitresses, for example. How do they treat you?"

"O.K."

"The blonde standing beside the back booth, who's she?"

"Millie. The other one's called Sunny, short for sunshine on account of she never smiles. She says, what's to smile at." Chico was relieved to have the conversation switched from himself, and he intended to keep it that way if he could. "Millie's real cool. She used to teach dancing at one of them schools, you know, like cha cha cha, but it was too hard on her feet. They were flat to begin with and got flatter."

"I thought there was a new girl around, Nita somebody-or-other."

"Oh, her. She's a funny one. One minute you're her best friend—good morning, Chico, ain't it a beautiful morning, Chico—and the next minute she looks at me like I'm the thing from outer space. She's a snappy waitress, though. Real jet. Her and the old bird"—he indicated Mrs. Brewster with a slight movement of his head—"are pretty palsy because the old bird knows her mother. I hear them talking about it a lot."

"Isn't Nita working today?"

"She was. She took off an hour ago with a guy. There was some trouble about a song, ended up with Mrs. Brewster and the guy singing this real square song with her name in it, Juanita. Nobody was drunk; it wasn't that kind of singing."

"Could the man have been her husband?"

"Naw. He's in hock. This other guy, he's the one put him here."

God, Fielding's back in town. I wonder if Daisy knows.

"I spotted him soon as he came in," Chico added with pride. "I got a good memory for faces. Maybe I don't dig that math bit so good, but faces I never forget."

"How old a man was he?"

"Old enough to be my father. Maybe even old enough to be *your* father."

"That's pretty old," Pinata said wryly.

"Sure. I know. I was kinda surprised Nita'd want to go out with him."

"Out where?"

"To the movies. Nita and the old bird had an argument about it, not a real fight like, just quiet. You go home to your mother, the old bird says, but Nita wasn't having any of that stuff, so she and the guy take off. Nita don't like to be told a thing. Like the other day it's raining, see, and I says to her, look, it's raining. That's all, nothing personal. But she gets sore as hell, like I'd told her her lipstick was on crooked or something. Me, I think she's *zafada*, she needs a headshrinker."

Mrs. Brewster turned suddenly and called out in a sharp, penetrating voice, "Chico, sweep!"

"Sure. Yes, ma'am," Chico said. "I got to get back to work now, Mr. Pinata. See you at the Y, huh?"

"I hope so. I'd hate to think you've given up everything merely to support a car."

"That's the way it is these days, if you dig me."

"Yes, I guess I dig you, Chico."

175

"You can't change it, I can't change it, that's the way it is."

"Chico!" Mrs. Brewster screamed. "Sweep!"

Chico swept.

The public phone booth on the corner smelled as if it were used during the dark hours for more personal communication and needs than the telephone company had planned on. The walls were covered with telephone numbers, initials, names, messages: WINSTON TASTES GOOD. WINSTON, 93446. SALLY M IS COOL. DON'T BE HAF SAFE. GREETINGS FROM JERSEY CITY. LIFE IS ROTTEN. YOU GUYS ARE ALL NUTZ. 24T, U4 ME. HELLO CRULE WORLD GOODBY.

Pinata dialed Daisy's number and received a busy signal. Then he called Charles Alston at his house.

Alston himself answered. "Hello?"

"This is Steve Pinata, Charley."

"Any luck?"

"That depends on what you mean by luck. I went to the Velada. Juanita wasn't on duty, but there's no doubt she's the girl."

Alston's heavy sigh could be heard even above the street noises coming through the open door of the telephone booth. "I was afraid of this. Well, I have no alternative. I'll have to let the Probation Department know about her. I hate the idea, but the girl's got to be protected and so do the children. Do you think—that is, you agree, don't you, that I should notify the Probation Department?"

"That's up to you. You know the circumstances better than I do."

"They're closed for the weekend, of course, but I'll call them first thing Monday morning."

"And meanwhile?"

"Meanwhile we wait."

"Meanwhile you wait," Pinata said. "I don't. I'm going to try and find her."

"Why?"

"She happens to be out with an ex-client of mine. I'd like to see him again for various reasons."

"When you find her, go easy on her. For her sake," Alston added, "not yours. I assume you can take care of yourself. Where's she staying?"

"With her mother, I think. At least she's in contact with her, so I'll try there first. Where does Mrs. Rosario live?"

"When I knew her, she was living in a little house on Granada Street. It's very likely she's still there, since the house belongs to her. She bought it a long time ago. She used to be the housekeeper on the old Higginson ranch. When Mrs. Higginson died, she left Mrs. Rosario a few thousand dollars, as she did all her other employees. By the way, if Juanita is out with this ex-client of yours, why do you expect to find her at the house on Granada Street? Believe me, she isn't the type to bring the boys home to mother."

"I have a hunch she might have dropped in to change her clothes. She was working, in uniform, until two o'clock. She wouldn't be likely to keep a date while wearing a uniform."

"Definitely not. So?"

"I thought I'd try to get some information from Mrs. Rosario."

Alston's laugh was loud and brief. "You may or may not get it. It depends on whether you have a *mal ojo*. By the way, I set up your appointment with Roy Fondero for three o'clock."

"It's almost that now."

"Then you'd better get over there. He's driving down to L.A. for the game tonight. Oh yes, one more word of advice, Steve: in dealing with Mrs. Rosario, play up the clean-living, high-thinking angle. You never swear, drink, smoke, blaspheme, or fornicate. You go to Mass and confession and observe saints' days. You don't happen to have a brother or uncle who's a priest?"

"I might have."

"That would help," Alston said. "Incidentally, do you speak Spanish?"

"Some."

"Well, don't. Many Spanish Americans who've been here a long time, like Mrs. Rosario, resent people addressing them in Spanish, although they may use the language themselves with their friends and families."

A dozen Doric columns entwined with giant Burmese honeysuckle made the front of Fondero's place look like an old southern mansion. The impression was destroyed by the long black hearse parked by the side door. In the driveway behind the hearse stood a small bright red sports car. The incongruity of the two vehicles amused Pinata. *The death and the resurrection,* he thought. *Maybe that's how modern Americans imagine resurrection, as a bright red sports car whitewalling them along a Styrofoam road to a nylon-Orlon-Dacron nirvana.*

Pinata went in the side door and turned right.

Fondero was watering a planter full of maranta. He was a man of massive proportions, as if he'd been built to withstand the weight and pressure of other people's griefs.

"Sit down, Mr. Pinata. Charley Alston called me to say you want some information."

"That's right."

"What about?"

"You may recall Carlos Camilla?"

"Oh yes. Yes, indeed." Fondero finished watering the maranta and put the empty pitcher on the window ledge. "Camilla was my guest, shall we say, for over a month. As you know, the city has no official morgue, but Camilla's body had to be kept, pending investigation of the source of the money that was found on him. Nothing came of the investigation, so he was buried."

"Did anyone attend the funeral?"

"A hired priest and my wife."

"Your wife?"

Fondero sat down in a chair that looked too frail to bear him. "Betty refused to let Camilla be buried without mourners, so she acted as a substitute. It wasn't entirely acting, however. Camilla, perhaps because of the tragic circumstances of his death, perhaps because we had him around so long, had gotten under our skin. We kept hoping that someone would come along to claim him. No one did, but Betty still refused to believe that Camilla didn't have somebody in the world who cared about him. She insisted that the money found on Camilla be used for an imposing monument instead of an expensive coffin. She had the idea that someday a mourner might appear, and she wanted Camilla's grave to be conspicuous. As I recall, it is."

"It's conspicuous," Pinata said. *And a mourner did come along and find it, but the mourner was a stranger—Daisy.*

"You're a detective, Mr. Pinata?"

"I have a license that says so."

"Then perhaps you have some theory of how a man like Camilla got hold of $2,000."

"A holdup seems the most likely source."

"The police were never able to prove that," Fondero said, taking a gold cigarette case from his pocket. "Cigarette? No? Good for you. I wish I could give them up. Since this lung cancer business, some of the local wits have started calling cigarettes Fonderos. Well, it's publicity of a kind, I suppose."

"Where do you think Camilla got the money?"

"I'm inclined to believe he came by it honestly. Perhaps he saved it up, perhaps it was repayment of a loan. The latter theory is more logical. He was a dying man. He must have been aware of his condition, and knowing how little time he had left, he decided to collect money owing to him to pay for his funeral. That would explain his coming to town—the person who owed him money lived here. Or lives here."

"That sounds plausible," Pinata said, "except for one thing. According to the newspaper, the police made an appeal to the public for anyone who knew Camilla to come forward. No one did."

"No one came forward in person. But I had a peculiar telephone call after Camilla had been here a week or so. I told the police about it, and they thought, as I did at the time, it was the work of some religious crank."

The expression on Fondero's face as he leaned forward was an odd mixture of amusement and irritation. "If you want to hear from every crackpot and prankster in town, try going into this business. At Halloween it's the kids. At Christmas and Easter it's the religious nuts. In September it's college boys being initiated. Any month at all is good for a lewd suggestion from a sex deviate as to what goes on in my lab. I received the call about Camilla just before Christmas, which made it the right timing for one of the religious crackpots."

"Was it from a man or a woman?"

"A woman. Such calls usually are."

"What kind of voice did she have?"

"Medium in all respects, as I recall," Fondero said. "Medium-pitched, medium-aged, medium-cultured."

"Any trace of an accent?"

"No."

"Could it have been a young woman, say about thirty?"

"Maybe, but I don't think so."

"What did she want?"

"I can't remember her exact words after all this time. The gist of her conversation was that Camilla was a good Catholic and should be buried in consecrated ground. I told her about the difficulties involved in such an arrangement, since there was no evidence that Camilla had died in the Church. She claimed that Camilla had fulfilled all the requirements for burial in consecrated ground. Then she hung up. Except for the degree of self-control she displayed, it was an ordinary run-of-the-mill crank call. At least I thought so then."

"Camilla is buried in the Protestant cemetery," Pinata said.

"I talked it over with our parish priest. There was no alternative."

"Did the woman mention the money?"

"No."

"Or the manner of his death?"

"I got the impression," Fondero said cautiously, "from her insistence on Camilla being a *good* Catholic, that she didn't believe he had killed himself."

"Do you?"

"The experts called it suicide."

"I should think by this time you'd be something of an expert yourself along those lines."

"Experienced. Not expert."

"What's your private opinion?"

Outside the window Fondero's son had begun to whistle, loudly and off-key, "Take Me Out to the Ball Game."

"I work very closely with the police and the coroner's office," Fondero said. "It wouldn't be good business for me to have an opinion contrary to theirs."

"But you have one anyway?"

181

"Not for the record."

"All right, for me. Top secret."

Fondero went over to the window and then returned to his chair, facing Pinata. "Do you happen to recall the contents of the note he left?"

"Yes. 'This ought to pay my way into heaven, you stinking rats... Born, too soon, 1907. Died, too late, 1955.'"

"Now everybody seemed to take that as a suicide note. Perhaps that's what it was. But it could also be the message of a man who knew he was going to die, couldn't it?"

"I guess so," Pinata said. "The idea never occurred to me."

"Nor to me, until I made my own examination of the body. It was that of an old man—prematurely aged if we accept the date of his birth as given, and I see no reason why he should lie about it under the circumstances. Many degenerative processes had taken place: the liver was cirrhotic, there was considerable hardening of the arteries, and he was suffering from emphysema of the lungs and an advanced case of arthritis. It was this last thing that interested me the most. Camilla's hands were badly swollen and out of shape. I seriously doubt whether he could have grasped the knife firmly enough to have inflicted the wound himself. Maybe he could. Maybe he did. All I'm saying is, I doubt it."

"Did you express your doubts to the authorities?"

"I told Lieutenant Kirby. He wasn't in the least excited. He claimed that the suicide note was more valid evidence than the opinion of a layman. Although I don't hold a pathologist's degree, I hardly consider myself a layman after some twenty-five years in the business. Still, Kirby had a point: opinions don't constitute evidence. The police were satisfied with a suicide verdict, the coroner was satisfied, and if Camilla had any friends who weren't, they didn't bother complaining. You're a detective, what do you think?"

"I'd be inclined to agree with Kirby," Pinata said carefully, "on the basis of the facts. Camilla had good reason to kill himself. He wrote, if not a suicide note, at least a farewell note. He left money for his funeral expenses. The knife used had his own initials on it. In the face of all this, I can't put too much stock in your opinion that Camilla's hands were too crippled to have wielded the knife. But of course I've had no experience with arthritis."

"I have."

Fondero leaned forward, holding out his left hand as if it were some specimen from his lab. Pinata saw what he hadn't noticed before: that Fondero's knuckles were swollen to twice normal size, and the fingers were bent and stiffened into a claw.

"That," Fondero said, "used to be my pitching hand. Now I couldn't even field a bunt if the World Series depended on it. I sit in the stands as a spectator, and when Wally Moon belts one over the fence, I can't even applaud. All my lab work these days is done by my assistants. Believe me, if I wanted to kill myself, it would have to be with something other than a knife."

"Desperation often gives a man additional strength."

"It may give him strength, yes, but it can't loosen up fused joints or restore atrophied muscles. It's impossible."

Impossible. Pinata wondered how often the word had already come up in connection with Camilla. Too many times. Perhaps he'd been the kind of man destined for the impossible, born to botch up statistics and defy the laws of physics. The evidence of motive, weapon, suicide note, and funeral money was powerful enough, but fused joints couldn't be loosened overnight, nor atrophied muscles restored on impulse or by desire.

Fondero was still holding out his hand for exhibit like a freak at a sideshow. "Are you still inclined to believe Kirby, Mr. Pinata?"

"I don't know."

"I don't actually know, either. All I can say is that if Camilla grasped that knife with those hands of his, I wish he'd have stayed alive long enough to tell me how he did it. I could use some advice on the subject."

He hid his deformed hand in his pocket. The show was over; it had been an effective one.

"Kirby's a sharp man," Pinata said.

"That's right, he's a sharp man. He just doesn't happen to have arthritis."

"Wouldn't Camilla's condition have prevented him from writing the suicide note?"

"No. It was printed, not written. This is common among arthritics. It's a good deal easier to print legibly."

"From your examination of the body, what general information did you get about Camilla's manner of living?"

"I won't go into further medical details," Fondero said, "but the evidence indicates that he was a heavy drinker, a heavy smoker, and at some time in his life a heavy worker."

"Was there any clue about what kind of work?"

"One, although some orthopedists might not agree with me. He had a bone malformation known as *genu varum*, less politely called bowlegs. Now bowlegs can be caused by a number of things, but if I had to make a wild guess about Camilla's occupation, I'd say that, beginning early in his youth, he had a lot to do with horses. He may have worked on a ranch."

"Ranch," Pinata said, frowning. Someone had recently mentioned a ranch to him, but it wasn't until he got back to his car that he recalled the circumstances: Alston on the telephone had said that Mrs. Rosario, Juanita's mother, had been housekeeper on a ranch and had inherited enough money, when the owners died, to buy the house on Granada Street.

14

The hotel guests are looking at me queerly while I write this, as if they are wondering what a tramp like me is doing in their lobby where I don't belong, writing to a daughter who has never really belonged to me...

Granada was a street of small frame houses built so closely together that they seemed to be leaning on each other for moral and physical and economic support against the pressures from the white side of town. The pomegranate trees, for which the street was named, were fruitless now, but at Christmas time the gaudy orange balls of fruit hung from the branches looking quite unreasonable, as if they had not grown there at all but had been strung up to decorate the street for the holiday season.

Five-twelve hid its age and infirmities—and proclaimed its independence from its neighbors—with a fresh coat of bright pink paint that seemed to have been applied by a child or a near-sighted amateur. Blotches of paint stained the narrow sidewalk, the railing of the porch, the square yard of lawn; the calla lilies, the leaves of the holly bush and the pittosporum hedge, were pimpled with pink as if they'd broken out with some strange new plant disease. Pink footsteps, belonging to a child or a very small woman, led up the gray porch steps and disappeared in the coarse bristles of the coca mat outside the front door. These footsteps were the only evidence that a child or children might be living in the house. There were no toys or parts of toys on the porch or lawn, no discarded shoes or sweaters, no half-eaten oranges or jelly sandwiches. If Juanita and her six children had taken up residence here, someone was being careful to hide the fact, perhaps Juanita herself, perhaps Mrs. Rosario.

Pinata pressed the door buzzer and waited, trying to figure out why Juanita had suddenly decided to come back to town after an absence of more than three years. She must have known she'd be in trouble with the authorities for breaking probation when she disappeared in the first place. On the other hand, Juanita didn't behave on the logical level, so the reason for her return could be something quite trivial and capricious, or purely emotional: homesickness, a desire to see her mother again or to show off her latest husband and youngest child to her friends, perhaps a quarrel with a neighbor, wherever she'd been living, followed by a sudden violent desire to get away. It was difficult to guess her motives. She was like a puppet operated by dozens of strings; some of them had broken, and others had become so inextricably twisted that not one of them functioned as it was intended to. To remove these knots and tangles, and to splice the broken ends together, was the job of Alston and his staff. So far, they had failed. Juanita's soarings and somersaults, her leaps and landings were beyond the control of any puppeteer.

The door opened to reveal a short, thin middle-aged woman with black, expressionless eyes like ripe olives. She held her body so rigidly straight that she appeared to be wearing an iron brace on her back. Everything about her was stretched taut; her skin looked as if it had been starched, her hair was drawn back from her face in a tight and tidy little bun, and her mouth was compressed into a hard line. Pinata was surprised when it opened with such ease.

"What do you want?"

"Mrs. Rosario?"

"That is my name."

"I'm Steve Pinata. I'd like to talk to you for a minute, if I may."

"If it's about old Mr. Lopez next door, I have nothing more to say. I told the lady from the Department of Health yesterday, they had no right to take him away like that against his will. He's had that same cough all his life, and it's never done him a bit of harm. It's as natural to him as breathing. As for the rest of the neighborhood getting into that ray machine, free or not, I refused and so did the Gonzales and the Escobars. It's against nature, getting your lungs choked up with all those rays."

"I'm not connected with the Department of Health," Pinata said. "I'm looking for a man who may be calling himself Foster."

"Calling himself? What is this business, calling himself?"

"Your daughter knows him as Foster, let's put it that way."

Mrs. Rosario took a tuck in her mouth, like a sailor reefing a mainsail at the approach of a storm. "My daughter, Juanita, lives down south."

"But she's here now for a visit, isn't she?"

"Whose concern is it if she comes here for a visit? She has done no harm. I keep a sharp eye on her, she stays out of trouble. Who are you anyway to come asking questions about my Juanita?"

"My name is Stevens Pinata."

"So? What does that tell me? Nothing. It tells me nothing. I don't care about names, only people."

"I'm a private investigator, Mrs. Rosario. My job right now is to keep track of Foster."

The woman clapped one hand to her left breast as if something had suddenly broken under her dress, a heart or perhaps merely the strap of a slip. "He's a bad man, is that what you're saying? He's going to cause trouble for my Juanita?"

"I don't think he's a bad man. I can't guarantee there won't be trouble, though. He can be a little impulsive at times. Did he come here with your daughter, Mrs. Rosario?"

"Yes."

"And they went off together?"

"Yes. Half an hour ago."

A thin, red-cheeked girl about ten came out on the porch of the house next door and started rotating a hula hoop around her hips and chewing a wad of gum in matching rhythm. She appeared to be completely oblivious to what was taking place on the adjoining porch, but Mrs. Rosario said in a hurried whisper, "We can't talk out here. That Querida Lopez, she hears everything and tells more."

Still not looking in their direction, Querida announced to the world in a loud, bright voice, "I am going to the hospital. None of you can come and see me either, because I've got spots on my lungs. I don't care. I don't like any of you anyway. I'm going to the hospital like Grandpa and I'll have lots of toys to play with and ice cream to eat, and I don't have to do any more dishes forever and ever. And don't any of you come and see me, because you can't, ha ha."

"Querida Lopez," Mrs. Rosario said sharply, "is this true?"

The only sign that the girl had heard was the increased speed of the hula hoop.

Mrs. Rosario's dark skin had taken on a yellowish tinge, and when she stepped back into her front room, it was as if Querida had pushed her in the stomach. "The girl lies sometimes. Perhaps it isn't true. If she is so sick as to go to a hospital, how could she be out playing like this? She coughs, yes, but all children cough. And you see for yourself what a fine, healthy color she has in her cheeks."

188

Pinata thought that the color might be caused by fever rather than health, but he didn't say so. He followed Mrs. Rosario into the house. Even after he closed the door behind him, he could hear Querida's rhythmic chanting: "Going to the hospital—I don't care. Can't come and see me—I don't care. Going in an ambulance..."

The rays of sun coming in through the lace curtains scarcely lightened the gloom of the small square parlor. All four walls were covered with religious ornaments and pictures, crucifixes and rosaries, Madonna's with and without child, heads of Christ, a little shrine presided over by the Holy Mother, haloed angels and blessed virgins. Many of these objects, which were intended to give hope and comfort to the living, had the effect of glorifying death while at the same time making it seem repulsive.

In this room, or another one just like it, Juanita had grown up, and this first glimpse of it did more to explain her to Pinata than all the words Alston had used. Here she had spent her childhood, surrounded by constant reminders that life was cruel and short, and the gates to heaven bristled with thorns, nails, and barbed wire. She must have looked a thousand times at the haloed mothers with their plump little babies, and unconsciously or deliberately, she had chosen this role for herself because it represented aliveness and creativity as well as sanctity.

Mrs. Rosario crossed herself in front of the little shrine and asked the Holy Mother for assurance that Querida Lopez, with her fine, healthy color, was lying. Then she tucked her thin body neatly into a chair, taking up as little space as possible because in this house there was hardly any room left for the living.

"Sit down," she said with a stiff nod. "I don't expect strangers to come into my house asking personal questions, but now you are here, it is only polite to ask you to sit down."

"Thanks."

The chairs all looked uncomfortable, as if they had been selected to discourage people from sitting. Pinata chose a small, wooden-backed, petit-point couch, which gave off a faint odor of cleaning fluid. From the couch he could look directly into what appeared to be Mrs. Rosario's bedroom. Here, too, the walls were crowded with religious paintings and ornaments, and on the night-stand beside the big carved double bed a candle was burning in front of the photograph of a smiling young man. Obviously, the young man had died, and the candle was burning for his soul. He wondered whether the young man had been Juanita's father and how many candles ago he had died.

Mrs. Rosario saw him staring at the photograph and immediately got up and crossed the room. "You must excuse me. It is not polite to display the sleeping quarters to strangers."

She pulled the bedroom door shut, and Pinata could see at once why she had left it open in the first place. The door looked as if it had been attacked by someone with a hammer. The wood was gouged and splintered, and one whole panel was missing. Through the jagged aperture, the young man continued to smile at Pinata. The flickering light of the candle made his face appear very lively; the eyes twinkled, the cheek muscles moved, the lips expanded and contracted, the black curls stirred in the wind behind the broken door.

"One of the children did it," Mrs. Rosario explained in a quiet voice. "I don't know which one. I was at the grocery store when it happened. I suspect Pedro, being the oldest. He's eleven, a boy, but the devil gets into him sometimes, and he plays rough."

Very rough, indeed, Pinata thought. *And playing isn't quite the word.*

"Pedro's down at the lumber mill now, seeing about a new door. For punishment, I made him take the other children with him.

Then he's got to paint and hang the new door by himself. I'm a poor woman. I can't afford painters and carpenters with such prices they charge."

It was obvious to Pinata that she wasn't rich. But he could see no signs in the house of extreme poverty, and the religious items alone had cost quite a bit of money. Mrs. Rosario's former employer on the ranch must have been generous in his will, or else she earned extra money doing odd jobs.

He glanced at the door again. *Some of the hammer marks were at the very top; if an eleven-year-old boy did the damage, he must be a giant for his age. And what would be his motive for such an act? Revenge? Destruction for its own sake? Or maybe,* Pinata thought, *the boy had been trying to break down a door locked against him.*

It didn't occur to him that Mrs. Rosario was lying…

She'd seen them coming up Granada Street, Juanita in her green uniform and an older man. Mrs. Rosario didn't recognize the man, but the two of them were laughing and talking, and that was enough: they were up to no good.

She called the children in from the backyard. They were old enough now to notice things, to wonder, yes, and to talk, too. Pedro had the eyes and ears of a fox and a mouth like a hippopotamus. Even in church he talked out loud sometimes and had to be punished afterward with adhesive tape.

She gave them each an apple and took them all into the bedroom. If they were very good, she promised, if they sat quietly on the bed and said their beads to themselves, later they would all go over to Mrs. Brewster's to watch the television.

She had just locked the bedroom door when she heard Juanita's quick, light step on the porch and the sound of laughter. She took the key out of the lock and put her eye to the keyhole. Juanita

191

was coming in the front door with the stranger, looking flushed and restless.

"Well, sit down," she said. "Take a look around. Some dump, eh?"

"It's different."

"I'll say it's different. Don't touch anything. She'll throw a fit."

"Where is your mother?"

Juanita raised her eyebrows, the corners of her mouth, and her shoulders in an elaborate combination of shrug and grimace. "How should I know? Maybe she dragged the kids over to church again."

"That's too bad."

"So what's too bad about it?"

"I was hoping to meet them." Fielding made his tone casual, as if he were expressing a polite desire instead of a deadly serious purpose. "I like children. I only had one of my own, a girl. She's about your age now."

"Yeah? How old do you think I am?"

"If you hadn't told me about the six children, I'd say about twenty."

"Sure," Juanita said. "I bet."

"I mean it. That goo you put on your eyes makes you look older, though. You should stop using it."

"It enhances them."

"They don't need enhancing."

"You can sure throw the bull around." But she began rubbing her eyelids with her two forefingers, as if she had more respect for his opinion than she cared to admit. "Is she pretty? Your kid, I mean."

"She was. I haven't seen her for a long time."

"How come you haven't seen her for a long time if you like children so much?"

It was a question with a hundred answers. He picked a couple at random. "I've been moving around. I've got itchy feet."

"So've I. Only I can't do much about it, saddled with six kids and an old lady that watches me like I got two heads." She flung herself almost violently on the couch, rolled over, and stared up at the ceiling. "Sometimes I wish a big wind would come along and blow this house away and me in it. I wouldn't care where I blew to. Even a foreign country would be O.K."

From the bedroom came the sudden, sharp cry of a child, followed immediately by a noisy babble of voices, as if that first single cry had been the signal for a whole chorus to begin.

Juanita glanced toward the door, looking angry but not surprised. "So she's in there spying on me again. I should've guessed."

The noise from the bedroom had increased to a roar. Fielding could scarcely hear his own voice above it. "We'd better leave. I don't want to get mixed up in another brawl."

"I haven't changed my clothes."

"You look fine. Come on, let's go. I need a drink."

"You can wait."

"For Pete's sake, someone might call the police like last time. Two hundred bucks that cost me."

"I don't like being spied on."

She jumped off the couch and moved swiftly toward the bedroom, yanking a large crucifix off the wall as she passed.

"What are you doing in there?" She banged on the door with the crucifix. "Open this up, you hear me? Open it up!"

There was a sudden silence. Then one of the children began to wail, and another answered in a scared voice, "Grandma won't let us."

Finally Mrs. Rosario herself spoke. "The door will be opened when the gentleman leaves."

"It'll be opened *now.*"

"When the gentleman leaves, not before. I will not allow the children to see their mother consorting with a strange man while her husband is away."

"Listen to me, you old spook!" Juanita screamed. "You know what I got here in my hand? I got Jesus Christ himself. And you know what I'm going to do with him? I'm going to pound him against this door—"

"You will not blaspheme in my house."

"—and pound him and pound him, until there's nothing left of him or it. Hear that, you witch? For once, Jesus is going to do me a good turn. He's going to break down this door."

"If there is any violence, I will take steps."

"He's on *my* side for a change, see? It's him and *me*, not you." She let out a brief, excited laugh. "Come on, Jesus baby, you're on my side."

She began striking the door with the crucifix, as rhythmically as a skilled carpenter driving nails. Fielding sat, his face frozen in a grimace of pain, listening to the sound of splintering wood and sobbing children. Suddenly the crucifix broke at the top, and the metal head flew through the air, narrowly missing Fielding's, and ricocheted off a table onto the floor.

The same blow that broke the crucifix had shattered one of the panels in the door, so that Mrs. Rosario could see what had happened. The door opened then, and the children scrambled out like cattle from a boxcar, confused and terrified.

With a cry of rage Mrs. Rosario darted across the room and picked up the head of Jesus.

"That'll teach you to spy on me," Juanita said triumphantly. "Next time it'll be more than Jesus; it'll be every lousy piece of junk in the house."

"Wicked girl. Blasphemer."

"I don't like being spied on. I don't like doors locked against me."

Three of the children had run directly out the front door. To the others, one hidden behind the couch and two clinging to Juanita's skirt, Mrs. Rosario said in a trembling voice, "Come. We must kneel together and ask forgiveness for your mother's sin."

"Pray for yourself, you old spook. You need it as bad as anybody."

"Come, children. To keep your mother's soul from the torments of eternal hell—"

"Leave my kids alone. If they don't want to pray, they don't have to."

"Marybeth, Paul, Rita…"

None of the children moved or uttered a sound. They seemed suspended in midair like aerialists aware of an imminent fall and not sure which side would be safer to fall on—God and Grandma's, or Juanita's. It was the youngest, Paul, who decided first. He pressed his dark, moist face against Juanita's thigh and began to wail again.

"Stop slobbering," Juanita said, and gave him a casual push in Fielding's direction.

Fielding found himself in the position of a spectator at a ball game who sees the ball suddenly coming off the field in his direction and has no choice but to catch it. He picked the child up and carried him into the bedroom to get him away from the screaming women.

"You'll go to hell, you wicked girl."

"That's O.K. by me. I got relatives there."

"Don't you dare speak his name. He is not in hell. The priest says by this time he is with the angels."

"Well, if he can get to be with the angels, so can I."

"'Hi diddle diddle,'" Fielding whispered in the boy's ear. "'The cat and the fiddle. The cow jumped over the moon. The little dog laughed to see such sport, and the dish ran away with the spoon.' Did you ever see a cow jump over the moon?"

The boy's black eyes looked grave, as if this were a very important question that deserved something better than a snap answer. "I saw a cow once."

"Jumping over the moon?"

"No, he was giving milk. Grandma took us to see a big ranch, and there was cows giving milk. Grandma says cows work hard to give milk, so I mustn't spill mine on the table."

"I had a job on a ranch once. And believe me, I worked harder than any old cows."

"Grandma's ranch?"

"No. This one was far away."

The noise from the next room stopped abruptly. Juanita had disappeared into another part of the house, and Mrs. Rosario was kneeling alone in front of the little shrine, the head of Jesus cradled in her left hand. She prayed silently, but from the vindictive look on her face Fielding thought she must be invoking punishment, not forgiveness.

"I want my daddy," the boy said.

"He'll be back one of these days. Now how about Miss Muffett, would you like to hear about her troubles? 'Little Miss Muffett sat on a tuffet, eating her curds and whey. Along came a spider and sat down beside her, and frightened Miss Muffett away.' Are you afraid of spiders?"

"No."

"Good boy. Spiders can be very useful."

Fielding's collar was damp with sweat, and every few seconds his heart gave a quick extra beat, as if it were being chased around inside his chest cavity. He often worried about having a heart attack, but when he was at home, he simply took a couple of drinks and forgot about it. Here he couldn't forget. It seemed, in fact, inevitable, a bang-up climax to the crazy afternoon of the broken crucifix and the shattered door, the grim praying woman and the terrified children, Juanita and Miss Muffett. *And now, ladies and gentlemen, for our grand finale of the day we give you Stanley Fielding and his death-defying coronary.*

"Miss Muffett," he said, listening to his heartbeat, "was a real little girl, did you know that?"

"As real as me?"

"That's right, just as real as you. She lived, oh, about two or three hundred years ago. Well, one day her father wrote a verse about her, and now children all over the world like to hear about little Miss Muffett."

"I don't." The boy shook his head, and his thick black curly hair tickled Fielding's throat.

"You don't, eh? What do you like to hear about? And not so loud; we mustn't disturb Grandma."

"Talk about the ranch."

"What ranch?"

"Where you worked."

"That was a long time ago." *Ladies and gentlemen, before our star performer does his death-defying act, he will entertain you with a few highlights from his life story.* "Well, I had a mare called Winnie. She was a cutting horse. A cutting horse has got to be fast and smart, and that's what she was. All I had to do was stay in the saddle, and Winnie could pick a cow from a herd as easy as you can pick an orange from a bowl of fruit."

"Grandma gave us an apple before you came. I hid mine. Want to know where?"

"I don't think you'd better confide in me. I'm not so good at keeping secrets."

"Do you tell?"

"Yeah. Sometimes I tell."

"I tell all the time. The apple is hid under the—"

"Shhh." Fielding patted his head. The boy, without speaking, had already told him what he'd come to find out. His black eyes and hair, his dark skin had spoken for him. One thing was clear now: a mistake had been made. But who had made it, and why? *My God, I need a drink. If I had a drink, I could think. I could think with a drink. Think…*

"What's your name?"

"Foster," Fielding said. He had used the name so often that it no longer seemed like lying. "Stan Foster."

"Do you know my daddy?"

"I'm not sure."

"Where is he?"

It was a good question, but an even better one was going around in Fielding's mind. Not where, but who. *Who's your daddy, kid?*

The boy was clinging to his neck so tightly that Fielding couldn't move his head even to look around the room. But he was suddenly aware of a peculiar odor which he'd been too excited to notice before. It took him a minute or two to identify it as burning wax.

Rising from the bed, he eased the child gently onto the floor. Then he turned and saw the picture of the curly-haired young man behind the flickering candle. His heart began to pound against his rib cage, and the noise of it seemed as loud as the noise Juanita had made banging on the door. Flashes of red struck his eyes, and his hands and legs felt numb and swollen to double size. *This is it,* he thought. *Ladies and gentlemen, this is it. Here I go…*

It was a trap.

He saw it now very clearly. The whole thing was a trap; it had been written, rehearsed, staged. Every line, even the little boy's, had been memorized. Every piece of business, including the shattering of the door, had been practiced over and over until it seemed real. And all of it had been leading up to this moment when he saw the picture.

He raised his swollen hand and wiped away the sweat that was dripping into his eyes, obscuring his vision.

They were in there now, in the other room, waiting to see what he would do, Mrs. Rosario pretending to pray, Juanita pretending to be getting ready to go out, the children pretending to be scared. They were in there listening, watching, waiting for him to give himself away, to make the wrong move. Even the little boy was a spy. Those innocent eyes looking up at him were not innocent at all, and the angelic mouth belonged to a demon.

"He is with the angels by this time," Mrs. Rosario had said. Fielding knew now whom she'd been talking about, and crazy laughter rose in his throat and stuck there until he began to choke. He loosened his tie to get more air but immediately tightened it again. He must not let the watchers see that the picture meant anything to him or that he was trying to find out about the little boy's father.

He was aware, in a vague way, that he wasn't thinking straight, but he couldn't clear his mind of the haze of suspicion that clouded it. In this haze, fact and fiction merged into paradox: a troubled girl became a master criminal, her mother a scheming witch, and the children were not children at all but adults whose bodies hadn't grown up.

"Hey, I'm ready," Juanita said.

Fielding whirled around so fast he lost his balance and had to steady himself by grabbing one of the bedposts.

"It's a brand-new dress. How do I look?"

He couldn't speak yet, but he managed to nod. The haze was beginning to lift, and he could see her quite clearly: a young woman, slim and pretty in a blue and white full-skirted dress, with a red sweater flung over her shoulders and red snakeskin shoes with heels like needles.

"Come on," she said. "Let's get out of this spookery."

He walked out of the bedroom, rubber-kneed, trembling with relief. There had been no plot, no trap. His mind had invented the whole business, molded it out of fear and guilt. Juanita, Mrs. Rosario, the children, they were all innocent. They didn't even know his real name or why he had come here. The picture beside the bed was one of those ugly coincidences that happen sometimes.

And yet...

I need a drink. My God, get me to a drink.

Mrs. Rosario crossed herself and turned from the little shrine. She still had made no acknowledgment of Fielding's presence, not even a casual glance in his direction. She looked over his shoulder, addressing Juanita. "Where are you going?"

"Out."

"You will buy me a new crucifix."

Juanita moistened a forefinger on her tongue and smoothed her eyebrows. "I will, eh? Fancy me being so bighearted."

"You are not bighearted," Mrs. Rosario said steadily. "But you're sensible enough to realize this is my house. If I lock the door against you, you'll be out on the street."

"You just tried the lock bit. See where it got you."

"If there's any more of that, I'll call the police. You'll be arrested, and the children will be taken to Juvenile Hall."

Juanita had turned quite pale, but she grinned and shrugged her shoulders so expressively that her sweater fell off onto the floor. When Fielding bent over to pick it up, she snatched it out of his hand. "So? The kids will be just as good off there as they are in this nuthouse with you crawling around on your knees half the time."

Mrs. Rosario for the first time looked directly at Fielding. "Where are you taking my daughter?"

"He's not taking me anyplace," Juanita said. "I'm taking him. I'm the one with the car."

"You leave that car in the garage. Joe says you're too wild to drive. You'll be killed. You can't afford to be killed with so many sins on your soul you haven't confessed."

"We had planned on going to a movie," Fielding said to Mrs. Rosario. "But if you don't approve—that is, I wouldn't want to be the cause of any family friction."

"Then you'd better leave. My daughter is a married woman. Married women don't go to movies with strangers, and gentlemen don't ask them to. I don't even know who you are."

"Stan Foster, ma'am."

"What does that tell me? Nothing."

"Leave him alone," Juanita said. "And keep your nose out of my business."

"This is my house; what goes on here is my business."

"O.K., take your damn house. Keep it. It's only a lousy little shack anyway."

"It's sheltered you and your children in times of trouble. You'd be out on the street if it wasn't for—"

"I *like* the street."

"Yes, sure, now that it's warm and sunny you like it. Wait till the night comes, wait till it's cold and maybe it starts to rain. You'll come crying."

"You'd love that, wouldn't you, me coming crying. All right, start praying for rain, see if I come crying." Juanita opened the front door and motioned to Fielding to go out ahead of her. "Just see if I come crying."

"Gypsy," Mrs. Rosario said in a soft, furious whisper. "You're no child of mine, gypsy. I found you in an open field. I took pity. There's none of my blood in you, gypsy."

Juanita slammed the door. The Madonnas on the wall shivered but continued to smile.

"I was born right here in St. Joseph's hospital," Juanita said. "It's on the records. You didn't believe that open field stuff, did you?"

"Let's go someplace and have a drink."

"Sure, but did you or didn't you?"

"What?"

"Believe that gypsy stuff."

"No." Fielding wanted to break into a run, to put as much distance as possible between himself and the weird house with the decapitated crucifix.

Juanita was tottering along beside him, crippled by her needle heels. "Hey, not so fast."

"I need a drink. My nerves are shot."

"She bugged you, eh?"

"Yeah."

"She didn't use to be so spooky when I lived at home before. Sure, she was religious, but it wasn't so bad until she started trying to get people into heaven. You saw the candle, didn't you?"

"I guess so."

"The car's just down here. I keep it in a separate garage so's the kids don't play around it and scratch the finish."

"We don't need a car," Fielding said. "I can't afford to be killed with all the sins on my soul, either."

"She's a crackpot."

"Yes. Only—"

"You heard that open field stuff, didn't you? That was all lies. It's on the records, how I was born in St. Joseph's hospital…"

Mrs. Rosario stood in front of the broken door as if she were trying to hide from Pinata the mortal wound of her house.

"Forgive me my curiosity," Pinata said. "But the young man in the picture, was he Juanita's father?"

"The name of Juanita's father has not been spoken in this house for twenty years. I would not waste good beeswax on his soul." She crossed her arms on her chest. "I must remind you that you were invited into my house to discuss Mr. Foster. No one else. Just Mr. Foster."

"All right. Where did he go when he left here with your daughter?"

"I don't know. They spoke of going to the movies. But Juanita hardly ever goes to the movies. She's afraid of being shut up in dark places."

"Well, what does she usually do when she gets off on a Saturday afternoon?"

"She shops or takes the children to the beach or maybe down to the wharf to fish. She likes being outdoors and talking and laughing with the fishermen that hang around the wharf. She can be a very happy girl sometimes." She studied her hands as if she were reading the past in their lines and finding it as inscrutable as the future. "Sometimes you never saw a happier girl."

"What does she do when she's miserable?"

"I don't follow her. I have the children to watch over."

"But you hear things?"

"Friends maybe tell me when they see her acting—acting, well, not so good."

"Does she do much drinking? I'm asking the question because Foster has a decided weakness in that direction. If Juanita shares it, it will give me some idea of where to start looking for them."

"She drinks sometimes."

"At the Velada?"

"No, never," Mrs. Rosario said sharply. "Never at the Velada. Mrs. Brewster wouldn't allow it, not even a glass of beer."

Strike the Velada, Pinata thought. That left some twenty-five or thirty places which could strictly be called taverns, and perhaps eighty or ninety restaurants in and around town which served liquor. A great many of these restaurants would be closed to Juanita because of her race, either obviously, with a quick brush-off at the door, or subtly, with small printed signs stating the proprietor's right to refuse service to anyone. The taverns, however, were mainly located in areas where discrimination would have meant bankruptcy. For this reason a tavern seemed the most logical place to look for Juanita. In spite of everything he'd been told about her aggressiveness, Pinata had a hunch that she was too timid to wander very far from the places where she felt welcome and at home.

"Mrs. Rosario," Pinata said, "Juanita left town nearly four years ago to live in Los Angeles. Why?"

"She got sick of being hounded by the police and the Probation Department and the people at the Clinic. Talk, talk, talk, that's all they did, tell her what was wrong with her, what to do, what to wear, how to manage the children."

"They were all trying to help her, weren't they?"

"It's a funny kind of help that hinders," she said scornfully. "The last time she was arrested, she wasn't doing any harm. It's hard, when you're young, always being followed by five children, never going anyplace alone. When she locked them in the apartment, it was for their own good, so they wouldn't run away or get in an accident. But the neighbors complained when they cried, and the police said what if there was a fire or an earthquake. So they arrested her and put the children in Juvenile Hall. Do you call this *helping?* I don't. If that's the only kind of help I can get, I'd rather fend for myself. Which is what she chose to do when she got out. She left right away, that same night. The children were in bed asleep, and I asked Mrs. Lopez to keep an eye on them while I went to church. When I came back, she was gone." She moved her head back and forth in remembered pain. "I didn't think she would leave so sudden, her with no husband, no friends, and another baby due in less than a month."

"Did she leave a message for you?"

"No."

"You didn't know where she was going?"

"No. I never heard from her or saw her again until two weeks ago. The Probation Department and someone from the Clinic came snooping around a few times. I told them just what I'm telling you now."

"I hear what you're telling me," Pinata said. "But is it the truth?"

Mrs. Rosario blinked, and the ripe-olive eyes disappeared for a fraction of a second under lids that looked withered from lack of tears. "Four years with no news of her, and suddenly comes a knock on the front door, and there she is, with six children and a husband and a car. She talked a blue streak telling me how happy she was, and didn't I think the baby was cute and the car beautiful and the husband handsome. But there was a look in her eye I didn't like, that restless look of hers. When she's like that, she hardly eats or sleeps, she just keeps on the go, day and night, one place to another, never getting tired."

One place to another, Pinata thought. *Twenty-five taverns, eighty restaurants, sixty thousand people. I'd better start moving.*

"This man she's with," Mrs. Rosario said, "this Mr. Foster, he is a drunk?"

"Yes."

"You find them and send Juanita home."

"I'll try."

"Tell her I'm sorry I called her a gypsy. I lost control of my tongue. She's no gypsy, my Juanita. I lost control—it's so easy sometimes. Afterwards I'm filled with such shame and sadness. You find her for me, will you? Tell her I'm sorry?"

"I'll do my best."

"Hurry up before this man gets her into trouble."

Pinata wasn't sure who was going to get whom into trouble, but he knew they made a bad combination, Juanita and Fielding. He wrote his name and the phone numbers of his office and residence on a slip of paper and gave it to Mrs. Rosario.

She held it at arm's length to read it. "Pinata," she said, nodding. "That's a good Catholic name."

"Yes."

"If my daughter went to church more often, she wouldn't suffer from this sickness."

"Perhaps not," Pinata said, knowing how useless it would be to argue the point. "I'd appreciate your letting me know right away if either Juanita or Fielding shows up here again."

"Fielding?"

"That's his real name."

"Fielding," she repeated quietly. Then she folded the piece of paper and tucked it into the pocket of her black dress. "I guess it doesn't matter what people call themselves. Fielding may not be his real name, either, maybe?"

206

"I'm sure it is."

"Well, it's no business of mine." She crossed the room and opened the front door. "You won't find Juanita, or Fielding, either. With a car, they could be anywhere by this time."

"I can try."

"Don't try for my sake."

"You asked me to find her and send her home."

"I'm tired," she said bitterly. "I'm *tired*. Let her stay lost."

"I have a job to do."

"Then do it. Good day to you, Mr. Pinata. If that is your name."

"It's the only one I have."

"I don't care anyway."

When he stepped across the threshold, she closed the door behind him so quickly that he felt he'd been forcibly ejected.

The porch of the Lopez house next door was empty, and Querida's purple hula hoop lay broken on the steps.

Mrs. Rosario waited until his car had turned the corner. Peering through the lace curtain, she felt faint and very cold, as if an iron hand had squeezed her heart and stopped its flow of blood. She touched the silver cross she wore at her throat, hoping it would warm and comfort her. But the metal was as cold as her skin. *Pinata. It sounded false. He hadn't even claimed that it was real, just that it was the only one he had.*

She went out into the kitchen and picked up the telephone directory. The name was listed. Stevens Pinata, and the phone numbers were the same ones he'd written on the slip of paper.

She stood leaning against the sink, paralyzed by indecision. She had orders not to call Mr. Burnett, the lawyer, at his office unless it was absolutely necessary, and never to call him at his home under any circumstances. But what right had he to give the orders? Maybe he'd even been the one who sent Pinata and Fielding to spy on her. Well, they had learned nothing, either of them. The picture had been taken thirty years ago and bore no resemblance to the way he'd looked when he died.

The minutes passed, ticking away like heartbeats. It had been a long, cruel day. So many of the days were long and cruel. Carlos was well out of it. He was with the angels by this time. No more candles would be necessary, the priest said. "He will certainly be in heaven by this time," the priest said. "You mustn't become a fanatic; it looks bad for the church. This has been going on long enough."

He was right, of course. Things had been going on long enough...

She picked up the phone.

15

Your mother kept her vow, Daisy. We are still apart, you and I.
She has hidden her shame because she cannot bear it the way we
weaker and humbler ones can and must and do...

On Saturday afternoon Ada Fielding had lunch at a downtown
restaurant with a group of friends. After lunch she found herself
being followed into the powder room by Mrs. Weldon, a member
of the group whom she didn't know very well and didn't like at all.
Mrs. Weldon's large, inquisitive eyes were always hidden by a veil,
like windows by a net curtain, and her thin, sharp mouth moved
constantly, even when she wasn't talking, as if she were chewing
on some little regurgitated seeds from the past.

Adjusting her veil in front of the mirror above the washbasin,
Mrs. Weldon said, "How's Daisy?"

"Daisy? Oh, fine, she couldn't be better, thanks."

"And Jim?"

She wasn't even aware that Mrs. Weldon knew the names of her
daughter and son-in-law, but she concealed her surprise, as she
had concealed a great many other things in her lifetime, under
a slow, placid smile. "Jim is very well, too. He'd planned on going
north this weekend to look at some land he's thinking of buying,
but he decided to wait until it was cooler. Hasn't it been a fantastic
year? All this heat and no rain to speak of."

But Mrs. Weldon did not intend to put up with weather-talk
when she'd planned on people-talk. "A friend of mine saw Daisy
the other day—Corinne, you've heard me mention Corinne, the

lovely girl that lives next door to us—well, not a girl, really, she's almost forty, but she's kept her figure like a girl. Of course she was born skinny; that helps. Corinne saw Daisy just the other day and said she was looking quite peaked."

"Indeed? I certainly haven't noticed."

"Thursday, it was. Thursday afternoon, walking along Piedra Street with a young man. I knew it couldn't be Jim. Jim's so blond and fair-skinned, and this man was quite—well, dark."

"Daisy is acquainted with a great many men," Mrs. Fielding said casually. "Dark and fair."

"I meant dark in you-know-what sense."

"I'm afraid I don't understand."

"Of course you're not a native Californian..." Mrs. Weldon stopped and shook her head helplessly; these nonnative Californians could be very dense. "I meant, this man wasn't one of *us.*"

Ada Fielding was well aware of her meaning, but it seemed advisable to feign innocence, to appear imperturbable; there was nothing a gossip enjoyed more than the signs of anxiety, a quickening of the breath, a sudden flush, a clenching of the hands. Mrs. Fielding's hands and breathing remained steady, and her flush was hidden by a layer of powder. Only she knew it was there, she could feel it in her cheeks and neck, and it annoyed her because there was nothing to get excited about. Daisy had been seen walking along a street with a dark young man. Very well, what of it? Daisy had all kinds of friends. Still, in a town like this, one had to be careful. There was a difference between being tolerant and being foolish, and Daisy, even with the best of intentions, could be quite foolish at times.

"No, I'm not a native Californian," she said blandly. "I was born in Colorado. Have you ever visited Colorado? The mountain scenery is perfectly magnificent."

But Mrs. Weldon was not interested in Colorado. "By a strange coincidence Corinne happened to recognize the man. She met him last year when she was in that little scrape with the police. All she had at the bridge party was one teensy cocktail, but when she ran through the red light—Corinne swears it was yellow—the police insisted she was drunk. She had a perfectly dreadful time. It was Saturday, the banks were closed, and her lawyer was out playing golf, and her parents were in Palm Springs for the weekend. And the poor girl is so delicate because she never eats anything. Anyway, along came this young man and bailed her out. Corinne can't recall his name, but she remembered his face because he was so good-looking—except of course he was—well, dark."

"That's a very interesting story about Corinne's scrape with the police," Mrs. Fielding said with a small, steely smile. "I must remember to pass it along."

For nearly a week Daisy had been trying to arrange to have the house to herself, and she had finally accomplished it. Her mother was downtown shopping, Stella had taken the weekend off after Daisy convinced her she wasn't feeling well, and Jim had gone out for a sail in Adam Burnett's new racing sloop. Both the invitation and its acceptance had been engineered by Daisy: Jim suffered from seasickness, and Adam, who wasn't accustomed to the new boat, would have preferred a more experienced crew, but neither man put up much of an argument.

From the kitchen window Daisy watched Jim's car until it disappeared around the first sharp turn of the road that wound down the canyon. Then she went down immediately to the lower part of the house. Here there was an extra bedroom and bath for guests; a lanai decorated in pale green and turquoise which, seen in a half-light, looked under water; Jim's hobby room; and, at the far end of the house off the lanai, Jim's den. The den was filled with various pieces of furniture Jim had made himself, some of it experimental and impractical, all of it modernistic in line. The largest object in the room looked incongruous beside the modern pieces: a huge, old-fashioned rolltop desk which Jim had bought at an auction so that he could study its design and work out an improved version. But the old desk had proved so useful and satisfactory that he'd never bothered trying to improve it.

The rolltop and the drawers were locked, though the key was in plain sight on the windowsill. Daisy thought how typical this was of Jim, to lock everything, as if he felt surrounded by thieves, then to leave the key available, as if he'd decided he had nothing worth stealing after all.

She unlocked the desk while the dog, Prince, stood in the doorway, his tail between his legs, his amber eyes indicating dis-approval of this change in routine. He knew Daisy didn't belong down here in this room, and he sensed her nervousness.

The top part of the desk was very neat, with separate little drawers for stamps and for paper clips, compartments for pencils, current bills, unanswered letters, bankbooks, clippings from out-of-town newspapers advertising land for sale. In contrast to the top of the desk, the larger drawers were crammed with stuff—old letters and postcards, bank statements, half-empty packets of matches and cigarettes.

She began going through the drawers, taking everything out and laying each item on a half-finished free-form table which Jim was making for her mother's cottage. She had no real hope of finding anything, but she kept on searching, her hands moving clumsily as if they were weighted down by feelings of guilt and shame at what she was doing. Jim had always trusted her, and she had trusted him. Now, she thought, after eight years of marriage, she was going through his private papers like a common thief. And, as any common thief deserved, she was finding nothing. The postcards were impersonal, the letters innocent. Already, in her mind, apologies were forming: *Jim dear, I'm terribly sorry. I didn't mean any harm...*

At the back of the left bottom drawer she came across a pile of used checkbooks. They were not arranged in order of date. The one on the top was from a year ago and covered a period of four months.

Without expecting to find anything important, she began to turn the tiny pages listlessly, as if she were reading a dull book with lots of characters but no plot. She knew most of the characters: the pharmacist, Stella, the owners of the bookstore and dress shop and building supply company, the dentist, the veterinarian, the gardener, the paperboy. The largest amount, $250, had gone to Stella for wages. The stub with the next largest amount bore the name Ab and the amount $200. It was dated September 1.

She checked the next month's stubs, and here again she discovered an identical notation for October 1. When she came to the end of the book, she'd found four of them altogether, each for $200, paid to Ab at the beginning of the month.

Ab. She knew no one by that name, no Abner, Abbott, Abernathy, Abigail. The closest was Adam. Adam Burnett. A.B.

She was not actually surprised at first: it was natural enough for Adam to be receiving money from Jim. He was Jim's lawyer and did all his tax work. But the amount—$200 a month, $2,400 a year for a tax consultant—seemed excessive, and she was puzzled by the fact that Jim had not paid it through his office as a business expense. Was it possible that Jim was paying off a debt, that he had borrowed money from Adam and wanted to keep it secret from his business associates? That he was not as well off as he pretended to be in front of her and her mother?

How foolish of him not to tell me, she thought. *I could easily economize. Mother and I got along on a shoestring when we had to. And we usually had to.*

The dog, Prince, suddenly let out a bark and bounded noisily through the lanai and up the stairs. Although Daisy could hear nothing from the upper floor, she knew someone must have come into the house, and she began frantically cramming everything back into the drawers. She might have had a chance to finish if Prince hadn't decided that it was his duty to guide Mrs. Fielding down to the den and Daisy.

The two women stared at each other for a moment in the silence of mutual confusion. Then Daisy said awkwardly, "I thought you were going to spend the afternoon shopping."

"I changed my mind. It was too hot downtown."

"Oh."

"It's nice and cool down here, though."

"Yes."

"Just what do you think you're doing?"

It was, for Daisy, like a scene from her childhood, with her mother standing over her, strong and angry and, above all, right, and herself cringing and scared and, beneath all, wrong. But she was older now; she knew better than to sound scared or admit she was wrong. "I was looking for something I thought Jim might have put in his desk."

"Something so important that you couldn't wait until he comes home to ask him about it?"

"On the contrary, it's so trivial I wouldn't bother him about it. Jim has a lot on his mind."

"You should know. You put it there."

"Oh, Mother, for heaven's sake, don't. Don't start anything."

"Something has already been started," Ada Fielding said harshly. "You started it last Monday morning when you allowed yourself to get hysterical over some absurd little dream. That's how it all began, with a dream, and since then everything's been going to pieces. There have been times when I actually thought you were losing your mind—crying and carrying on, wandering around a cemetery alone looking for a tombstone you saw in a dream, cross-examining us all, even Stella, about a dead Mexican none of us ever heard of—it's sheer madness."

"If it's madness, it's mine, not yours. Don't worry about it."

"And now *this*, this sneaking around going through Jim's private papers, what does it mean? What are you looking for?"

"You know what I'm looking for. Jim must have told you. He tells you everything else."

"Only because you won't talk to him anymore."

Daisy stared at a section of the wall, wondering how many times during the past week Jim and her mother had discussed the situation. Perhaps they had a conference about her whenever she was absent, like two doctors in consultation over a very sick patient whose symptoms they didn't understand. *"She's looking for a lost day, Dr. Fielding." "That sounds pretty serious, Dr. Harker." "Oh, it is. First case I've ever had quite like it." "We may have to operate." "Good idea. Splendid. If the lost day is anywhere, it's inside her. We'll dig it out and dispose of it. Can't leave it in there festering."*

"You seem," Mrs. Fielding said, "to resent the fact that Jim confides in me."

"Not at all."

"Most young women are grateful for a decent relationship between in-laws. Jim and I have many differences of opinion, but we try to overlook them for your sake, because we both love you."

Mrs. Fielding's eyes were moist, and the corners of her mouth turned down as if she was going to cry. She pressed her fingertips against her mouth to steady it. "You know that, don't you? That we both love you?"

"Yes." She knew they both loved her, each in a different way, neither of them completely. Jim loved her insofar as she fitted his conception of the ideal wife. Her mother loved her as a projection of herself, but the projected part must be without the flaws of the original. Oh yes, certainly, she was loved. Being loved was not the problem. The problem, when you were the focus of two such powerful people as Jim and her mother, was the loss of spontaneity, of being able to love.

She thought, suddenly and disturbingly, of Pinata, of the drive back to the city from the cemetery, how old and tormented his face had looked in the dashlights as if he thought no one was watching him and it was safe to show his sorrow.

She turned her head and saw her mother looking at her, and she knew she'd better stop thinking about Pinata. It was frightening the way her mother could read her mind sometimes. *But then I am her projection machine. She just sits back and watches the pictures, censoring, editing. She can't see Pinata, though. She doesn't even know about him. No one does.* Pinata was hers, locked up in a secret drawer inside herself.

She finished replacing the papers. Then she locked the desk and put the key back on the windowsill. Everything looked exactly the same as when she had come in. Jim need never know she'd searched the desk and found out about the monthly payments to Adam. Unless her mother told him.

"I suppose," Daisy said, "you'll tell him?"

"I consider it my duty."

"Do you have any duty to me?"

216

"If I thought you were acting in a logical and rational matter, I wouldn't dream of mentioning this episode to Jim. Yes, I have a duty to you, and that is to protect you from the consequences of your own irresponsibility."

"I'm irresponsible," Daisy repeated. "I'm illogical and irrational and irresponsible. Just like my father. Go on, say it. I'm just like my father."

"I don't have to say it. You did."

"In exactly what ways have I been irresponsible?"

"Several that I know of. One that I'd like to find out about."

"You could ask me."

"I'm going to."

Mrs. Fielding sat down, holding her back straight and her hands crossed on her lap. It was a posture Daisy had come to know well through the years. It indicated seriousness of purpose, great patience, maternal affection (this hurts me more than it does you), and anger with its bile so finely distilled that it was almost palatable. Wry whiskey.

"I had lunch with Mrs. Weldon today," Mrs. Fielding said. "Do you remember her?"

"Vaguely."

"She's an impossible woman, but she has a way of finding out odd bits of information. This time the information was about you. Perhaps you'll consider it trivial. I don't. It's an indication that you're not being as careful as you should be. You can't afford to get yourself talked about. Jim is becoming a prominent man in this town. And he's a devoted husband as well. There isn't a woman who knows him who doesn't envy you."

Daisy had heard it all before. The tone varied, the clichés varied, but the message was always the same: that she, Daisy, was a very lucky girl, who ought to be grateful every day of her life that

Jim remained married to her even though she was sterile. Mrs. Fielding was too subtle to say any of this outright, but the implication was clearly made: Daisy had to be a super wife because she couldn't be a mother. The marriage was the important thing, not the individuals who contracted it. And the marriage was important, not for any religious or moral reasons, but because it meant, for Mrs. Fielding, the only real security she'd ever had. Daisy understood this and felt both sympathetic, because her mother had worked very hard to keep the family going, and resentful, because it seemed to Daisy that it wasn't her own life or marriage or husband; half, or more than half, belonged to her mother.

"Are you listening to me, Daisy?"

"Yes."

"On Piedra Street?"

"I may have been on Piedra Street. Why? What difference does it make?"

"Someone saw you," Mrs. Fielding said. "A next-door neighbor of Mrs. Weldon's, called Corinne. She claims you were walking with a good-looking dark young man who has some connection with jails or the Police Department. Were you, Daisy?"

She was tempted to lie about it, to keep Pinata safely and secretly locked inside her private drawer, but she was afraid that a lie would be more damaging than the truth. "Yes, I was there."

"Who was the man?"

"He's an investigator."

"Do you mean a *detective?*"

"Yes."

"Why on earth would you be walking around town with a detective?"

"Why not? It was a nice day, and I like walking."

218

There was a silence, then Mrs. Fielding's voice, as smooth and chilling as liquid air. "I warn you not to be flippant with me. How did you meet this man?"

"Through my—through a friend. I didn't know he was an investigator at the time. When I found out, I hired him."

"You hired him? What for?"

"To do a job. Now that's all I have to say on the subject."

She started toward the door, but her mother called her back with an urgent "Wait."

"I prefer not to discuss—"

"*You* prefer, do you? Well, *I* prefer to get this settled between the two of us before Jim finds out about it."

"There's nothing to settle," Daisy said, keeping her voice calm because she knew her mother was waiting for her to lose her temper. Her mother was always at her best when other people lost their tempers. "I hired Mr. Pinata to do some work for me, and he's doing it. Whether Jim finds out about it doesn't matter. He hires people at the office all the time. I don't make an issue of it, because it's none of my business."

"And you think it's none of Jim's business that you should go traipsing all over town with a Mexican?"

"Whether Mr. Pinata is a Mexican or not is beside the point. I hired him for his qualifications, not his racial background. I know nothing about him personally. He doesn't volunteer any information, and I don't ask for any."

"Tolerance is one thing. Foolishness is another." There was a curious rasp in Mrs. Fielding's voice, as if her fury, which had been denied admittance into words, had broken in through the back door of her larynx. "You know nothing about such people. They're cunning, treacherous. You're a babe in the woods. If you let him, he'll use you, cheat you—"

"Where did you learn so much about a man you've never even seen?"

"I don't have to see him. They're all alike. You must put a stop to this relationship before you find yourself in serious trouble."

"Relationship? For heaven's sake, you're talking as if he were my lover, not someone I happened to hire." She took a deep breath, fighting for control. "As for traipsing all over town, I didn't. Mr. Pinata escorted me to my car at the conclusion of our business appointment. Now does that satisfy you, *and* Mrs. Weldon, *and* Corinne?"

"No."

"I'm afraid it will have to. I have nothing farther to say on the subject."

"Sit down," Mrs. Fielding said sharply. "Listen to me."

"I've already listened."

"Forget I'm your mother for a minute."

"All right." It was easy, she thought. The green watery light coming in through the doorway from the lanai made Mrs. Fielding's face look strange and opalescent, like something that lived in the depths of the sea.

"For your own sake," Mrs. Fielding said, "I want you to tell me what you hired this Pinata to do."

"I'm trying to reconstruct a certain day in my life. I needed someone—someone objective—to help me."

"And that's all? It has nothing to do with Jim?"

"No."

"What about this other man, the one whose name is on the tombstone?"

"I've found out nothing further about him," Daisy said.

"Are you trying to?"

"Of course."

220

"Of course," Mrs. Fielding repeated shrilly. "What do you mean, *of course*? Are you still being foolish enough to believe that his tombstone is the same one you saw in your dream?"

"I know it's the same one. Mr. Pinata was with me at the cemetery. He recognized the tombstone before I did, from the description I'd given him from my dream."

There was a long silence, broken finally by Mrs. Fielding's painful whisper. "Oh, my God. What will I do? What's happening to you, Daisy?"

"Whatever is happening, it's to me, not to you."

"You're my only child. Your welfare and happiness are more important to me than my own. Your life is my life."

"Not anymore."

"Why have you changed like this?" Her eyes filled with tears of disappointment and anger and self-pity, all mixed up together and inseparable. "What's *happened* to us?"

"Please don't cry," Daisy said wearily. "Nothing's happened to us except that we're both getting a little older, and you want a little more of my life than I'm willing to give."

"God knows I only try to make things easier for you, to protect you. What's the use of my having gone through everything I did if I can't pass on to you the benefit of my experience? My own marriage was broken. Can you blame me for trying to keep yours from turning out the same way? Perhaps if I'd had someone to guide me, as I've guided you, I'd never have married Stan Fielding in the first place. I'd have waited for someone reliable and trustworthy, like Jim, instead of tying myself to a man who never told a straight story or did a straight thing from the day he was born."

She went on talking, pacing up and down the room as though it were the prison of the past. Daisy listened without hearing, while she tried to remember some of the lies her father had told her. But

221

they hadn't been lies, really, only bits of dreams that hadn't come true. *Someday, Daisy baby, I'm going to take you and your mother to Paris to see the Eiffel Tower.* Or to Kenya on a safari, or London for the coronation, or Athens to see the Parthenon.

If they were lies, they belonged as much to life as to Fielding. No one believed them anyway.

"Daisy, are you paying attention to me?"

"Yes."

"Then you must stop all this nonsense, do you understand? We're not the kind of people who hire detectives. There's something squalid about the very word."

"I'm not sure what kind of people we are," Daisy said. "I know what we pretend to be."

"Pretense? Is that what you call putting up a good front to the world, pretense? Well, I don't. I call it simple common sense and self-respect." Mrs. Fielding pressed one hand to her throat as if she were choking on the torrent of words gushing up inside her. "What's your idea of how to get along in life—hiring a hall and shouting your secrets to the whole city?"

"I have no secrets."

"Haven't you? *Haven't you?* You fool. I despair of you." She fell into a chair like a stone falling into a pond. "Oh God. I despair." The words rose from the very bottom of the pond. "I'm so— tired."

Daisy looked at her with bitterness. "You have reason to be tired. It takes a lot of energy to lead two lives, yours and mine."

The only noise in the room was the nervous panting of the collie and the tea tree pawing at the windowpane as if it wanted to get in.

"You must leave me alone," Daisy said softly. "Do you hear me, Mother? It's very important, you must leave me alone."

"I would if I thought you were strong enough to do without me."

"Give me a chance to try."

"You've picked a bad time to declare your independence, Daisy. Worse than you realize."

"Any time would be a bad time as far as you're concerned, wouldn't it?"

"Listen to me, you little fool," Mrs. Fielding said. "Jim's been a wonderful husband to you. Your marriage is a good one. Now, for the sake of some silly whim, you're putting it in jeopardy."

"Are you trying to tell me that Jim would actually divorce me simply because I've hired a detective?"

"All I meant—"

"Or could it be that you're afraid the detective might find out something Jim doesn't want found out?"

"If you were younger," Mrs. Fielding said steadily, "I'd wash your mouth out with soap for that remark. Your husband is the most decent, the most moral man I've ever met. Someday, when you're mature enough to understand, I'll be able to tell you some things about Jim that will surprise you."

"One thing about him surprises me right now. And I discovered it without the help of any detective." Daisy glanced briefly at the rolltop desk. "He's been paying Adam Burnett $200 a month. I found the check stubs."

"So?"

"It seems peculiar, doesn't it?"

"Obviously it does to you."

"You sound as if you know something about it."

"I know everything about it," Mrs. Fielding said dryly. "Jim bought some acreage Adam owned up near Santa Inez Pass. He intended to build a mountain hideaway on it as a surprise anniversary present for you. I'm sorry I've been forced to tell. But it seemed wiser to spoil the surprise than to let your suspicions keep on growing. You must have a guilty conscience, Daisy, or you wouldn't be so quick to accuse others."

"I didn't accuse him. I was simply curious."

"Oh? Just what did you think Adam was being paid for?" Mrs. Fielding got up out of the chair as though her joints had stiffened during the hour. "This man Pinata is obviously a bad influence on you to have affected your thinking like this."

"He has nothing to do with—"

"I want you to call him immediately and tell him he is no longer in your employ. Now I'm going over to my cottage and get some rest. The doctor says I must avoid scenes like this. The next time I see you, I hope the cause of them will have been removed."

"You think firing Pinata will solve everything?"

"It will be a start. Someone has to start somewhere."

She walked to the door with brisk, determined steps, but there was a weary stoop to her shoulders that Daisy had never seen before. "I despair," her mother had said.

Why, it's true, Daisy thought. *She despairs. How extraordinary to despair on a bright, sunny afternoon with Pinata somewhere in the city.*

She looked across the room at the telephone. Its shiny black cord seemed like a lifeline to her. All she had to do was pick up the receiver and dial, and even if she couldn't reach him personally, he would get her message through his answering service: *Call me, meet me, I want to see you.*

The phone began to ring while the sound of her mother's step was still on the stairs. She crossed the room, forcing herself to walk slowly because she wanted to run.

"Hello?"

"Long distance for Mrs. Daisy Harker."

"This is Mrs. Harker."

"Go ahead, ma'am. Your party's on the line."

Daisy waited, still hoping, though she had no reason to hope, that it was Pinata, that this was his way of reaching her in the event Jim or her mother might be around when he called.

But the voice was a woman's, high-pitched and nervous. "I know I shouldn't be phoning you like this, Mrs. Harker, or maybe I should say Daisy, though it don't seem socially proper to call you Daisy when we never even been introduced yet—"

"Who is this calling, please?"

"Muriel. Your new—new stepmother." Muriel let out an anxious little giggle. "I guess this is kind of a shock to you, picking up the phone and hearing a perfect stranger say she's your stepmother."

"No. I knew my father had married again."

"Did he write and tell you?"

"No. I heard it the way I hear everything else about my father— not from him but from somebody else."

"I'm sorry," Muriel said in her quick, nervous voice. "I told him to write. I kept reminding him."

"It's certainly not your fault. You have my best wishes, by the way. I hope you'll both be very happy."

"Thank you."

"Where are you calling from?"

"I'm in Miss Wittenburg's apartment across the hall. Miss Wittenburg promised not to listen; she has her fingers in her ears."

To Daisy it was beginning to sound like an April Fools' joke: *I am your new stepmother—Miss Wittenburg has her fingers in her ears...* "Is my father there with you?"

"No. That's why I decided to phone you. I'm worried about him. I shouldn't have let him go off by himself the way he did. Hitchhiking can be dangerous even when you're young and strong and have no outstanding weaknesses. I guess," Muriel added cautiously, "being as you're his daughter, you know he drinks?"

"Yes. I know he drinks."

"He's been pretty good lately, with me to keep an eye on him. But today he wouldn't take me along. He said we didn't have the money for bus fare for both of us, so he was going to hitchhike up alone."

"Do you mean up here, to San Félice?"

"Yes. He wanted to see you. His conscience was bothering him on account of he walked out on you last time when he lost his nerve. Stan has a very strong conscience; it drives him to drink. It's like he always has a bad pain that has to be numbed."

"I haven't seen him or heard from him," Daisy said. "Are you sure he intended to come right here to the house?"

"Why, yes. Why, he even mentioned how maybe you'd all have some champagne to celebrate being together again."

Daisy thought how typical it was of her father: *to Paris to see the Eiffel Tower, to London for the coronation, to San Félice for a champagne celebration.* Her sorrow and anger met and merged in a relationship that weakened them both and conceived a monster child. This child, half formed, tongueless, without a name, lay heavy inside her, refusing to be born, refusing to die.

"Stan wouldn't like me phoning you like this," Muriel said, "but I just couldn't help it. Last time he was up there, he got involved with that waitress, Nita."

"Nita?"

"Nita Garcia. That's what he called her."

"The report in the paper said her name was Donelli."

"It said Stan's name was Foster. That don't make it true." Muriel's dry little laugh was like a cough of disapproval. "Sure, I'm suspicious—women are—but I can't help thinking he's going to see her again, maybe get in some more trouble. I was hoping—well, that maybe he'd be in touch with you by this time and you could set him straight about associating with the wrong people."

"He hasn't been in touch," Daisy said. "And I'm afraid I couldn't set him straight if he were."

"No. Well. Well, I'm sorry to have bothered you." She seemed ready to hang up.

Daisy said hurriedly, "Just a minute, Muriel. I wrote my father a special delivery letter on Thursday night asking him an important question. Was this the reason he suddenly decided to come and see me?"

"I don't know about any special delivery letter."

"I sent it to the warehouse."

"He didn't mention it to me. Maybe he never got it. He was reading some other letters from you, though, just before he decided to leave. He kept them in his old suitcase. You know that old suitcase of his that he lugs around full of junk?"

Daisy remembered the suitcase. It was the only thing he'd taken with him when he'd left the apartment in Denver on a winter afternoon: "Daisy baby, I'm going to take a little trip. Don't you stop loving your daddy." The trip had lasted fifteen years, and she hadn't stopped.

"He was reading a letter of yours," Muriel said, "when he suddenly got the blues."

"How do you know it was from me?"

"Right away he started talking about how he'd failed as a father. Besides," she added bluntly, "nobody else writes to him."

"Did he mention what was in the letter?"

"No."

"Did he put it back in the suitcase?"

"No. I looked right after he left, and it wasn't there, so I guess he took it with him." Muriel sounded both apologetic and defensive. "He doesn't keep the suitcase *locked*, just chained."

"How did you know what particular letter to look for?"

"It was in a pink envelope."

Daisy was on the point of saying she didn't use colored stationery when she remembered that a friend of hers had given her some for her birthday several years ago. "What was the address on the envelope?"

"Some hotel in Albuquerque."

"I see." The Albuquerque address and the pink stationery dated the letter positively as being written in December of 1955. Her father had moved from Illinois to New Mexico at the end of that year, but he had stayed barely a month. She recalled sending his Christmas presents and check to a hotel in Albuquerque and receiving a postcard from Topeka, Kansas, a couple of weeks later thanking her for the gifts and saying he didn't like New Mexico, it was too dusty. There'd been a doleful quality about the postcard, and the handwriting was shaky, as if he'd been ill or on a drinking spree or, more likely, both.

"Stan will be awful mad about me phoning you like this," Muriel said nervously. "Maybe you just sort of keep it a secret when you see him?"

"I may not see him. He may not be anywhere near San Félice."

"But he said—"

"Yes. He said." He'd said, too, that he was taking a little trip, and the trip had lasted fifteen years. Perhaps he'd started on another little trip, and Muriel, as naive as Daisy had been in her early teens, would walk up and down the city streets searching for him in crowds of strangers; she would catch a glimpse of him passing in a speeding car or walking into an elevator just before the door

228

closed. Daisy had seen him a hundred times, but the car was too fast, the face in the crowd too far away, the elevator door too final.

"Well, I'm sorry to have bothered you," Muriel repeated.

"It was no bother. In fact, I'm very grateful for the information."

"Stan gave me another number to call in case of emergency, a Mr. Pinata. But I didn't want to call a stranger about—well, about Stan's certain weakness."

Daisy wondered how many strangers, the length and breadth of the country, knew about Stan's certain weakness and how many more were finding out right now. "Muriel?"

"Yes."

"Don't worry about anything. I'm going to get in touch with Mr. Pinata. If my father's in town, we'll find him and look after him."

"Thank you." There were tears in Muriel's voice. "Thank you ever so much. You're a good girl. Stan's always said you were a real good girl."

"Don't take everything my father says too seriously."

"He really meant it. And I do, too. I'm ever so grateful for all the things you've done for him. I don't mean just the money. Having somebody who really cares about him, that's what's important."

Oh yes, I care, Daisy thought bitterly when she'd hung up. *I still love Daddy after his little trip of fifteen years. And if he's in town, I'll find him. I'll get to the elevator door before it closes; the speeding car will be stopped by a red light, a policeman, a flat tire; the face in the crowd will be his.*

The wind had increased, and the air was filled with the rush of birds and flying leaves, and the scratching of the tea tree against the window sounded like the paws of a dozen animals.

Daisy sat with the phone in her hands, shivering, as if there were no glass between her and the cold wind. She could barely dial Pinata's number, and when she was told he wasn't in, she wanted to scream at the girl on the other end of the line and accuse her of bungling or fraud.

She took a deep breath to steady herself. "When do you expect him?"

"This is his answering service. He left word that he'd be in his office at seven. He'll check in for his calls before that, though. Is there any message?"

"Tell him to call..." She stopped, dubious about leaving her name, even more dubious about Pinata phoning the house when her mother or Jim might be present. "I'll meet him at his office at seven."

"What name shall I put on that?"

"Just say it's about a tombstone."

16

Shame—it is my daily bread. No wonder the flesh is falling off my bones...

Jim had been waiting at the dock for nearly an hour when Adam Burnett finally showed up. He came running along the seawall, moving heavily but quietly in his sailing sneakers.

"Sorry I'm late. I was delayed."

"Obviously."

"Don't get sore. I couldn't help it." The lawyer sat down beside Jim on the seawall. "The sail's off, anyway. They've raised a small-craft warning at the end of the wharf."

"Well, I suppose I might as well go home, then."

"No, you'd better wait a minute."

"What for?"

Although there was no one within hearing distance, Adam kept his voice low. "I had a phone call half an hour ago from Mrs. Rosario. Juanita's back in town. What's worse, so is Fielding."

"Fielding? Daisy's father?"

"What's worse still, the two of them are together."

"But they don't even know each other."

"Well, they're getting acquainted in a hurry, if Mrs. Rosario can be believed."

"It just doesn't make sense," Jim said in a bewildered voice. "Fielding had nothing to do with the—the arrangements."

"Mrs. Rosario somehow got the impression that you—or I—sent him to spy on her."

"I haven't seen Fielding for years."

"And I never have. I pointed these facts out to her, but she was pretty excited, almost incoherent toward the end. She insisted I swear on the soul of her dead brother that I had nothing to do with Fielding's going to her house." Adam squinted out at the whitecaps, multiplying under the wind. "Know anything about a dead brother?"

"No."

"His name was Carlos, apparently."

"I said I knew nothing about a dead brother, didn't I?"

"Well, don't get waspish. I was just asking."

"You asked twice," Jim said curtly. "That's once too often. My relationship with Mrs. Rosario has been brief and impersonal. You should be aware of that better than anyone."

"Impersonal isn't quite the word, surely?"

"As far as I'm concerned, it is. I wouldn't recognize her if I met her on the street."

A fishing boat was coming into port, her catch measurable by the squat of her stern and the number of gulls quarreling in her wake, trying to snatch pieces of fish from each other's beaks.

"What does she want?" Jim said. "More money?"

"Money wasn't mentioned. Apparently there'd been some violence when Fielding was at the house, though he didn't have anything to do with it as far as I was able to make out. Mrs. Rosario was upset and needed reassurance."

"You gave it to her, I hope?"

"Oh, certainly. I swore on the soul of her dead brother. Whom you don't know."

"Whom I don't know. As I have now stated three times. Why the persistence, Adam?"

"She kept raving about him, and I'm curious, that's all. How does a dead brother fit into the arrangements we made about Juanita?"

"The woman's obviously unstable."

"I agree. But I wonder how unstable."

Jim got up and stretched his arms. "Well, I'll leave you to your wonderings. I must get home. Daisy will think we've both drowned."

"I don't believe," Adam said carefully, "that Daisy is thinking about us at all."

"What's that supposed to mean?"

"Just before I left the house, I had a phone call from Ada Fielding. She asked me to tell you that Daisy had hired a detective a few days ago, a man named Pinata."

"Oh, for God's sake."

"Mrs. Fielding thinks you ought to do something about it."

"She does, eh?" Jim's face was grim and weary. "Such as what?"

"I gather she meant unhire him. After all, it's your money he's getting." Adam paused, watching the fishing boat as it tied up to the dock, wishing he were on it. "There's more if you want to hear it."

"I'm not sure I do."

"You'd better listen anyway. Daisy's meeting this man at his office tonight at seven o'clock. She promised Fielding's new wife that she and Pinata would go looking for Fielding."

"Fielding's new wife? How the hell did she come into it?"

"She was worried about Fielding getting into trouble and phoned Daisy from Los Angeles."

"What's it all about anyway?"

"I was hoping that you'd tell me."

Jim shook his head. "I can't. I have no idea how Fielding got involved in this thing, if he is involved. As for his wife, I didn't know of her existence until Daisy informed me this week. I'm at a complete loss, I tell you."

"You tell me, yes."

"Your tone suggests disbelief."

"Let's put it this way. It's better to lie to your wife than to your lawyer."

"I play it safe," Jim said, "by not lying to either."

"What about the girl?"

"I told Daisy all about that when it happened—names and everything—and she took it very calmly. She seems to have forgotten now, and that's not my fault. I told her."

"Why?"

"Why? Because it was the reasonable, the honorable, thing to do."

"It may have been honorable as all get-out," Adam said with a cryptic little smile. "But reasonable, no."

"She'd have found out sooner or later anyway."

"Your logic reminds me of the first time I took my brother-in-law sailing. It was a brisk day, we were going along at a nice clip with just the right angle of heel, but Tom was so afraid we'd tip that he jumped overboard and swam to shore. I know you don't enjoy sailing much, so you probably think Tom did the sensible thing. It wasn't, though. It was both silly and dangerous. He almost didn't make it to shore, and of course, the boat didn't tip."

"She'd have found out eventually," Jim repeated.

"How? The girl left town and remarried. She'd have nothing to gain by talking. As for the mother, all arrangements were made by me. You were never brought into it except as a name. I don't want to pry"—he leaned over to remove a pebble caught in the tread of his sneakers—"but I've often wondered why you didn't let me take the case into court, especially since you never intended to keep it secret from Daisy."

"I couldn't afford the scandal."

"But I'm sure we could have won it."

"The scandal would still be there. Besides, the child was—and is—mine. Would you ask me to perjure myself?"

"Of course not. But the girl's reputation alone would certainly have cast doubt on the legitimacy of her claim."

"In other words, I should have stayed on the boat until it tipped?"

"It didn't tip," Adam said.

"Well, this one would have."

"You didn't wait around to find out. You jumped overboard."

"Oh, stop it, Adam. It happened. It happened a long time ago. Why go into it all over again now?"

"Do you remember exactly how long ago it happened?"

"No. I try not to think about it."

"It was four years ago. To be precise, it was on December 2, 1955, that I made the first payment to Mrs. Rosario in my office. I looked it up before I left." He pulled the hood of his sea jacket over his head. "You'd better go home and have a talk with Daisy."

"Yes, I guess so."

"Well, I'll see you later. I want to stay down and make sure everything's tight and tidy on the sloop. I don't like the size of those swells. Sorry we missed our sail, by the way."

"I'm not. I didn't want to go anyway."

"As a matter of fact, I didn't want to ask you, either."

"So Daisy arranged it."

"Yes."

"Daisy's getting to be quite an arranger." Jim turned abruptly and walked toward the parking lot.

But he was not thinking of Daisy as he climbed into his car. He was thinking of the boat that hadn't tipped, and of the man who'd jumped overboard and almost hadn't made it to shore. A silly and dangerous thing, Adam had called it. Sometimes, though, silly and dangerous things were necessary. Sometimes people didn't jump; they were pushed.

She pretended, in case any of the fishermen or the dockhands were observing her, that she was standing against the wall of the harbormaster's office for shelter from the wind. She made a show of being cold—shivering, pulling up her coat collar, rubbing her hands together—until, as time passed, the show became real and the coldness penetrated every tissue of her body.

She watched the two of them talking on the seawall fifty yards away. They looked as though they might have been discussing the weather, but Daisy knew it couldn't have been the weather when Jim suddenly turned and walked away in a peculiarly abrupt manner, as if he and Adam had been quarreling. She waited until Jim got into his car. Then she started running toward Adam, who was going down the floating ramp to the mooring slips.

"Adam."

He turned and came back up the ramp to the guardrail, swaying with the movement of the waves. "Hello, Daisy. You missed Jim by a couple of minutes. He just left."

"That's too bad." There was nothing in her voice to indicate how long she had waited for Jim to leave.

"I may be able to catch him for you."

"Oh no, don't bother."

"He told me he was going home."

"I'll see him there, then," Daisy said. "You didn't stay out very long, did you?"

"We didn't get out at all. The storm warnings are up."

"That's a pity."

"Jim didn't seem to mind," Adam said dryly. "By the way, next time you arrange a sailing partner for me, make it someone who likes water, will you?"

"I'll try." Daisy leaned against the guardrail and looked down at the crabs scuttling around the rocks as if they were trying to find the biggest and safest one to weather out the storm. "Since you couldn't sail, what did you and Jim do?"

"We talked."

"About me?"

"Certainly. We always talk about you. I ask Jim how you are, and he tells me."

"Well, how am I? I'd like Jim's version of the state of my health, mental and otherwise."

Adam's smile was imperturbable. "Obviously, you're a little cranky today. That's my version, not Jim's."

"Did he tell you his plans for our anniversary?"

"We discussed a great many—"

"He's made some lovely plans, only I'm not supposed to know about them."

"Only you do."

"Oh yes. Word gets around. I must say you've kept the secret from me very well, considering the fact that you must have been the first to know."

"Keeping secrets," Adam said coolly, "is part of my job."

"How large is it going to be, my surprise, I mean?"

"Large enough but not too large."

"And the style?"

"The style will be stylish. Naturally."

"And you haven't the faintest notion what I am talking about, have you?"

He took her arm. "Come on, I'll buy you a cup of coffee at the Yacht Club."

"No."

"You don't have to snap at me. What's the matter with you today?"

"I'm glad you asked. I intended to tell you anyway. I found some check stubs this afternoon in Jim's desk. They indicate that he's been paying you $200 a month for some time."

"Well?"

"I asked my mother about it, and she claimed the money was for some acreage Jim was buying from you to build a mountain cabin on. I gather she was lying?"

"She may have been lying," Adam said with a shrug. "Or she may actually believe it's the truth."

"It isn't, of course."

"No."

"What was that money for, Adam?"

"To pay for the support of Jim's child by another woman." He deliberately looked away from her as he spoke because he didn't want to see the pain and shock in her face. "You were told about it at the time, Daisy. Don't you remember?"

"Jim's—child. How funny that sounds. So f-funny." She was clutching the guardrail as if she were afraid she was going to fling herself into the sea against her own will. "Was it—is it a boy or a girl?"

"I don't know."

"You don't *know*? Haven't you even asked him?"

"That wouldn't do much good. Jim doesn't know, either."

She turned to Adam, and her eyes looked blind, as if a film of ice had formed over the pupils. "You mean he hasn't even seen the child?"

"No. The woman left town before her delivery. Jim hasn't heard from her since."

"Surely she must have written him a letter when the baby was born."

"There was a mutual agreement between the two parties involved that no contact be made, and no correspondence entered into."

"But what a terrible thing, not to see your own child. It's inhuman. I can't believe that Jim would evade his responsibilities like—"

"Now wait a minute," Adam said crisply. "Jim evaded nothing. In fact, if he'd taken my advice, he wouldn't have admitted paternity at all. The woman had a flock of other children whose paternity was in question. She also had a husband, although he was allegedly out of the country at the time. If she had brought charges against him—and I doubt that she'd have had the nerve—she would have had a tough time proving anything. As things turned out, Jim quietly admitted paternity, and financial arrangements were made with Mrs. Rosario, the girl's mother, through me. That's all there was to it."

"All there was to it," she repeated. "You talk like a lawyer, Adam, in terms of cases and bringing charges, of proving or not proving. You don't talk about justice."

"In this case, I think justice was done."

"Do you call it justice that Jim, who so desperately wanted to father a child, should cut himself off from his own flesh and blood?"

"The arrangements were his."

"I can't believe that."

"Ask him."

"I can't believe that any man, let alone Jim, wouldn't want to see his own child at least once."

"Jim did the only sensible thing under the circumstances," Adam said. "And the circumstances weren't in the least what you seem to imagine in your sentimental way. No sentiment was involved. The girl thought nothing of Jim personally, nor he of her. The child was not the product of love. If it's still alive—and neither Juanita nor Mrs. Rosario would be in a hurry to inform us otherwise—it's half Mexican, its mother is mentally unstable—"

"Stop it. I don't want to hear anymore."

"I must present the facts bluntly to prevent you from sentimentalizing and perhaps doing something foolish which you might regret."

"Foolish?"

Adam pushed back the hood of his sea jacket, as if the day had suddenly turned warm. "I think you hired the detective to find that child."

"So you know about Pinata?"

"Yes."

"Does Jim know, too?"

"Yes."

"Well, I don't care," she said listlessly. "I don't really care. I guess it's time we laid our cards on the table. You're wrong, though, about my reason for hiring Pinata. Why should I hire someone to find a child I didn't even know existed?"

"You knew. You were told."

"I can't remember."

"You were told."

"Stop repeating it like that, as if forgetting were a cardinal sin. All right, I was told. I forgot. It's not the kind of thing a woman likes to remember about her husband."

"Some part of you remembered," Adam said. "Your dream shows that. The date on your tombstone was the day the first payment

240

was made to Mrs. Rosario. It was also the day that Juanita left town, and, possibly, the day Jim confessed the affair to you. Was it?"

"I don't—I don't know."

"Try to think about it. Where were you that day?"

"Working. At the Clinic."

"What happened when you had finished working?"

"I went home, I guess."

"How?"

"I drove the car—no. No, I didn't." She was looking down at the water as if it were the deep dark well of memory. "Jim called for me. He was waiting in the car when I went out the back door. I started to cross the parking lot. Then I saw this young woman getting out of Jim's car. I'd seen her around the Clinic before. She was one of the regular patients, but I'd never paid much attention to her. I wouldn't have then either, if she hadn't been talking to Jim and if she hadn't been so terribly pregnant. Jim opened the door for me…"

"Who was the girl?" Daisy said.

"Her name's Juanita Garcia."

"I hope she has her hospital reservations all set."

"Yes, so do I."

"You look pale, Jim. Are you feeling sick?"

He reached out and took her hand and held it so tightly that it began to feel numb. "Listen to me, Daisy. I love you. You won't ever forget that, will you? I love you. Promise never to forget it. There's nothing in the world I wouldn't do to make you happy."

"You don't very often talk like this, as if you were going to die or something."

"The girl—the child—I've got to tell you—"

"I don't want to hear." She turned and looked out of the car window, smiling the little smile she put on in the morning and washed off at

241

night. "It gets dark so early, it's a pity we don't have daylight saving time all year."

"Daisy, listen, nothing's going to happen. She won't cause any trouble. She's going away."

"The paper says there'll be snow on the mountains again tomorrow."

"Daisy, give me a chance to explain."

"The mountains always look so much prettier with a little snow on them..."

THE STRANGER

17

I have nothing to live for. Yet, as I move through the days, shackled to this dying body, I yearn to step free of it long enough to see you again, you and Ada, my beloved ones still…

They had already visited five taverns, and Fielding was getting tired of moving from place to place. But Juanita was all set to go again. She sat on the very edge of the stool as though she were waiting for some whistle to blow inside her as a signal to take off. *Aawouhee…*

"For Pete's sake, can't you settle down?" Fielding said. He was beginning to feel the drinks, not in his head, which was marvelously clear and sharp and full of wit and information, but in his legs, which were getting older and heavier and harder to drag in and out of doors. His legs wanted to sit down and rest while his head informed and amused Juanita or the bartender or the guy on the next stool. None of them was in his class, of course. He had to talk down to them, way down. But they listened; they could see he was a gentleman of the old school.

"What old school?" the bartender said, and his left eye closed in a quick, expert wink directed at Juanita.

"You miss the point, old chap," Fielding said. "No particular school is involved. It's a figure of speech."

"It is, eh?"

"Precisely. Speaking of old schools, Winston Churchill went to Harrow. You know what people who went to Harrow are called?"

"I guess they're called the same names as the rest of us."

"No, no, no. They are Harrovians."

"You don't say."

"It's God's truth."

"Your friend's getting crocked," the bartender told Juanita.

Juanita gave him a blank stare. "No, he's not. He always talks that way. Hey, Foster, are you getting crocked?"

"Absolutely not," Fielding said. "I'm feeling absolutely shape-ship. How are you feeling, my dear?"

"My feet hurt."

"Take off your shoes."

Juanita began tugging at her left shoe, using both hands. "They're genuine snakeskin. I paid $19 for them."

"Your tips must be good."

"No. I got a rich uncle."

She put the sharp-toed, needle-heeled shoes side by side on the counter in front of her. She had ordinary-sized feet, but out of their proper place the shoes looked enormous and misshapen, as if they belonged to some giant with a taste for pain.

Fielding's drink seemed extremely small in comparison with the shoes, and he pointed this out to the bartender, who told Juanita to put the shoes on again and quit messing around.

"I'm not messing around."

"When I come over to your joint for a drink, I don't undress and leave my clothes on the counter."

"Well, why don't you?" Juanita said. "I think it'd be a riot. I can just see Mrs. Brewster swelling up and turning blue."

"If you want to do a striptease, sit in the back booth so the police patrol can't see you. Saturday night they go past maybe ten times."

"I'm not scared of the cops."

"Yeah? You want to know what happened up in Frisco the other day? I read it in the paper. This girl wasn't doing nothing except walking around in her bare feet, and by God, the cops arrested her."

Juanita said she didn't believe it, but she picked up the shoes and her half-finished drink and headed for the back booth, trailed by Fielding.

"Hurry up and finish your drink," she said as she sat down. "I'm sick of this place."

"We just got here."

"I want to go where we can have some fun. Nobody's having any fun around here."

"I am. Can't you hear me laughing? Ho ho ho. Ha ha ha."

Juanita was sitting with both hands clenched around her glass as if she were trying to crush it. "I hate this town. I wish I'd never've come back. I wish I was a million miles away and never had to see my old lady again or anyone else. I'd like to go where everybody is a stranger and don't know anything about me."

"They'd find out soon enough."

"How?"

"You'd tell them," Fielding said. "Just the way I did. I've hit a hundred towns as a stranger, and inside of ten minutes I was talking to somebody about myself. Maybe I wasn't speaking the truth, and maybe I was using a false name, but I was talking, see? And talking is telling. So pretty soon you're no stranger any longer, so you head for the next town. Don't be a patsy, kid. You stick around here, close to that rich uncle of yours."

Juanita let out an unexpected little giggle. "I can't very well stick close to him. He's dead."

"He is, eh?"

"You sound like you don't believe I ever had a rich uncle."

"Did you ever see him?"

"When I was a kid, he came to visit us. He brought me a silver belt, real silver made by the Indians."

"Where did he live?"

"New Mexico. He had important cattle interests there. That's how he made all his money."

He didn't have any money, Fielding thought, *except a few bucks on Saturday, which were gone by Sunday because he couldn't help drawing to an inside straight.* "And he left this money of his to you?"

"To my mother, on account of she was his sister. Every month she gets a check from the lawyer, regular as clockwork, out of the—I guess you call it the trust fund."

"Did you ever see any of these checks?"

"I saw the money. My mother sent me some every month to help feed the kids. Two hundred dollars," she added proudly. "So in case you think I've *got* to work in a crummy dive like the Velada, you got another think coming. I do it for the kicks. It's more fun than sticking around the house watching a bunch of kids."

To Fielding, the story was getting crazier by the minute. He signaled the bartender to bring another round of drinks while he did some rapid calculation. An income of $200 a month would mean a trust fund of around $50,000. The last time he'd seen Camilla, the man had been unemployed and trying desperately to raise the money for some food and clothing. Yet Juanita didn't appear to be lying. Her pride in having a rich uncle with important cattle interests was as obviously genuine as her pride in the $19 snakeskin shoes. The whole thing was beginning to smell like a shakedown, but Fielding felt almost certain that if Juanita was part of it, she had no knowledge of her role. The girl was being used by someone more intelligent and cunning than she was. *But that's crazy,* he thought. *She's the one who gets the money; she's admitted it.*

"What was the name of the lawyer?" he said.

"What lawyer?"

"The one who sends the checks?"

"Why should I tell you?"

"Because we're friends, aren't we?"

"I don't know if we're friends or not," Juanita said with a shrug. "You ask a lot of questions."

"That's because I'm interested in you."

"A lot of people have been interested in me. It never got me nowhere. Anyhow, I don't know his name."

"Does he live in town?"

"Are you deaf or something? I told you I never saw the checks, and I don't know the lawyer. My old lady sent me the money every month from my uncle's trust fund."

"This uncle of yours, how did he die?"

"He was killed."

"What do you mean, killed?"

Juanita's mouth opened in a yawn a little too wide and loud to be genuine. "What do you want to talk about an old dead uncle for?"

"Old dead uncles intrigue me, if they happen to be rich."

"There's nothing in it for you."

"I know that. I'm just curious. How did he die?"

"He got in an automobile accident in New Mexico about four years ago." In an attempt to appear detached, Juanita stared at a patch of grimy pink roses on the wallpaper. But Fielding had the idea that this was a subject which interested and puzzled her and which she actually wanted to discuss in spite of her apparent reluctance. "He was killed right away, before the priest could give him the last rites. That's why my old lady's always praying and burning candles for him, so he'll get into heaven anyway. You saw the candle, didn't you?"

"Yes."

"It's funny her making such a fuss over a brother she never saw for years. It's like she did something wrong to him and is trying to make up for it."

"If she did something wrong to him, he surely wouldn't have left her his money."

"Maybe he didn't know about whatever she'd done." She reached out and began tracing the outlines of one of the pink roses on the wallpaper. Her sharp fingernail cut a path through the grease. "It's like he only got to be important by dying and leaving the money. She didn't even talk about him when he was alive."

He didn't talk about her, either, Fielding thought. Only once, right at the end: "I'd like to see my sister Filomena before I go." "You can't do it, Curly." "I want her to pray for me; she's a good woman." "You're crazy to take a chance seeing anyone now. It's too dangerous." "No. I must say good-bye to her." At the time he'd barely had a voice to say good-bye, let alone a cent to leave anyone.

"Did he make a will?" Fielding asked.

"I never saw it. She says he did."

"Don't you believe her?"

"I don't know."

"When did you first hear about it?"

"One day before Paul was born, she suddenly announced that Uncle Carl had died and left a will. If I did this and that, I would get $200 a month."

"And what was 'this and that'?"

"Mostly I was to leave town right away and have the baby born in L.A. It seemed kind of crazy him being interested in the baby when he never even sent the other kids anything at Christmastime. When I asked my old lady about it, she said Uncle Carl wanted the baby born in L.A. because that's where he was born. For sentimental reasons, like."

He was born in Arizona, Fielding thought. *He must have told me a dozen times. Flagstaff, Arizona. And nobody knows better than me that he didn't die in any automobile accident in New Mexico. He died right here, less than a mile from this very spot, with his own knife between his ribs.*

Only on one count was the girl's story correct: there had been no last rites for Camilla.

"I guess he must have been very sentimental," Juanita said. "So's my old lady sometimes. A funny thing, there I was in L.A. with everything going pretty good, and suddenly she gets this idea she wants to see me again, me and the kids. She wrote me a letter how she was getting old and she had a bad heart and she was lonely all by herself and she wanted me to come visit her for a while. Well, Joe had just lost his job, and it seemed like a good time to come. I must've been crazy. An hour after I stepped inside that door, she was screaming at me and I was screaming back. That's the way it is. She wants me around, and she wants me far away. How the hell can I be both? Well, this time I'm going to settle it for good. I'm never coming back once I get out of this town again."

"Just make sure you get out."

"Why?"

"Be careful."

"What's to be careful about?"

"Oh, things. People." He would have liked to tell her the truth at this point, or as much of it as he knew. But he didn't trust her not to talk. And if she talked in front of the wrong people, she would put herself in danger as well as him. Perhaps she was already in danger, but she certainly seemed unaware of it. She was still busy outlining the wallpaper roses with her fingernail, looking as rapt and dedicated as an artist or a child.

Fielding said, "Stop that for a minute, will you?"

"What?"

"Stop fooling around with the wallpaper."

"I'm making it prettier."

"Yeah, I know that, but I want you to listen to me. Are you listening?"

"Well, sure."

"I came to town to see Jim Harker." He leaned across the table and repeated the name carefully. "Jim Harker."

"So what?"

"You remember him, don't you?"

"I never heard of him before."

"Think."

Her two eyebrows leaped at each other into the middle of her forehead, like animals about to fight. They didn't quite meet. "I wish people would quit telling me to think. I think. Thinking's easy. It's *not* thinking that's hard. I think all the time, but I can't think about Jim Harker if I never even heard of Jim Harker. Think, hell."

The single monosyllable had destroyed her creative impulse as well as her good mood. She turned from the wall and began wiping the grime off her hands with a paper napkin. When she had finished, she crumpled the napkin into a ball and threw it on the floor with a sound of despair, that she had ever tried to make things prettier in the world.

The bartender came around the end of the counter, frowning as if he intended to rebuke her for messing up his place. Instead, he said, "Mrs. Brewster just called, wanted to know if you were here."

Juanita's face immediately assumed the peculiarly bland expression that indicated she was interested. "What'd you say to her?"

"That I'd keep an eye out for you, and if you showed up, I'd tell you to call her back. So now I'm telling you."

"Thanks," Juanita said without moving.

"You gonna do it?"

252

"So she can go blabbing to my old lady? What do you think I am, like stupid?"

"You better call her," the bartender said stubbornly. "She's at the Velada."

"So she's at the Velada. And I'm here, at—what's the name of this dump?"

"El Paraiso."

"The Paradise. Hey, Foster, ain't that a laugh? You and me are strangers in paradise."

The bartender turned to Fielding. One of his eyelids was twitching in unexpressed irritation. "If you're a friend of hers, you better persuade her to talk to Mrs. Brewster. There've been a couple of men looking for her at the Velada. One of them was a private detective."

A detective, Fielding thought. *So Pinata was in on this, too.*

He wasn't exactly surprised. He'd been half expecting it ever since Daisy's letter was delivered to him at the warehouse. There was no other way for her to have found out where he was working except through Pinata. Obviously, if Pinata was looking for Juanita, that was what Daisy had hired him to do. But how did Camilla come into it? As far as Fielding knew, the name hadn't been mentioned in Daisy's presence; she was unaware such a man had ever existed.

He realized suddenly that both Juanita and the bartender were staring at him as if they were waiting for an answer. He hadn't heard any question.

"Well," the bartender said.

"Well, what?"

"You know any private detective around town?"

"No."

"That's funny, because he was looking for you, too."

253

"Why me? I haven't done anything."

Juanita protested shrilly that she hadn't done anything, either, but neither of the men paid any attention.

Fielding was squinting up at the bartender as if he found it difficult to focus his eyes. "You said two men came to the Velada. Who was the other one?"

"Search me."

"A cop?"

"Mrs. Brewster would have mentioned it if he'd been a cop. All she told me, he was a big man with blond hair and he acted funny. Jumpy, like. You know anybody like that?"

"Sure, lots of them." *One in particular,* Fielding thought. *He wasn't jumpy the last time I saw him, in Chicago, but now he has reason to be.* "Some of my best friends are jumpy."

"Yeah, I bet." The bartender glanced briefly at Juanita. "I gotta get back to work. Don't say I didn't warn you."

When he had gone, Juanita leaned across the table and said confidentially, "I think Mrs. Brewster was making it all up so I'll get scared and go home. I don't believe there's any detective looking for me, or any big blond man, either. Why would they want to see me for?"

"Maybe they have some questions."

"What about?"

He hesitated a minute. He wanted to help the girl because in a disturbing way she reminded him of Daisy. It was as if some perverse fate had singled them both out to be victims, Daisy and Juanita, who had never met and perhaps never would, although they had so much in common. He felt sorry for them. But Fielding's pity, like his love and even his hate, was a variable thing, subject to changes in the weather, melting in the summer, freezing in the winter, blowing away in a high wind. Only by a miracle did it survive at all.

Proof of its survival was in the single monosyllable he spoke now. "Paul."

"Paul who?"

"Your son."

"Why would they ask questions about him? He's too young to be in any trouble. He's not even four. All he can do is maybe break windows or steal a little."

"Don't be naive, girl."

"What's that mean?"

"Innocent."

Juanita's eyes widened in outrage. "I'm not innocent. I may be dumb, but I'm not innocent."

"All right, all right, skip it."

"I'm not going to skip it. I want to know how come two men are so interested in my kids all of a sudden."

"Not the others, just Paul."

"Why?"

"I think they're trying to find out who his father is."

"Well, of all the goddamn nerve," Juanita said. "What business is it of theirs?"

"I can't answer that."

"Not that it's any of your business, either, but it so happens I was *married* at the time. I had a *husband.*"

"What was his name?"

"Pedro Garcia."

"And that's who Paul's father is?"

Juanita picked up one of the snakeskin shoes, and Fielding thought for a moment that she was going to hit him with it. Instead, she began pushing it on her left foot. "By God, I don't have to sit here and be insulted by no lousy imitation district attorney."

"I'm sorry, I have to ask these questions. I'm trying to help you, but I've got my own hide to save, too. What happened to Garcia?"

"I divorced him."

Fielding knew that at least this part of her story was a deliberate lie. After he'd left Pinata's office the previous Monday, he'd gone to City Hall to check the records. It was Garcia who'd brought the divorce suit; Juanita had not contested it or asked for alimony or child support, a curious omission if the child was actually Garcia's. It occurred to Fielding now, not for the first time, that perhaps Juanita herself didn't know who the boy's father was and didn't care much, either. He might have been someone she picked up in a bar or on the street, or a sailor from a ship visiting the harbor or an airman down from Vandenberg. Juanita's pregnancies were inclined to be casual. One thing was certain: the little boy Paul bore no resemblance to Jim Harker.

Juanita finished squeezing her feet into the shoes and tucked her purse under her arm. She seemed ready to leave, but she made no move to do so. "What do you mean, you got your own hide to save?"

"The detective's looking for me, too."

"That's funny when you come to think of it. Someone must've told him we were together."

"Mrs. Brewster maybe."

"No." Her tone was positive. "She wouldn't give a detective the time of day."

"No one else knows except her and your mother."

"By God, that's it. That's who told him, my old lady."

"But first someone else must have given him your address," Fielding said. "Maybe the busboy or one of the waitresses."

"They don't know my address. I never tell people like that nothing personal about myself."

"He found out from somewhere."

"All right, so he found out from somewhere. What do I care? I haven't committed any crime. Why should I run away?"

"It's possible," Fielding said carefully, "that you're a part of something you're not fully aware of."

"Like what?"

"I can't explain it to you." He couldn't explain it to himself, either, because there were gaps in his knowledge that must be filled in. Once they were filled in, his duty would be done and he could be on his away again. The important thing now was to get rid of the girl. She was too conspicuous, and he had to travel light and fast and, if he was unlucky, far.

Luck. Fielding believed in it as some men believed in God, country, or mother. To luck he credited his triumphs; on lack of it he blamed his misfortunes. Several times a day he rubbed the tiny rabbit's foot that dangled from his watch chain, always expecting miracles from the fragile inert scrap of bone and fur, but not complaining if a miracle failed to occur. It was this quality of fatalism that always baffled his second wife and enraged his first. He knew now, for example, that he was inviting disaster in the same way that he knew he was getting drunk. He accepted both as things over which he personally had no control. Whatever happened, how the dice rolled, the ball bounced, the cookie crumbled, would be a matter of luck or lack of it. His sense of responsibility was no greater than that of the severed paw he wore on his watch chain.

"Why can't you explain things to me?" Juanita said.

"Because I can't."

"All this hinting around like I was going to be killed or something—well, it don't scare me. Nobody'd want to kill me. Why, nobody even hates me except my old lady and sometimes Joe and maybe a few others."

"I didn't say you were going to be killed."

"It sounded like that."

"I just warned you to be careful."

"How the hell can I be careful if I don't know who of or what of?" She leaned across the table, studying him soberly and carefully. "You know what I think? I think you're a crackpot."

"That's your considered opinion, eh?"

"It sure is."

Fielding wasn't offended. He was, in fact, quite pleased because once again luck had taken charge of his affairs. By calling him a crackpot the girl had relieved him of any sense of responsibility toward her. It made what he intended to do to her easier, even inevitable: *She called me a crackpot, therefore it's all right to steal her car.*

The immediate problem was to get her away from the table for a few minutes and make sure she left her purse behind with the keys in it.

He said abruptly, "You'd better call Mrs. Brewster."

"Why?"

"For your own sake—leaving me out of it entirely—you should find out everything you can about the two men who are looking for you."

"I don't want to talk to her. She's always telling me what to do."

"Well, in case you change your mind..." He took a dime out of his pocket and laid it on the table in front of her.

Juanita stared at the coin with a child's petty avarice. "I don't know what to say to her."

"Let her do the talking."

"Maybe it's all lies about the two men. She wants me to get scared and go home."

"I don't think so. It strikes me she's a pretty good friend of yours."

It was the dime that clinched her decision. She slid it off the table with the casual ease of an experienced waitress. "Watch my purse, will you?"

"All right."

"I'll be back."

"Sure."

She teetered across the floor to the phone booth, which was jammed in a corner between the end of the bar and the door to the kitchen. Fielding waited, stroking his little rabbit's foot with affection as one might stroke a living pet. Once again it was a matter of luck whether Juanita could remember Mrs. Brewster's phone number or whether she would have to look it up in the directory. If she had to look it up, he would have thirty seconds or more to open the purse, search through all Juanita's junk to find the keys, and reach the front door. If she dialed the number directly, he'd be forced to grab the purse and run, taking a chance on getting past the bartender and the half-dozen customers he was serving. The sentimental side of Fielding's nature, always erratic after a few drinks and apt to disappear entirely after a few more, balked at the idea of stealing a woman's purse. The car was a different matter. He'd stolen quite a few cars in his lifetime; he had also put the bite on a great many women. But he had never actually stolen a purse from any of them. Besides, there were the risks involved: the thing was too large to put in his pocket or hide under his coat. There seemed only one other alternative—to dump its contents out of sight on the seat beside him, pick out the car keys, and replace the purse on the table. The whole operation would require no more than four or five seconds...

Juanita was dialing.

The purse lay within reach of his hand, a black plastic rectangle with a gold clasp and handle. The plastic was so shiny that Fielding could see in miniature the reflection of his own face. It looked curiously young and unlined and innocent, not the image that stared back at him in the mornings between flyspecks and dabs of toothpaste and other unidentified residues of life. This face in the plastic belonged to his youth, as the picture in Mrs. Rosario's bedroom belonged to Camilla's youth. *Camilla*, he thought, and the knife of pain that stabbed him between the ribs seemed as real as the *navaja* that had so senselessly killed his friend. *We were both young together, Curly and I. It's too late for him now, but there's still a chance for me.*

He wanted suddenly and desperately to take the purse, not for the money or for the car keys which were in it, but for that reflection of his own face, that innocence intact, that youth preserved in plastic and protected from the sins of time.

He glanced across at the phone booth. Juanita, scowling, was in the act of hanging up. He thought that his opportunity was lost, that she had reached the Velada and been told Mrs. Brewster had gone. Then he saw her pick up the directory chained to the wall, and he knew she must have received a busy signal and decided to recheck the phone number. Luck was giving him another chance.

His eyes returned to the purse, but this time his angle of vision was different and the image that stared back at him was like the images in a fun house. The forehead projected out to the right and the jaw to the left, and in between was a distorted nose and two malevolent slits of eyes. With a little cry of rage he grabbed the purse off the table and dumped its contents on the seat beside him. The car keys were on a small chain separate from Juanita's other keys. He slid them into his pocket, stood up, and walked toward the front door. He didn't hurry. The trick was to appear casual. It was the kind of thing he'd done a hundred times before, the friendly, final good-bye-see-you-later to the landlady or grocer

260

or hotel clerk or liquor dealer whom he had no intention of paying or ever seeing again.

He smiled at the bartender as he passed. "Tell Juanita I'll be back in a few minutes, will you?"

"You didn't pay for the last round of drinks."

"Oh, didn't I? Terribly sorry." It was a delay he hadn't anticipated, but he kept the smile on his face as he fished around in his pocket for a dollar. The only sign of his anxiety was a brief, nervous glance in the direction of the phone booth. "Here you are."

"Thanks," the bartender said.

"Juanita's talking to Mrs. Brewster. I thought I'd take a little walk to clear my head."

"You do that."

"See you later."

As soon as Fielding was outside, he dropped the pretense of being casual. He hurried along the sidewalk, the cold brisk air slapping his face with a wintry hand.

At this point he had no clear or extensive plan of action. Impulsively and without thought of the consequences, he had rushed into the middle of something he only half understood. Getting the car and going to Daisy's house—this was as far ahead as he could see. At Daisy's house he would almost inevitably run into Ada, and the idea excited him. At this stage he was quite ready to meet her. Sober, he couldn't have faced her; drunk, he would certainly pick a quarrel, perhaps a very violent one. But right now, somewhere in between, he felt able to deal with her, confront her without malice, expose her without cruelty. Right now he could teach her a few lessons in civilization, in manners: *My dear Ada, it grieves me to bring this to your attention but in the interests of justice, I must insist you reveal the truth about your part in this devious little scheme…*

It didn't even seem ironic to him that he should be planning remarks about truth and justice when, in fact, his whole life had been a marathon race, with truth a few jumps ahead of him and justice a few jumps behind. He had never caught up with the one, and the other had never caught up with him.

The car was at the end of the block, parked in front of a long frame building with a dimly lit sign announcing its function: *billar*. The sign, printed only in Spanish, made it clear that whites were not welcome. Although the place was jammed, the noise coming out of the open door was subdued, punctuated by the click of balls and score racks. A group of young Negroes and Mexicans were hanging around outside, one of them with a cue in his hand. He was using the cue like a drum major, raising it and lowering it in time to some rhythms he heard in his head or felt in his bones.

As Fielding approached, the boy pointed the cue at him and said, "Rat ta ta ta ta. Man, you're dead."

Sober, Fielding might have been a little intimidated by the group; drunk, he would certainly have made trouble. But in between, right now—"That's pretty funny, kid. You ought to be on TV"—and he brushed past the boy with a grin and made his way to the car.

There were two keys on the ring he'd taken from Juanita's purse—one for the luggage compartment, the other for the doors and ignition. He tried the wrong key on the door first. It was a bad start, made worse by the fact that the boys were watching him with sober interest, as if they knew perfectly well what he intended to do and were waiting to see how he did it and if he would get caught. Later—if there was a later—they would be able to give a good description of both him and the car. Or perhaps Juanita had already called the police, and they had a description on the radio right now. He had counted on her distrust of officials to prevent such a move, but Juanita was unpredictable.

Once inside her car, he had a moment of panic when he looked at the dashboard. He hadn't driven a car for a long time, and never one like this, with so many buttons and switches that he couldn't tell which was supposed to turn on the lights. Even without lights, though, he knew where to find the most important object in the car—the half-pint of whiskey he'd bought at one of the bars and later hidden on the floorboard under the seat. The bottle had hardly touched his lips before he began feeling the effects of its contents. First there was a fleeting moment of guilt, followed by the transition of guilt to blame, blame to revenge, revenge to power: *By God, I'm going to teach all of them a lesson.*

In an ordinary person these changes of emotion would take time to evolve. But Fielding was like a man who's been hypnotized so often that a snap of the fingers will put him under. A smell of the cork, a tilt of the bottle, and *By God, I'll teach those smug, hypocritical, patronizing bastards.*

One of the young Negro men had approached the car and was kicking the right rear tire absently, as if he had no motive other than that the tire was there to kick and he didn't have anything more important to do.

Fielding shouted through the closed window, "Get your black feet off that tire, coon boy!" He knew these were fighting words, but he knew, too, in that corner of his mind which still had access to the real world, that the insult had been muffled by the window glass and scrambled by the wind.

He pressed the starter button. The car gave a couple of forward lurches, then the engine died, and he saw that he hadn't released the emergency brake. He released it, started the engine again, and looked in the rearview mirror to make sure the road was clear of traffic behind him. There were no nearby cars, and he was on the point of pulling away from the curb when he saw two Juanitas running down the middle of the road, barefooted, their arms flailing like windmills in a gale, their skirts ballooning around their thighs.

The sight of these two furies coming at him made him panic. He pressed the accelerator right down to the floorboard. The engine flooded and died again, and he knew that he had no choice but to wait.

He turned down the window and looked back at the road, narrowing his eyes until the two Juanitas merged into one. He could hear her screaming twenty yards away. A scream in this part of town was interpreted not as a cry for help, but as a sign of impending trouble: the group of young Negroes and Mexicans had disappeared without a trace, and the doors below the sign *billar* had closed as if in response to an electronic ear, alert to the decibels of danger. When and if the police arrived, nobody would know anything about a car thief and a screaming woman.

Fielding glanced at the clock on the dashboard. It was 6:30. There was still plenty of time. All he had to do was keep his head, and the girl would be handled easily enough. The fact that she was running toward the car indicated that she hadn't called the police. The important thing was to stay calm, play it cool...

But as he watched her approach, rage beat against his temples and exploded behind his eyes with flashes of colored lights. Between flashes Juanita's face appeared, streaked with black tears, red from cold and exertion.

"You—sonna bitch—stole my car."

"I was coming to pick you up. I told the bartender I'd be right back."

"Dirty—liar."

He reached across the seat and unlocked and opened the right front door. "Get in."

"I'm gonna—calla cops."

"Get in."

The repetition of the direct order and the opening of the door had the same effect on her as his putting the dime on the table in the café. The dime was there to be picked up; the door was there to be entered. She went around the front of the car, keeping her eyes fixed steadily on Fielding as if she suspected he might try to run her down.

She got in, still breathing hard from her sprint down the road. "You sonofabitch, what've you got to say?"

"Nothing you'd believe."

"I wouldn't believe nothing you said, you—"

"Take it easy." Fielding lit a cigarette. The flare of the match blended with the lights flashing behind his eyes, so that he wasn't quite sure which was real. "I'm going to make a bargain with you."

"*You* make a bargain with *me?* That's a laugh. You've got more guts than a sausage factory."

"I want to borrow your car for a couple of hours."

"Oh, you do, eh? And what do I get out of it?"

"Some information."

"Who says I want information from an old crackpot like you?"

"Watch your language, girl."

Although he didn't raise his voice, she seemed to sense the force of his anger, and when she spoke again, she sounded almost conciliatory. "What kind of information?"

"About your rich uncle."

"Why should I want to hear about him for? He's been dead and buried for four years. Besides, how would you know anything about him that my old lady didn't tell me already?"

"There's no similarity between what your old mother told you and what I'm going to tell you. If you cooperate. All you have to do is lend me your car for a couple of hours. I'll drive you home now and bring the car back to your house when I've finished my errand."

Juanita rubbed her cheeks with the back of her hand, looking surprised to find tears there, as if she'd already forgotten that she had wept and why. "I don't want to go home."

"You will."

"Why will I?"

"You're going to be curious to find out why your mother has been lying through her teeth all these years."

He started the car and pulled away from the curb. Juanita seemed too astonished to object. "Lying? My old lady? You must be crazy. Why, she's so pure she…" Juanita used an ancient and earthy figure of speech without embarrassment. "I don't believe you, Foster. I think you're making all this up so you can get the car."

"You don't have to believe me. Just ask her."

"Ask her what?"

"Where your rich uncle got his money."

"He had cattle interests."

"He was a cowhand."

"He owned—"

"He owned nothing but the shirt on his back," Fielding said, "and ten chances to one he'd stolen that." This was not true, but Fielding couldn't admit it, even to himself. He had to keep himself convinced that Camilla had been a liar, a thief, and a scoundrel.

Juanita said, "Then where did the money come from that he left to me in the trust fund?"

"That's what I'm trying to tell you—there is no trust fund."

"But I get $200 regular every month. Where does it come from?"

"You'd better ask your mother."

"You talk like she's a crook or something."

"Or something."

He turned left at the next corner. He wasn't familiar with the city, but in his years of wandering, he had taught himself to observe landmarks carefully so he could always find his way back to his hotel or rooming house. He did it now automatically, like a blind man counting the number of steps between places.

Juanita was sitting on the edge of the seat, tense and rigid, one hand clutching her plastic purse and the other the snakeskin shoes. "She's no crook."

"Ask her."

"I don't have to. Her and me, maybe we don't get along so buddy-buddy, but I swear she's no crook. Unless she was doing something for somebody else."

"Unless that, yes," Fielding said blandly.

"How come you pretend to know so much about my uncle and my old lady?"

"Camilla was a friend of mine once."

"But you never even saw my old lady till this afternoon." She paused to give this some thought. "Why, you never even saw *me* till that day you got in the fight with Joe."

"I'd heard about you."

"Where? How?"

He was tempted, momentarily, to tell her where and how, to show her the letter from Daisy he'd taken out of the old suitcase that morning. It was this letter, dated almost four years previously, that had sent him to the Velada in the first place, in the hope of finding, or getting some information about, a young woman called Juanita Garcia. That she happened to be there at the time was luck, but he still wasn't sure whether it was good luck or bad luck.

That her husband happened to drop in and started the quarrel was pure bad luck: it had put Fielding's timing off, it had temporarily dislodged his whole purpose in coming to town, and, what might turn out to be the worst misfortune yet, it had brought Pinata into the affair. Pinata, and then Camilla. One of the most terrible shocks in Fielding's life occurred at the moment he looked across Mrs. Rosario's bedroom and saw the picture of Camilla.

That's when I should have stopped, he thought. *I should have walked away right then.*

Even now he didn't know why he hadn't stopped; he was just aware that the gnawing restlessness inside him disappeared when he was playing a game of danger, whether it was a simple matter of cheating at cards or defrauding a landlady, or whether it involved, as it did now, his own life or death.

"I don't believe you ever heard of me before," Juanita said, and it was obvious from her tone that she wanted to believe it, that she was flattered by the notion of being recognized by strangers, like a movie star. "I mean, I'm not famous or anything, so how could you?"

"Well, I did."

"Tell me about it."

"Some other time."

The idea of showing her the letter and watching her reactions appealed to his sense of dramatic irony. But the references to herself were decidedly unflattering, and he was afraid to take a chance on making her angry again. Besides, the letter was, in its way, a very special one. Of all the times that Daisy had written to him, this was the only time she had ever expressed genuine and deep emotions.

·   ·   ·

Dear Daddy, I wish you were here tonight so you and I could talk about things the way we used to. Talking to Mother or Jim isn't the same. It always ends up not as a conversation, but as their telling me.

Christmas is nearly here. How I've always loved it, the gaiety and the singing and the wrapping of presents. But this year I feel nothing. There is no good cheer in this childless house. I use that word, childless, with bitter irony: I found out a week ago today that another woman is giving—or has already given—birth to a baby fathered by Jim. I can almost see you now as you read this, and hear you saying, Now Daisy baby, are you sure you've got the facts straight? Yes, I'm sure. Jim has admitted it. And here's the awful thing about it—whatever I'm suffering, Jim is suffering twice as much, and neither of us seems able to help the other. Poor Jim, how desperately he's wanted children, but he will never even see this one. The woman has left town, and arrangements for her support have been made through Adam Burnett, Jim's lawyer.

After this letter is written, I will do my utmost to forget what has happened and to go on being a good wife to Jim. It's over and done with. I can't change anything, so I must forgive and forget. The forgiving is easy; the other might be impossible, but I'll try. After tonight, I'll try. Tonight I feel like wallowing in this ugly thing like a pig in a mudhole.

I've seen the woman many times. (How the ironies pile up once they start! It's as if they're self-multiplying like amoebae.) She has been a patient at the Clinic for years, off and on. Perhaps this is where Jim first met her while he was waiting for me. I haven't asked him, and he hasn't told me. Anyway, her name is Juanita Garcia, and she's been working as a waitress at the Velada Café, which is owned by a friend of her mother. She is married and has five other children. Jim didn't tell me this, either; I looked up her file at the Clinic. Also from her file I found out something else, and if you aren't already choking on ironies, try swallowing this one:

269

Mrs. Garcia was arrested last week on charges of child neglect. I hope to God Jim never finds this out; it would only increase his misery to think of the kind of life his own child will have.

I haven't told Mother, but I suspect Jim has. She's going around with that kind of desperate, determined cheerfulness she puts on in emergencies. Like last year when I found out I was sterile, she drove me crazy counting blessings and pointing out silver linings.

One question keeps going through my mind: why did Jim have to tell me the truth? His confession hasn't lessened his own suffering. It has, in fact, added mine to his. Why, if he never intended to see the woman again, and the child, didn't he keep them both a secret? But I mustn't dwell on such things. I have promised myself I will forget, and I will. I must. Pray for me, Daddy. And please answer this. <u>Please</u>.

Your loving daughter, Daisy

He hadn't answered it. At the time there were a dozen reasons why not, but as the years passed, he'd forgotten the reasons and only the fact remained: he hadn't answered this simplest of requests. Every time he opened the old suitcase, that word *please* flew up out of it and struck him in the face...

Well, he was answering it now, and at a much greater risk than if he'd done it in the first place. It was a stroke of incredibly bad luck that the sister Camilla had referred to before he died had turned out to be Mrs. Rosario. And yet Fielding realized now that if he'd been thinking logically, he should have made some connection between Camilla, on the one hand, and Juanita, on the other. Daisy's letter was dated December 9. In it she stated she'd first heard about Juanita's child a week before, which would make it December 2. This was also the day Camilla had died and Juanita had left town. A connection between the two events was inescapable. And the link must be Mrs. Rosario, who, behind her

270

crucifixes, madonnas, and shrines, seemed as devious an operator as Fielding himself.

"Ask your mother," he said, "how she wangled that money."

Juanita was stubborn. "Maybe someone gave it to her."

"Why?"

"There's some people that *like* to give away money."

"They do, eh? Well, I hope I meet one before I die."

They had reached Granada Street. It was lined on both sides with cars parked for the night; garages were a luxury in this part of town.

Fielding remembered the house not by number, but by its bright pink paint. As he braked the car, he noticed a new blue and white Cadillac pulling away from the curb with an anxious shriek of rubber.

"I'll be back in two hours," he told Juanita.

"You better be."

"I give you my word."

"I don't want your word. I want my car."

"You'll have it. In two hours."

He had no idea whether he'd be back in two hours, two days, or ever. It would all be a matter of luck.

18

I came here to see you, but I lack the courage. That is why I am writing, to feel in touch with you for a little, to remind myself that my death will be only partial; you will be left, you will be the proof that I ever lived at all. I leave nothing else…

The blue and white Cadillac was just as conspicuous on Opal Street as it had been on Granada, but there was no one around to notice. At the first drop of rain the sidewalks had emptied. Jim turned off the windshield wipers and the lights and waited in the cold darkness. Although he didn't look either at his watch or the clock on the dashboard, he knew it was five minutes to seven. During this week of crisis he seemed to carry around inside him his own clock, and he could hear the seconds ticking off with ominous accuracy. Time had become a living, breathing thing, attached to him as inexorably as a remora to a shark's belly, never sleeping or relaxing its grip, so that even when he awoke in the middle of the night, it would communicate to him the exact hour and minute.

Across the street the lights were on in Pinata's office, and a man's shadow was moving back and forth past the window. An overpowering hatred surged up Jim's body like a bore tide up a river, roiling his reason, muddying his perceptions. The hatred was divided equally between Pinata and Fielding—Pinata because he had dredged up the business about Carlos Camilla, Fielding because he had, in his impulsive, irresponsible manner, caused the events of the past week. It was his seemingly innocent phone call on Sunday night that had triggered Daisy's dream. If it hadn't been for the dream, Camilla would still be dead, Juanita forgotten, Mrs. Rosario unknown.

He had questioned Ada Fielding thoroughly about the phone call from Fielding, trying to make her remember exactly what she'd said that evening that might have disturbed Daisy and started the train of thought that led to the dream. "What did you say to her, Ada?" "I told her it was a wrong number." "What else?" "I said it was some drunk. God knows that part of it was true enough." "There must be something more." "Well, I wanted to make it sound realistic, so I told her the drunk had called me baby…"

Baby. The mere word might have caused the dream and led to Daisy's recollection of the day she'd forced herself to forget, the day Jim had told her about Juanita's baby. So it was Fielding who had started it, that unpredictable man whose friendship could be more disastrous than his enmity. Questions without answers dangled in Jim's mind like kites without strings. What had brought Fielding to San Félice in the first place? What were his intentions? Where was he now? Was the girl still with him? Mrs. Rosario hadn't been able to answer any of these questions, but she'd answered another before it was asked: Fielding had seen the boy, Paul.

Jim watched the raindrops zigzagging across the windshield, and he thought of Daisy walking in the rain on Laurel Street trying to find her lost day as if it were something that was still there in the old house. Tears came into his eyes, of love, of pity, of help-lessness. He could no longer keep her safe and protect her from knowledge about her father that would cause her pain for the rest of her life. Yet he knew he must keep on trying, right to the end. "We can't let her find out now, Jim," Ada Fielding had said, and he had replied, "It's inevitable." "No, Jim, don't talk like that." "You shouldn't have lied to her in the first place." "I did it for her own

273

good, Jim. If she'd had children, they might have been like him. It would have killed her." "People don't die so easily."

He realized now how true this was. He'd died a little more each day, each hour, of the past week, and there was still a long way to go.

He blinked away his tears and rubbed his eyes with his knuckles as if he were punishing them for having seen too much, or too little, or too late. When he looked up again, Daisy was coming down the street, half running, her dark hair uncovered and her raincoat blowing open. She appeared excited and happy, like a child walking along the edge of a steep precipice, confident that there would be no landslide, no loose stones under her feet.

Carrying the landslide and the loose stones in his pockets, he got out of the car and crossed the road, head bowed against the wind.

"Daisy?"

She gave a little jump of fright, as if she were being accosted by a strange man. When she recognized him, she didn't say anything, but he could see the happiness and excitement drain out of her face. It was like watching someone bleed.

"Have you been following me, Jim?"

"No."

"You're here."

"Ada told me you had an appointment at—at his office." He didn't want to say the name Pinata. It would have made the shadow moving behind the window too real. "Please come home with me, Daisy."

"No."

"If I have to plead with you, I will."

"It won't do the slightest good."

"I must make the attempt anyway, for your sake."

She turned away with a skeptical little smile that was hardly more than a twist of the mouth. "How quick people are to do things for *my* sake, never their own."

"Married people have a mutual welfare that can't be divided like a pair of towels marked His and Hers."

"Then stop talking about *my* sake. If you mean for the sake of our marriage, say so. Though of course it doesn't sound quite so noble, does it?"

"Please don't be ironic," he said heavily. "The issue is too important."

"What is the issue?"

"You don't realize the kind of catastrophe you're bringing down on yourself."

"But *you* realize?"

"Yes."

"Then tell me."

He was silent.

"Tell me, Jim."

"I can't."

"You see your own wife headed for a catastrophe, as you put it, and you can't even tell her what it is?"

"No."

"Does it have anything to do with the man in my grave?"

"Don't talk like that," he said harshly. "You have no grave. You're alive, healthy—"

"You aren't answering my question about Camilla."

"I can't. Too many people are involved."

She raised her eyebrows, half in surprise, half in irony. "It sounds as if there's been some giant plot going on behind my back."

"It's been my duty to protect you. It still is." He put his hand on her arm. "Come with me now, Daisy. We'll forget this past week, pretend it never happened."

She stood silent in the noisy rain. It would have been easy, at that moment, to yield to the pressure of his hand, follow him across the street, letting him guide her back to safety. They would take up where they left off; it would be Monday morning again, with Jim reading aloud to her from the *Chronicle.* The days would pass quietly, and if they promised no excitement, they promised no catastrophe, either. It was the nights she feared, the return of the dream. She would climb back up the cliff from the sea and find the stranger under the stone cross, under the seamark tree.

"Come home with me now, Daisy, before it's too late."

"It's already too late."

He watched her disappear through the front door of the building. Then he crossed the road and got into his car, without looking up at the shadow behind the lighted window.

The noise of the rain beating on the tile roof was so loud that Pinata didn't hear her step in the corridor or her knocking at the door of his office. It was after seven o'clock. He'd been chasing around after Juanita and Fielding for three hours until he'd reached the point where all the bars, and the people in them, looked alike. He was feeling tired and irritable, and when he looked up and saw Daisy standing in the doorway, he said brusquely, "You're late."

He expected, in fact wanted, her to snap back at him and give him an excuse to express his anger.

She merely looked at him coolly. "Yes. I met Jim outside."

"Jim?"

"My husband." She sat down, brushing her wet hair back from her forehead with the back of her hand. "He wanted me to go home with him."

"Why didn't you?"

"Because I found out some things this afternoon that indicate we've been on the right track."

"What are they?"

"It won't be easy or pleasant for me to tell you, especially about the girl. But of course you have to know, so you can plan what to do next." She blinked several times, but Pinata couldn't tell whether it was because the overhead lights were bothering her eyes or whether she was on the point of weeping. "There's some connection between the girl and Camilla. I'm pretty sure Jim knows what it is, although he wouldn't admit it."

"Did you ask him?"

"Yes."

"Did he indicate that he was acquainted with Camilla?"

"No, but I think he was."

She told him then, in a detached voice, about the events of the afternoon: her discovery of the check stubs in Jim's desk, the call from Muriel about Fielding, her talk with Adam Burnett at the dock, and finally her meeting Jim. He listened carefully, his only comments being the tapping of his heels as he paced the floor.

He said, when she'd finished, "What was in the letter in the pink envelope that Muriel mentioned to you?"

"From the date I know it could have been only one thing—the news about Juanita and the child."

"And that's what motivated his trip up here?"

"Yes."

"Why four years after the fact?"

277

"Perhaps it wasn't possible for him to do anything about it at the time," she said defensively. "I know he wanted to."

"Do anything such as what?"

"Give me moral support, or sympathy, or let me talk it out with him. I think the fact that he didn't come when I needed him has been bothering him all these years. Then when he finally settled nearby, in Los Angeles, he decided to satisfy his conscience. Or his curiosity. I don't know which. It's hard to explain my father's actions, especially when he's been drinking."

It's even harder to explain your husband's, Pinata thought. He stopped pacing and leaned against the front of the desk, his hands in his pockets. "What do you make of your husband's insistence that he is 'protecting' you, Mrs. Harker?"

"He appears to be sincere."

"I don't doubt it. But why does he think you need protection?"

"To avoid a catastrophe, he said."

"That's a pretty strong word. I wonder if he meant it literally."

"I'm sure he did."

"Did he indicate who, or what, would be the cause of this catastrophe?"

"Me," Daisy said. "I'm bringing it down on my own head."

"How?"

"By persisting in this investigation."

"Suppose you don't persist?"

"If I go home like a good little girl and don't ask too many questions or overhear too much, presumably I will avoid catastrophe and live happily ever after. Well, I'm not a good little girl anymore, and I no longer trust my husband or my mother to decide what's best for me."

She had spoken very rapidly, as if she were afraid she might change her mind before the words were all out. He realized the pressure she was under to go home and resume her ordinary life, and while he admired her courage, he doubted the validity of the reasons behind it. *Go back, Daisy baby, to Rainbow's End and the pot of gold and the handsome prince. The real world is a rough place for thirty-year-old little girls in search of catastrophe.*

"I know what you're thinking," she said with a frown. "It's written all over your face."

He could feel the blood rising up his neck into his ears and cheeks. "So you read faces, Mrs. Harker?"

"When they're as obvious as yours."

"Don't be too sure. I might be a man of many masks."

"Well, they're made of cellophane."

"We're wasting time," he said brusquely. "We'd better go over to Mrs. Rosario's house and clear up a few—"

"Why do you get so terribly embarrassed when I bring up anything in the least personal?"

He stared at her in silence for a moment. Then he said, with cold deliberation, "Lay off, Daisy baby."

He had meant to shock her, but she seemed merely curious. "Why did you call me that?"

"It was just another way of saying, don't go looking for two catastrophes."

"I don't understand what you mean."

"No? Well"—he picked up his raincoat from the back of the swivel chair—"are you coming along?"

"Not until you explain to me what you meant."

"Try reading my face again."

"I can't. You just look mad."

"Why, you're a regular face-reading genius, Mrs. Harker. I *am* mad."

"What about?"

"Let's just say I'm a sorehead."

"That's not an adequate answer."

"O.K., put it this way: I have dreams, too. But I don't dream about dead people, just live ones. And sometimes they do some pretty lively things, and sometimes you're one of them. To be any more explicit I would have to go beyond the bounds of propriety, and neither of us wants that, do we?"

She turned away, her jaws clenched.

"Do we?" he repeated.

"No."

"Well, that's that. To hell with dreams." He went to the door and opened it, looking back at her impatiently when she made no move to get up. "Aren't you coming?"

"I don't know."

"I'm sorry if I've frightened you."

"I'm—not frightened." But she hunched in her raincoat as if she had shrunk during the storm, the real one on the other side of the window or the more turbulent one inside herself. "I'm not frightened," she said again. "I just don't know what's ahead for me."

"Nobody does."

"I used to. Now I can't see where I'm going."

"Then you'd better turn back." There was finality in his voice. It was as if they had met, had come together, and had parted, all in the space of a minute, and he knew the minute was gone and would not return. "I'll take you home now, Daisy."

"No."

"Yes. The role of good little girl is better suited to you than this. Just don't listen too hard and don't see too much. You'll be all right."

She was crying, holding the sleeve of his raincoat against her face. He looked away and focused his eyes on an unidentifiable stain on the south wall. The stain had been there when he moved

280

in; it would be there when he moved out. Three coats of paint had failed to obscure it, and it had become for Pinata a symbol of persistence.

"You'll be all right," he repeated. "Going home again might be easier than you think. This past week has been like—well, like a little trip from reality, for both of us. Now the trip's over. It's time to get off the boat, or the plane, or whatever we were on."

"No."

He turned his eyes from the wall to look at her, but her face was still hidden behind his coat sleeve. "Daisy, for God's sake, don't you realize it's impossible? You don't belong in this part of town, on this street, in this office."

"Neither do you."

"The difference is, I'm here. And I'm stuck here. Do you understand what that means?"

"No."

"I have nothing to offer you but a name that isn't my own, an income that ranges from meager to mediocre, and a house with a leaky roof. That's not much."

"If it happens to be what I want, then it's enough, isn't it?"

She spoke with a stubborn dignity that he found both touching and exasperating.

"Daisy, for God's sake, listen to me. Do you realize that I don't even know who my parents were or what race I belong to?"

"I don't care."

"Your mother will."

"My mother has always cared about a lot of the wrong things."

"Maybe they're not wrong."

"Why are you trying so hard to get rid of me, Steve?"

She had never before called him Steve, and the sound of it coming from her made him feel for the first time that the name was finally and truly his own, not something borrowed from a parish priest and tacked on by a Mother Superior. Even if he never saw Daisy again, he would always be grateful to her for this moment of strong, sure identity.

Daisy was wiping her eyes with a handkerchief. The lids were faintly pink, but unswollen, and he wondered whether a really powerful emotion could have caused such dainty and restrained weeping. Perhaps it had been no more than the weeping of a child denied a toy or an ice cream cone.

He said carefully, "We'd better not discuss this anymore tonight, Daisy. I'll take you back to your car."

"I want to come with you."

"You're making this tough for me. I can't force you to go home, and I can't leave you alone in this part of town even with the door locked."

"Why do you keep referring to this part of town as if it were a corner of hell?"

"It is."

"I'm coming with you," she said again.

"To Mrs. Rosario's house?"

"If that's where you're going, yes."

"Juanita might be there. And the child."

A spasm of pain twisted her mouth, but she said, "It may be a necessary part of my growing up, to meet them both."

19

Memories—how she cried before you were born, day in, day out, until I wished there were a way of using all those tears to irrigate the dry, dusty rangeland…

She had taken the children to the Brewsters' house and left them without explanation, and Mr. Brewster, who was crippled and liked to have company while he watched television, had demanded none. On her return trip she avoided the lighted streets, using shortcuts across backyards and driveways, hunched under her umbrella like a gnome on night business. She was not afraid, either of the dark or its contents. She knew most of the people in the neighborhood stood in awe of her because of the candles she burned and the number of times she went to church.

The thin walls of poverty hold few secrets. Even before she reached the porch, she could hear Juanita slamming around inside the house as if she were looking for something. Mrs. Rosario shook the water off her umbrella and removed her dripping coat, thinking, *Maybe she's got it in her head that I am spying on her again, and she is looking for me all over the house, even in places I couldn't possibly be if I were a midget. I must hurry…*

But she couldn't hurry. Weariness dragged at her legs and arms, and ever since the scene with Juanita in the afternoon, there'd been a sickness in her stomach that didn't get worse but wouldn't go away. When she'd fed the children their supper, she had eaten nothing, just sipped a little lemon and anise tea.

She let herself quietly into the house and went to the bedroom to hang up her coat. With Pedro's help she had taken the broken door off its hinges and carried it out to the backyard, where it would lie, with other damaged pieces of her life, to warp in the rain and bleach in the sun. Next week she and Pedro would go to the junkyard and hunt for another door until they found one almost the right size. They would fix it up with sandpaper and a little paint…

"Next week," she said aloud, as if making a promise of improvement to someone who'd accused her of being slovenly. But the thought of the long trip to the junkyard, the grating of sandpaper, the smell of paint, increased her nausea. "Or the week after, when I am feeling stronger."

Even without the door, the bedroom was her sanctuary, the only place where she could be alone with her grief and guilt. The candle in front of Camilla's picture had burned low. She put a fresh one in its place and lit it, addressing the dead man in the language they had used as children.

"I am sorry, Carlos, little brother. I yearned to see justice done, out in the open, but I had my Juanita to think of. Just that very week you came here, she had been arrested again, and I knew wherever she went in this town from then on, she'd be watched; they'd never let her alone—the police, the Probation Department, and the Clinic. I had to get her away where she could start over and live in peace. I am a woman, a mother. No one else would look after my Juanita, who was cursed at birth by the evil eye of the *curandera* masquerading as a nurse at the hospital. Not a penny did I touch for myself, Carlos."

Every night she explained to Carlos what had happened, and every night his static smile seemed to indicate disbelief, and she was forced to go on, to convince him she had meant no wrong.

"I know you did not kill yourself, little brother. When you came to see me that night, I heard you telephoning the woman, telling her to meet you. I heard you ask for money, and I knew this was a bad thing, asking money from rich people; better to beg from the poor. I was afraid for you, Carlos. You acted so queer, and you would tell me nothing, only to be quiet and to pray for your soul.

"When the time came that you were to meet her, I went down to the jungle by the railroad tracks. I lost my way. I couldn't find you at first. But then I saw a car, a big new car, and I knew it must be hers. A moment later she came out from the bushes and began running towards the car, very fast, as if she was trying to escape. When I reached the bushes, you were lying there dead with a knife in you, and I knew she had put it there. I knelt over you and begged you to be alive again, Carlos, but you would not hear me. I went home and lit a candle for you. It is still burning, God rest your soul."

She remembered kneeling in the dark in front of the little shrine, praying for guidance. She couldn't confide in Juanita or Mrs. Brewster, because neither of them could be trusted with a secret, and she couldn't call in the police, who were Juanita's enemies and hence her own. They might even suspect she was lying about the woman in the green car in order to protect Juanita.

She'd prayed, and as she prayed, one thought grew in her mind and expanded until it pushed aside all others: Juanita and her unborn child must be taken care of, and there was no one else to do it but herself. She'd called the woman on the telephone, knowing only her name and the shape of her shadow and the color of her car…

"It is a bad and dangerous thing, Carlos, asking money from the rich, and I was afraid for my life knowing what she'd done to you. But she was more afraid because she had more to lose than I.

285

I did not tell her my name or where I lived, only what I had come across in the bushes and her running away to the car. I said I wanted no trouble, I was a poor woman, but I would never seek money for myself, only for my daughter, Juanita, with her unborn child that had no father. She asked me whether I'd told anyone else about you, Carlos, and I said no, with truth. Then she said if I gave her my telephone number, she would call me back; there was someone she had to consult. When she called back a little later, she told me she wanted to take care of my daughter and her child. She didn't even mention you, Carlos, or argue about the money, or accuse me of blackmail. Just 'I would like to take care of your daughter and her child.' She gave me the address of an office I was to go to the next day at 12:30. When I went in, I thought at first it was a trap for me—she wasn't there, only a tall blond man, and then later the lawyer. No one talked about you, no one spoke your name, Carlos. It was as if you had never lived…"

She turned away from the picture with a groan as another spasm of nausea seized her stomach. The lemon and anise tea had failed to ease her, although it was made from a recipe handed down by her grandmother and had never failed in the past. Clutching her stomach with both hands, she hurried out to the kitchen, with the idea of trying some of the medicine the school doctor had sent home to cure Rita's boils. The medicine had not been opened; Mrs. Rosario was treating the boils herself with a poultice of ivy leaves and salt pork.

She was so intent on her errand, and her pain, that she didn't notice Juanita standing at the stove until she spoke. "Well, are you all through talking to yourself?"

"I was not—"

"I got ears. I heard you mumbling and moaning in there like a crazy woman."

Mrs. Rosario sat down, hunched over the kitchen table. In spite of the pain crawling around inside her like a live thing with cruel legs, merciless arms, she knew she must talk to Juanita now. Mr. Harker had warned her; he'd been very angry that she had permitted Juanita to come back to town.

The room felt hot and airless. Juanita had turned the oven up high to cook herself some supper, and she hadn't opened the window as she was supposed to. Mrs. Rosario dragged herself over to the window and opened it, gasping in the cold fresh air.

"Where are my kids?" Juanita said. "What have you done with them?"

"They're at the Brewsters'."

"Why aren't they home in bed?"

"Because I didn't want them to overhear what I am going to say to you." Mrs. Rosario returned to her place at the table, forcing herself to sit erect because she knew the disastrous effects which a show of weakness on her part sometimes had on her daughter. "The man who was with you—where is he?"

"He had some business to look after, but he'll be back."

"Here?"

"Why not here?"

"You mustn't let him in. He's a bad man. He lies. Even about his name, which is not Foster but Fielding."

Juanita masked her annoyance with a shrug. "I don't care. What difference does it—"

"Did you tell him anything?"

"Sure. I told him my feet hurt, and he said take off your shoes. So I took—"

"There is no time for insolence." The strain of holding herself erect had weakened Mrs. Rosario's voice to a whisper, but even her whisper had a sting in it.

Juanita felt the sting and resented it. She was afraid of this old woman who could invoke saints and devils against her, and her fear was compounded by her knowledge that she had talked too much and too loosely to Fielding. "I never told him a thing, so help me God."

"Did he ask you any questions about your Uncle Carlos?"

"No."

"Or about Paul?"

"No."

"Juanita, listen to me—I must have the truth this time."

"I swear by Mary."

"What do you swear?"

Juanita's face was expressionless. "Whatever you want me to."

"Juanita, are you frightened of me? Are you afraid to tell the truth? I smell drink on your breath. Maybe the drink has made you forget what you said, eh?"

"I never said a word."

"Nothing about Paul or Carlos?"

"I swear by Mary."

Mrs. Rosario's lips moved silently as she bowed her head and crossed herself. The familiar gesture loosened angry memories in Juanita's mind, and they came crashing down like an avalanche of gravel, covering her fear with dust and noise.

"Do you call me a liar, you old witch?" she shouted.

"Shhhh. You must keep your voice down. Someone might—"

"I don't care. I got nothing to hide. That's more than you can say."

"Please. We must have a quiet talk, we—"

"For all your moaning and groaning to God Almighty, you're no better than the rest of us, are you?"

"No. I am no better than the rest of you."

Juanita's loud, harsh laughter filled the little room. "Well, that's the first thing you ever admitted in your whole damn life."

"You must be quiet a minute and listen to me," Mrs. Rosario said. "Sit down here beside me."

"I can listen standing up."

"Mr. Harker was here half an hour ago."

Juanita had a vague memory of Fielding mentioning the name to her. It had meant nothing to her then and meant nothing now. "What's that got to do with me?"

"Mr. Harker is Paul's father."

"Are you crazy? I never even heard of a guy called Harker."

"You are hearing now. He is Paul's father."

"By God, what are you trying to do? Prove I'm so spooky I can't even remember my own kid's father? You want me to get locked up so's you can keep the money from the trust fund for yourself?"

"There never was a trust fund," Mrs. Rosario said quietly. "Carlos was a poor man."

"Why did you lie to me?"

"It was necessary. If you told anyone about Mr. Harker, the money would stop."

"How could I tell anyone about Harker when I don't even know him?" Juanita pounded the table with her fist, and the salt-shaker gave a little jump, fell over on its side, and began spilling, as if it had been shot.

Hurriedly Mrs. Rosario picked up a pinch of the salt and put it under her tongue to ward off the bad luck that plagued a house where there was waste. "Please, there must be no violence."

"Then answer me."

"Mr. Harker has been supporting Paul because he is Paul's father."

"He's not."

"You are to say so, whether you remember or not."

"I won't. It's not true."

Mrs. Rosario's voice was rising in pitch as if it were competing with Juanita's. "You are to do as I tell you, without arguing."

"You think I can't even remember Paul's father? He was in the Air Force, he went to Korea. I wrote to him. We were going to get married when he got out."

"No, no! You must listen to me. Mr. Harker—"

"I never even heard of a guy called Harker. Never in my life, do you hear me?"

"Shhhh!" Mrs. Rosario's face had turned gray, and her eyes, darkened by fear, were fixed on the back door. "There's someone out on the porch," she said in an urgent whisper. "Quick, lock the door, close the window."

"I got nothing to hide. Why should I?"

"Oh God, will you never listen to your mother? Will you never know how much I've endured for you, how much I've loved you?"

She reached out to touch Juanita's hand with her own, but Juanita stepped back with a sound of contempt and disbelief, and went to the door.

She opened it. A man was standing on the threshold, and behind him, at the bottom of the porch steps, a woman, faceless in the shadows.

The man, a stranger to Juanita, was politely apologetic. "I knocked on the front door, and when I didn't get any answer, I came around to the back."

"Well?"

"My name is Steve Pinata. If you don't mind, I'd like to—"

"I don't know you."

"Your mother does."

"He's a detective," Mrs. Rosario said dully. "Tell him nothing."

"I've brought Mrs. Harker with me, Mrs. Rosario. She wants to talk to you about something that's of great importance to her. May we come inside?"

"Go away. I can't talk to anyone. I'm sick."

Pinata knew from her color and her labored breathing that she was telling the truth. "You'd better let me call a doctor, Mrs. Rosario."

"No. Just leave me alone. My daughter and I were having… a little argument. It is no business of yours."

"From what I overheard, it's Mrs. Harker's business."

"Let her talk to her husband about it. Not me. I can say nothing."

"Then I'm afraid I'll have to ask Juanita."

"No, no! Juanita is innocent. She knows nothing."

Using the table as support, Mrs. Rosario tried to push herself to her feet, but she fell back into the chair with a sigh of exhaustion. Pinata crossed the room and took her by the arm. "Let me help you."

"No."

"You'd better lie down quietly while I call a doctor."

"No. A priest—Father Salvadore…"

"All right, a priest. Mrs. Harker and I will help you to your bedroom, and I'll send for Father Salvadore." He motioned to Daisy to come into the house, and she started up the porch steps.

Up to this point Juanita had been standing, blank-faced, beside the open door, as if what was happening was of no concern or interest to her. It was only when Daisy reached the periphery of light that Juanita let out a gasp of recognition.

She began screaming at her mother in Spanish. "It's the woman I used to see at the Clinic. She's come to take me away. Don't let her. I promise to be good. I promise to buy you a new crucifix, and go to Mass and confession, and never break things anymore. Don't let her take me away!"

"Be quiet," Pinata said. "Mrs. Harker's had no connection with the Clinic for years. Now listen to me. Your mother's very ill. She belongs in a hospital. I want you to help Mrs. Harker look after her while I call an ambulance."

At the word *ambulance* Mrs. Rosario tried once more to get to her feet. This time she fell across the table. The tabled tilted, and she slid slowly and gracefully to the floor. Almost immediately her face began to darken. Bending over her, Pinata felt for a pulse that wasn't there.

Juanita was staring down at her mother, her fists clasped against her cheeks in an infantile gesture of fright. "She looks so funny."

Daisy put her hand on Juanita's shoulder. "We'd better go into the other room."

"But why does she look so black, like a nigger?"

"Mr. Pinata has called an ambulance. There's nothing else we can do."

"She isn't dead? She can't be dead?"

"I don't know. We—"

"Oh, God, if she'd dead, they'll blame me."

"No, they won't," Daisy said. "People die. There's no use blaming anyone."

"They'll say it's my fault because I was bad to her. I broke her crucifix and the door."

"No one will blame you," Daisy said. "Come with me."

It was only by concentrating on helping Juanita that Daisy was able to keep herself under control. She led Juanita into the front room and closed the door. Here, among the shrines and madonnas and thorn-crowned Christs, death seemed more real than it had in the presence of the dead woman herself. It was as if the room had been waiting for someone to die in it.

292

The two women sat side by side on the couch in awkward silence, like guests waiting for a tardy hostess to introduce them to each other.

"I don't know what it was all about," Juanita said finally in a high, desperate voice. "I just don't *know*. She asked me to lie, and I wouldn't. I never met any Mr. Harker."

"He's my husband."

"All right, then. Ask him. He'll tell you himself."

"He's already told me."

"When?"

"Four years ago," Daisy said. "Before your son was born."

"What did he say?"

"That he was the boy's father."

"Why, he's crazy." Juanita's fists were clenched so tight that the broad, flat thumbs almost covered the knuckles. "Why, the whole bunch of you are *crazy*. I don't even know any Mr. Harker!"

"I saw you getting out of his car at the parking lot outside the Clinic just before your baby was born."

"Maybe he just gave me a ride. A lot of people give me rides when I'm pregnant. I can't remember them all. Maybe he was one of them. Or maybe it wasn't even me you saw."

"It was you."

"All right, maybe I'm the one that's crazy. Is that what you're getting at? They oughta maybe come and take me away and lock me up someplace."

"That isn't going to happen," Daisy said.

"Maybe it'd be better if it did. I can't make sense of things like they are now. Like the business about my Uncle Carlos and the money—he said my mother had been lying about Uncle Carlos."

"Who said?"

"Foster. Or Fielding. He said Uncle Carlos was an old friend of his and he knew a lot about him and what my mother told me was all lies."

"Your uncle's name is—was Camilla?"

"Yes."

"And you think my fa—Mr. Fielding was telling you the truth?"

"I guess so. Why shouldn't he?"

"Where is he now, this Mr. Fielding?"

"He had an important errand, he said. He asked to borrow my car for a couple hours. We made like a bargain. I gave him the car; he gave me the dope on my uncle."

Daisy had no reason to doubt the statement: it sounded exactly like the kind of bargain her father would make. As for the important errand, there was only one logical place it could have taken him—to her own home. Fielding, Juanita, Mrs. Rosario, Jim, her mother, Camilla, they were all beginning to merge and adhere into a multiple-headed monster that was crawling inexorably toward her.

Outside the house the ambulance had come to a stop with one last suffocated wail of its siren.

Juanita began to moan, bent double, so that her forehead pressed against her knees. "They're going to take her away."

"They have to."

"She's scared of hospitals; hospitals are where you die."

"She won't be scared of this one, Juanita."

After a time the noises from the kitchen ceased. A door opened and banged shut again, and a minute later the ambulance pulled away from the curb. Its siren was mute. The time for hurrying had passed.

Pinata came in from the kitchen and looked across the room at the moaning girl. "I called Mrs. Brewster, Juanita. She's coming over to get you right away."

294

"I'm not going with her."

"Mrs. Harker and I can't leave you here alone."

"I got to stay here and wait, in case they send my mother home. There won't be anybody to look after her if I—"

"She's not coming home."

The strange blankness had come over Juanita's face again, as concealing as the sheet that was used to cover her mother's. Without a sound, she rose to her feet and walked into the bedroom. The candle in front of Camilla's picture was still burning. She leaned down and blew it out. Then she flung herself across the bed, rolled over on her back, and stared up at the ceiling. "It's just wax. It's just ordinary beeswax."

Daisy stood at the foot of the bed. "We'll stay with you until Mrs. Brewster gets here."

"I don't care."

"Juanita, if there's anything I can do, if there's any way I can help you—"

"I don't want no help."

"I'm putting my card with my telephone number on it here on the bureau."

"Leave me alone. Go away."

"All right. We're leaving."

Their departure was marked by the same words as their arrival had been: *Go away.* Between the two, a woman had died and a monster had come to life.

20

Dust and tears, these are what I remember most about the day of your birth, your mother's weeping, and the dust sifting in through locked windows and bolted doors and the closed draft of the chimney…

The drapes were drawn across all the windows as if there was no one at home, or the people who were at home didn't want to advertise the fact. A car, unfamiliar to Daisy, was parked beside the garage. Pinata opened the door and examined the registration card while Daisy stood waiting under a eucalyptus tree that towered a hundred feet above the house. The pungent odor of the tree's wet bark, half bitter, half sweet, stung her nostrils.

"It's Juanita's car," he said. "Your father must be here."

"Yes. I thought he would be."

"You look pale. Are you feeling all right?"

"I guess so."

"I love you, Daisy."

"Love." The sound of the word was like the scent of eucalyptus, half bitter, half sweet. "Why are you telling me that now?"

"I wanted you to know, so that no matter what happens tonight in connection with your father or mother or Jim—"

"An hour ago you were trying to get rid of me," she said painfully. "Have you changed your mind?"

"Yes."

"Why?"

"I saw a woman die." He couldn't explain to her the shock he'd had of complete realization that this was the only life he was given to live. There would be no second chance, no certificate of merit to be awarded for waiting, no diploma for patience.

She seemed to understand what he meant, without explanation. "I love you, too, Steve."

"Then everything will work out all right. Won't it?"

"I guess so."

"We don't have time for guessing, Daisy."

"Everything will work out," she said, and when he kissed her, she almost believed herself.

She clung to his arm as they walked toward the house where the dream had begun and where it was now to end. The front door was unlocked. When she opened it and went into the foyer, there was no sound from the adjoining living room, but the silence was curiously alive; the walls seemed to be still echoing with noises of anger.

Her mother's sharp voice sliced the silence. "Daisy? Is that you?"

"Yes."

"Is there anyone with you?"

"Yes."

"We are having a *private* family discussion in here. You must ask our guest to excuse you. Immediately."

"I won't do that."

"Your—your father is here."

"Yes," Daisy said. "Yes, I know."

She went into the living room, and Pinata followed her.

A small woman who looked like Daisy was huddled in a chair by the picture window, a handkerchief pressed tightly against her mouth as if to stem a bloody flow of words. Harker sat by himself on the chesterfield, an unlit pipe clenched between his teeth. His glance at Daisy was brief and reproachful.

Standing on the raised hearth, surveying the room like a man who'd just bought the place, was Fielding. Pinata realized immediately that Fielding was drunk on more than liquor, as if he'd been waiting for years for this moment of seeing his former wife cringing in fear before him. Perhaps this was his real motive for coming to San Félice, not any desire to help Daisy, but a thirst for revenge against Ada. Revenge was heady stuff; Fielding looked delirious, half mad.

Daisy was crossing the room toward him, slowly, as if she wasn't quite sure whether this strange man was her father or not. "Daddy?"

"Yes, Daisy baby." He seemed pleased, but he didn't step off the raised hearth to go and meet her. "You're as pretty as ever."

"Are you all right, Daddy?"

"Certainly. Certainly I am. Never better." He bent to touch her forehead lightly with his lips, then straightened up again quickly, as though he was afraid a usurper might steal his position of power. "So you've brought Mr. Pinata with you. That's unfortunate, Daisy baby. This is entirely a private family affair, Pinata wouldn't be interested."

"I was hired," Pinata said, "to make an investigation. Until it's concluded, or until I'm dismissed, I'm under Mrs. Harker's orders." He glanced at Daisy. "Do you want me to leave?"

She shook her head. "No."

"You might regret it, Daisy baby," Fielding said. "But then regrets are a part of life, aren't they, Ada? Maybe the main part, eh? Some regrets, of course, are slower in coming than others, and harder to take. Isn't that right, Ada?"

Mrs. Fielding spoke through the handkerchief she held to her mouth. "You're drunk."

"In wine is truth, old girl."

"Coming from you, truth is a dirty word."

"I know dirtier ones. Love, that's the dirtiest of all, isn't it, Ada? Tell us about it. Give us the lowdown."

"You're a—an evil man."

"Don't antagonize him, Ada," Jim said quietly. "There's nothing to be gained."

"Jim's right. Don't antagonize me, Ada, and maybe I'll go away like a good lad without telling any tales. Would you like that? Sure you would. Only it's too late. Some of your little tricks are catching up with you. My going away can't stop them."

"If there were any tricks, they were necessary." Her head had begun to shake, as if the neck muscles that held it up had suddenly gone flabby. "I was forced to lie to Daisy. I couldn't permit her to have children who would inherit certain—certain characteristics of her father."

"Tell Daisy about these characteristics. Name them."

"I—please, Stan. Don't."

"She's got a right to know about her old man, hasn't she? You made a decision that affected her life. Now justify it." Fielding's mouth cracked open in a mirthless smile. "Tell her about all the little monsters she might have brought into the world if it hadn't been for her wise, benevolent mother."

Daisy was standing with her back against the door, her eyes fixed, not on her father or mother, but on Jim. "Jim? What are they talking about, Jim?"

"You'll have to ask your mother."

"She was lying to me that day in the doctor's office? It's not true I can't have children?"

"No, it's not true."

"Why did she do it? Why did you let her?"

"I had to."

"You *had* to. Is that the only explanation you can offer me?" She crossed the room toward him, the rain dripping soundlessly from her coat onto the soft rug. "What about the girl, Juanita?"

"I only met her once in my life," he said. "I picked her up on the street and drove her three or four blocks to the Clinic. Deliberately. I knew who she was. I kept her talking in the car until you came out because I wanted you to see us together."

"Why?"

"I intended to claim her child."

"You must have had a reason."

"No man would take a drastic step like that without having reasons."

"I can think of one," she said in a brittle voice. "You wanted to make sure I kept on believing that our lack of children was my fault and not yours. You're admitting now that it has been your fault, right from the beginning."

"Yes."

"And the reason you and my mother lied to me and that you claimed Juanita's child was to make sure I'd never suspect you were the sterile one in our marriage."

He didn't try to deny it, although he knew it was only a small portion of the truth. "That was a factor, yes. I didn't originate the lie; your mother did. I went along with it when I found out—when it became necessary."

"Why did it become necessary?"

"I had to protect your mother."

Mrs. Fielding sprang out of her chair like a runner at the sound of the starter's gun. But there was nowhere to run; the course had no beginning and no ending. "Stop it, Jim. Let me tell her, please."

"You?" Daisy turned to face her mother. "I wouldn't believe you if you told me it was Saturday night and raining outside."

"It *is* Saturday night and it *is* raining outside. You'd be a fool not to believe the facts just because they came from me."

"Tell me some facts, then."

"There's a stranger present." Mrs. Fielding glanced at Pinata, then at Fielding. "Two strangers. Must I talk in front of them? Can't we wait until—"

"I've done enough waiting. Mr. Pinata can be trusted to be discreet, and my father wouldn't do anything to harm me."

Fielding nodded and smiled at her—"You bet I wouldn't, Daisy baby"—but there was a derisive, cynical quality about the smile that worried Pinata because he couldn't understand it. He wished the alcohol, and whatever other intoxicant was at work in Fielding's system, would wear off and leave him less sure of himself. One sign of its wearing off was already apparent, the fine tremor of Fielding's hands, which he attempted to cover up by hiding them in his pockets.

Mrs. Fielding had begun to talk again, her eyes on Daisy. "No matter what you think now, Daisy, Jim has done everything possible for your happiness. Remember that. The first lie was mine. I've already told you why it was necessary—your children would be marked by a stigma that must not be passed on. I can't talk about it in front of a stranger. Later, you and I will discuss it alone." She took a long breath, wincing as if it hurt her lungs, or heart, to probe so deep. "Four years ago, without warning, I received a telephone call from a man I hadn't seen for a very long time and never expected to see again. His name was Carlos Camilla, and Stan and I had known him as Curly when we were first married in New Mexico. He was a close friend to us both. You've always accused me of race prejudice, Daisy. But in those days Camilla was our friend; we went through bad times together and helped each other.

"He didn't mince words when he called. He said he had only a short time to live and needed money for his funeral. He reminded me of—of old times, and I—well, I agreed to meet him and give him some money."

"Two thousand dollars?" Pinata said.

"Yes."

"That's a lot to pay for memories of old times, Mrs. Fielding."

"I felt an obligation to help him," she said. "He sounded so terribly ill and broken, I knew he must be telling the truth about his approaching death. I asked him if I could send him the money instead of meeting him, but he said there wasn't time, and he had no address for me to send it to."

"Where did you get the money?"

"From Jim. I knew he had a lot of cash in the safe at his office. I explained the situation to him, and he thought it would be advisable to pay what Camilla asked."

"Advisable?" It seemed, to Pinata, a curious word to use under the circumstances.

"Jim is a very generous man."

"Obviously there were reasons for his generosity?"

"Yes."

"What were they?"

"I must refuse to answer."

"All right," Pinata said. "You went to meet Camilla. Where?"

"At the end of Greenwald Street, near the signalman's shack. It was very late and dark. I couldn't see anyone, and I thought I had misunderstood his instructions. I was about to leave when I heard him call my name, and a shadow stepped out from behind a bush. 'Come here and look at me,' he said. He lit a match and held it in front of his face. I'd known him when he was young and lively and handsome; the man in the matchlight was a living corpse, emaciated, misshapen. I couldn't speak. There were so many things to say, but I couldn't speak. I gave him the money, and he said, 'God bless you, Ada, and God bless me, Carlos.'"

The funereal words seemed, to Pinata, to contain a curious echo of another ceremony: *I, Ada, take thee, Carlos...*

"I thought I heard someone coming," Mrs. Fielding went on. "I panicked and ran back to my car and drove off. When I returned to the house, the phone was ringing. It was a woman."

"Mrs. Rosario?"

"Yes, although she didn't tell me her name then. She said she had found Carlos dead and that I had killed him. She wouldn't listen to my denials, my protests. She just kept talking about her daughter, Juanita, who needed taking care of because she was going to give birth to a fatherless child. She seemed obsessed with this single idea of money for her daughter and the baby. I said I would call her back, that I had to consult someone. She gave me her phone number. Then I went to Jim's room and woke him up."

She paused, looking at Daisy half in sorrow, half in reproach. "You'll never know how many times Jim has taken a burden off my shoulders, Daisy. I told him the situation. We both agreed that it was impossible for me to be dragged through a police investigation. Too many suspicious things would come out: that I knew Camilla, that I'd given him two thousand dollars. I couldn't face it. I realized I had to keep Mrs. Rosario quiet. The problem was how to pay her so that even if someone found out about the payments, the real reason for them would remain secret. The only possible way was to concoct a false reason and make it known to someone in a key position, like Adam Burnett."

"And the false reason," Pinata said, "was support for Juanita's child?"

"Yes. It was Mrs. Rosario who inadvertently suggested it by insisting that she wanted no money for herself, only for Juanita. So we decided that was how it would be done. Jim was to claim the child and pay for its support. It seemed, in a way, like a stroke of fate that the lie should fit in so perfectly with the lie I was forced to tell Daisy in the first place. It was all arranged in Adam Burnett's office the next day, by Adam and Jim and Mrs. Rosario. Adam was never told the truth. He even wanted to fight Juanita's 'claim' in court, but Jim managed to convince him that he must keep quiet. The next step was convincing Daisy. That was easy enough. Jim found out through Mrs. Rosario that Juanita was to go to the Clinic late that afternoon. He picked her up in his car and kept her talking in the parking lot until Daisy came out and saw them together. Then he made his false confession to her.

"Cruel? Yes, it was a cruel thing to do, Daisy. But not as cruel as others, perhaps—and not as cruel as some of the real tricks life plays on us. The next days were terrible ones. Although the coroner's inquest ruled Camilla's death was a suicide, the police were still investigating the source of the money found on him and still trying to establish who Camilla was. But time passed and nothing happened. Camilla was buried, still unknown."

Pinata said, "Did you ever visit his grave, Mrs. Fielding?"

"I passed it several times when we went to leave flowers for Jim's parents."

"Did you leave flowers for Camilla, too?"

"No, I couldn't. Daisy was always with me."

"Why?"

"Because I—I wanted her along."

"Was there any display of emotion on these occasions?"

"I cried sometimes."

"Wasn't Daisy curious about the reason for your tears?"

"I told her that I had a cousin buried there, of whom I'd been very fond."

"What was this cousin's name?"

"I…"

Fielding's sudden fit of coughing sounded like stifled laughter. When he had finished, he wiped his eyes with his coat sleeve. "Ada has a very sentimental nature. She weeps at the drop of a dead cousin. The only difficulty in this instance is that neither of her parents had any siblings. So where did the cousin come from, Ada?"

She looked at him, her mouth moving in a soundless curse.

Pinata said, "There was no cousin, Mrs. Fielding?"

"I—no."

"The tears were for Camilla?"

"Yes."

"Why?"

"He died alone and was buried alone. I felt guilty."

"Guilt as strong as that," Pinata said, "makes me wonder whether Mrs. Rosario's accusation against you might not have some basis in fact."

"I had nothing whatever to do with Camilla's death. He killed himself, with his own knife. That was the coroner's verdict."

"This afternoon I talked to Mr. Fondero, the mortician in charge of Camilla's body. It's his opinion that Camilla's hands were too severely crippled by arthritis to have used that knife with the necessary force."

"When I left him," Mrs. Fielding said steadily, "he was still alive."

"But when Mrs. Rosario arrived—and let's assume that her coming was the noise you heard which frightened you away—he was dead. Suppose Fondero's opinion about Camilla's incapacity to handle the knife is correct. As far as we know, only two people were with Camilla that night, you and Mrs. Rosario. Do you think Mrs. Rosario killed her brother?"

"It's more reasonable than to think I did."

"What would her motive have been?"

"Perhaps a deliberate scheme to get money for the girl. I don't know. Why don't you ask her, not me?"

"I can't ask her," Pinata said. "Mrs. Rosario died tonight of a heart attack."

"Oh God." She dropped back into the chair, her hands pressing against her chest. "Death. It's beginning to surround me. All this death, and nothing to take the curse off it, no new life coming to take its place. This is my punishment, no new life." She gazed at Fielding with dull eyes. "Revenge is what you wanted, isn't it, Stan? Well, you have it. You might as well leave now. Go back to whatever hole you crawled out of."

Fielding's smile wobbled at the corners, but it stayed with him. "You won't be living so fancy yourself from now on, will you, Ada? Maybe you'll be glad to find a hole to crawl into. Your passport to the land of gracious living expires when Daisy leaves."

"Daisy won't leave."

"No? Ask her."

The two women looked at each other in silence. Then Daisy said, with a brief glance at her husband, "I think Jim already knows I won't be staying. I think he's known for the past few days. Haven't you, Jim?"

"Yes."

"Are you going to ask me to stay?"

"No."

"Well, *I* am," Mrs. Fielding said harshly. "You can't walk out now. I've worked so hard to keep this marriage secure—"

Fielding laughed. "People should work on their *own* marriages, my dear. Take yours, for instance. This man Fielding you married, he wasn't a bad guy. Oh, he was no world-beater. He could never have afforded a split-level deal like this. But he adored you, he thought you were the most wonderful, virtuous, truthful—"

"Stop it. I won't listen."

"Most truthful—"

"Leave her alone, Fielding," Jim said quietly. "You've drawn blood. Be satisfied."

"Maybe I've developed a taste for it and want more."

"Any more will be Daisy's. Think about it."

"Think about Daisy's blood? All right, I'll do that." Fielding put on a mock-serious expression like an actor playing a doctor on a television commercial. "In this blood of hers there are certain genes which will be transmitted to her children and make monsters out of them. Like her father. Right?"

"The word monster doesn't apply, as you well know."

"Ada thinks it does. In fact, she's not quite sane on the subject. But then perhaps guilt makes us all a little crazy eventually."

Pinata said, "You know a lot about guilt, Fielding."

"I'm an expert."

"That makes you a little crazy, too, eh?"

Fielding grinned like an old dog. "You have to be a little crazy to take the risks I took in coming here."

"Risks? Did you expect Mrs. Fielding or Mr. Harker to attack you?"

"You figure it out."

"I'm trying." Pinata crossed the room and stood beside Mrs. Fielding's chair. "When Camilla telephoned you that night from Mrs. Rosario's house, you said the call was a complete surprise to you?"

307

"Yes. I hadn't seen him or heard from him for many years."

"Then how did he find out that you were living in San Félice and that you were in a position where you could help him financially? A man in Camilla's physical state wouldn't start out across the country in the vague hope of locating a woman he hadn't seen in years and finding her prosperous enough to assist him. He must have had two facts before he decided to come here—your address and your financial situation. Who told him?"

"I don't know. Unless..." She stopped, turning her head slowly toward Fielding. "It was—it was you, Stan?"

After a moment's hesitation, Fielding shrugged and said, "Sure. I told him."

"Why? To make trouble for me?"

"I figured you could afford a little trouble. Things had gone pretty smooth for you. I didn't actually plan anything, though. Not at first. It happened accidentally. I hit Albuquerque the end of that November. I decided to look Camilla up, thinking there was an off-chance he had struck it rich and wouldn't mind passing some of it around. It was a bum guess, believe me. When I found him, he was on the last skid. His wife had died, and he was living, or half living, in a mud shack with a couple of Indians."

His mouth stretched back from his teeth with no more expression or purpose than a piece of elastic. "Oh yes, it was quite a reunion, Ada. I'm sorry you missed it. It might have taught you a simple lesson, the difference between poorness and destitution. Poorness is having no money. Destitution is a real, a positive thing. It lives with you every minute. It eats at your stomach during the night, it drags at your arms and legs when you move, it bites your hands and ears on cold mornings, it pinches your throat when you swallow, it squeezes the moisture out of you, drop by drop by drop. Camilla sat there on his iron cot, dying in front of my eyes. And you think, while I stood and watched him, that I was worried about making trouble for *you?* What an egotist you are, Ada. Why, you didn't even exist as a person anymore, for Camilla or for me. You were a possible source of money, and we both needed it desperately—Camilla to die with, and I to live with. So I said to him, why not put the bite on Ada? She's got Daisy fixed up with a rich man, I told him; they wouldn't miss a couple of thousand dollars."

Mrs. Fielding's face had stiffened with pain and shock. "And he agreed to—to put the bite on me?"

"You or anyone else. It hardly matters to a dying man. He knew he wasn't going to make it in this life, and he'd gotten obsessed with the idea of the next one, having a fine funeral and going to heaven. I guess the idea of getting money from you appealed to him, particularly because he had a sister living here in San Félice. He thought he'd kill two birds: get the money and see Mrs. Rosario again. He had an idea that Mrs. Rosario had influence with the Church that would do him some good when he kicked off."

"Then you were aware," Pinata said, "when you arrived here, that Camilla was Juanita's uncle?"

"No, no," said Fielding. "Camilla had never called his sister anything but her first name, Filomena. It was a complete surprise to me seeing his picture when I took Juanita home this afternoon. But that's when I began to be sure some dirty work was going on. Too many coincidences add up to a plan. Whose plan I didn't know. But I did know my former wife, and plans are her specialty."

"They've had to be," Mrs. Fielding said. "I've had to look ahead if no one else would."

"This time you looked so far ahead you didn't see the road in front of you. You were worried about your grandchildren; you should have worried about your child."

309

"Let's get back to Camilla," Pinata said to Fielding. "Obviously you expected a share of whatever money he could pry out of your former wife?"

"Of course. It was my idea."

"You were pretty sure she'd pay up?"

"Yes."

"Why?"

"Oh, auld lang syne, and that sort of thing. As I said, Ada has a very sentimental nature."

"And as I said, two thousand dollars is a heap of auld lang syne."

Fielding shrugged. "We were all good friends once. Around the ranch they called us the three musketeers."

"Oh?" It was difficult for Pinata to believe that Mrs. Fielding, with her strong racial prejudices, should ever have been one of a trio that included a Mexican ranch hand. But if Fielding's statement was untrue, Ada Fielding would certainly deny it, and she made no attempt to do so.

All right, so she's changed, Pinata thought. *Maybe the years she spent with Fielding embittered her to the point where she's prejudiced against anything that was a part of their life together. I can't blame her much.*

"The idea, then," he said, "was for Camilla to come to San Félice, get the money, and return to Albuquerque with your share of it?"

Fielding's hesitation was slight, but noticeable. "Sure."

"And you trusted him?"

"I had to."

"Oh, not necessarily. You could, for example, have accompanied him here. That would have been the logical thing to do under the circumstances, wouldn't it?"

"I don't care."

It seemed to Pinata a strangely inept answer for a glib man like Fielding. "As it turned out, you didn't receive your share of the money because he killed himself?"

"I didn't get my share," Fielding said, "because there wasn't anything to share."

"What do you mean?"

"Camilla didn't get the money. She didn't give it to him."

Mrs. Fielding looked stunned for a moment. "That's not true. I handed him two thousand dollars."

"You're lying, Ada. You promised him that much but you didn't come across with it."

"I swear I gave him the money. He put it in an envelope, then he hid the envelope under his shirt."

"I don't believe—"

"You'll have to believe it, Fielding," Pinata said. "That's where it was found, in an envelope inside his shirt."

"It was *on* him? It was there *on* him, all the time?"

"Certainly."

"Why, that dirty bastard…" He began to curse, and each word that damned Camilla damned himself, too, but he couldn't stop. It was as if he'd been saving up words for years, like money to be spent all at once, on one vast special project, his old friend, old enemy, Camilla. The violent emotion behind the flow of words surprised Pinata. Although he knew now that Fielding was responsible for Camilla's death, he still didn't understand why. Money alone couldn't be the reason: Fielding had never cared enough about money even to pursue it with much energy, let alone kill for it. Perhaps, then, he had acted out of anger at being cheated by Camilla. But this theory was less likely than the other. In the first place, he hadn't found out until now that he'd been cheated; in the second, he wasn't a stand-up-and-fight type of man. If he was

311

angry, he would walk away, as he'd walked away from every other difficult situation in his life.

A spasm of coughing had seized Fielding. Pinata poured half a glass of whiskey from the decanter on the coffee table and took it over to him. Ten seconds after Fielding had gulped the drink, his coughing stopped. He wiped his mouth with the back of his hand, in a symbolic gesture of pushing back into it words that should never have escaped.

"No temperance lecture?" he said hoarsely. "Thanks, preacher man."

"You were with Camilla that night, Fielding?"

"Hell, you don't think I'd have trusted him to come all this way alone? Chances were he wouldn't have made it back to Albuquerque even if he wanted to. He was a dying man."

"Tell us what happened."

"I can't remember it all. I was drinking. I bought a bottle of wine because it was a cold night. Curly didn't touch any of it; he wanted to see his sister, and she didn't approve of drinking. When he came back from his sister's house, he told me he'd called Ada and she was going to bring the money right away. I waited behind the signalman's shack. I couldn't see anything; it was too dark. But I heard Ada's car arrive and leave again a few minutes later. I went over to Camilla. He said Ada had changed her mind and there was no money to share after all. I accused him of lying. He took the knife out of his pocket and switched the blade open. He threatened to kill me if I didn't go away. I tried to get the knife away from him, and suddenly he fell over and—well, he was dead. It happened so fast. Just like that, he was dead."

Pinata didn't believe the entire story, but he was pretty sure a jury could be convinced that Fielding had acted in self-defense. A strong possibility existed that the case wouldn't even reach a

312

courtroom. Beyond Fielding's own word there was no evidence against him, and he wasn't likely to talk so freely in front of the police. Besides, the district attorney might be averse to reopening, without strong evidence, a case closed four years previously.

"I heard someone coming," Fielding went on. "I got scared and started running down the tracks. Next thing I knew I was on a freight car heading south. I kept going. I just kept going. When I got back to Albuquerque, I told the two Indians Camilla had been living with that he had died in L.A., in case they might get the idea of reporting him missing. They believed me. They didn't give a damn anyway. Camilla was no loss to them, or to the world. He was just a lousy no-good Mexican." His eyes shifted back to Mrs. Fielding. He was smiling again, like a man enjoying a joke he couldn't share, because it was too special or too involved. "Isn't that right, Ada?"

She shook her head listlessly. "I don't know."

"Oh, come on now, Ada. Tell the people. You knew Camilla better than I did. You used to say he had the feelings of a poet. But you've learned better than that since, haven't you? Tell them what a mean, worthless hunk of—"

"Stop it, Stan. Don't."

"Then say it."

"All right. What difference does it make?" she said wearily. "He was a—a worthless man."

"A lazy, stupid *cholo*, in spite of all your efforts to educate him. Isn't that correct?"

"I—yes."

"Repeat it, then."

"Camilla was a—a lazy, stupid *cholo.*"

"Let's drink to that." Fielding stepped down off the hearth and started across the room toward the decanter. "How about it,

313

Pinata? You're a *cholo* too, aren't you? Have a drink to another *cholo*, one who didn't play it so smart."

Pinata felt the blood rising up into his neck and face. *Cholo, cholo, grease your bolo…* The old familiar word was as stinging an insult now as it had been in his childhood… *Take a trip to the northern polo…* But the anger Pinata felt was instinctive and general, not directed against Fielding. He realized that the man, for all his blustering arrogance, was suffering, perhaps for the first time, a moral pain as intense as the mortal pain Mrs. Rosario had suffered; and the exact cause of the pain Pinata didn't understand any more than, as a layman, he understood the technical cause of Mrs. Rosario's. He said, "You'd better lay off the liquor, Fielding."

"Oh, preacher man, are you going to go into that routine again? Pour me a drink, Daisy baby, like a good girl."

There were tears in Daisy's eyes and in her voice when she spoke. "All right."

"You've always been a good Daddy-loving girl, haven't you, Daisy baby?"

"Yes."

"Then hurry up about it. I'm thirsty."

"All right."

She poured him half a glass of whiskey and turned her head away while he drank it, as if she couldn't bear to witness his need and his compulsion. She said to Pinata, "What's going to happen to my father? What will they do to him?"

"My guess is, not a thing." Pinata sounded more confident than the circumstances warranted.

"First they'll have to find me, Daisy baby," Fielding said. "It won't be easy. I've disappeared before. I can do it again. You might even say I've developed a real knack for it. This Eagle Scout here"—he pointed a thumb contemptuously at Pinata—"he can blast off to the police till he runs out of steam. It won't do any good. There's no case against me, just the one I'm carrying around inside. And that—well, I'm used to it." He put his hand briefly and gently on Daisy's hair. "I can take it. Don't worry about me, Daisy baby. I'll be here and there and around. Someday I'll write to you."

"Don't go away like this, so quickly, so—"

"Come on now, you're too big a girl to cry."

"Don't. Don't go," she said.

But she knew he would and that her search must begin again. She would see his face in crowds of strangers; she would catch a glimpse of him passing in a speeding car or walking into an elevator just before the door closed.

She tried to hold on to his arm. He said quickly, "Good-bye, Daisy," and started across the room.

"Daddy..."

"Don't call me Daddy anymore. That's over. That's gone."

"Wait a minute, Fielding," Pinata said. "Off the record, what did Camilla say or do to you that made you furious enough to knife him?"

Fielding didn't reply. He just turned and looked at his former wife with a terrible hatred. Then he walked out of the house. The slam of the door behind him was as final as the closing of a crypt.

"Why?" Daisy said. "*Why?*" The melancholy little whisper seemed to echo around the room in search of an answer. "Why did it have to happen, Mother?"

Mrs. Fielding sat, mute and rigid, a snow statue awaiting the first ominous rays of the sun.

"You've got to answer me, Mother."

"Yes. Yes, of course."

"Now."

"All right."

With a sigh of reluctance Mrs. Fielding stood up. She was holding in her hand something she'd taken unobtrusively from her pocket. It was an envelope, yellowed by age and wrinkled as if it had been dragged in and out of dozens of pockets and drawers and corners and handbags. "This came for you a long time ago, Daisy. I never thought I'd have to give it to you. It's a letter from—from your father."

"Why did you keep it from me?"

"Your father makes that quite clear."

"Then you've read it?"

"Read it?" Mrs. Fielding repeated wearily. "A hundred times, two hundred—I lost count."

Daisy took the envelope. Her name and the old address on Laurel Street were printed in a shaky and unfamiliar hand. The postmark said, "San Félice, December 1, 1955."

As Pinata watched her unfold the letter, the malevolent chant from his childhood kept running through his head: *Cholo, cholo, grease your bolo.* He hoped that his own children would never have to hear it and remember. His children and Daisy's.

My beloved Daisy:

*It has been so many years since I have seen you. Perhaps, at this hour
that is very late for me, I should not step back into your life. But I cannot
help it. My blood runs in your veins. When I die, part of me will still be
alive, in you, in your children, in your children's children. It is a thought
that takes some of the ugliness out of these cruel years, some of the sting
out of the tricks of time.*

*This letter may never reach you, Daisy. If it doesn't, I will know why.
Your mother has vowed to keep us apart at any cost because she is
ashamed of me. Right from the beginning she has been ashamed, not
only of me but of herself too. Even when she talked of love, her voice
had a bitterness in it, as if the relationship between us was the result of
a physical defect she couldn't help, a weakness of the body which her
mind despised. But there was love, Daisy. You are proof there was love.*

*Memories are crowding in on me so hard and fast that I can barely
breathe. I wish they were good memories, that like other men I could sit
back in the security of my family and review the past kindly. But I cannot. I am alone, surrounded by strangers in a strange place. The hotel
guests are looking at me queerly while I write this, as if they are wondering what a tramp like me is doing in their lobby where I don't belong,
writing to a daughter who has never really belonged to me. Your mother
kept her vow, Daisy. We are still apart, you and I. She has hidden her
shame because she cannot bear it the way we weaker and humbler ones
can and must and do.*

*Shame—it is my daily bread. No wonder the flesh is falling off my
bones. I have nothing to live for. Yet, as I move through the days, shackled*

to this dying body, I yearn to step free of it long enough to see you again, you and Ada, my beloved ones still. I came here to see you, but I lack the courage. That is why I am writing, to feel in touch with you for a little, to remind myself that my death will be only partial; you will be left, you will be the proof that I ever lived at all. I leave nothing else.

Memories—how she cried before you were born, day in, day out, until I wished there were a way of using all those tears to irrigate the dry, dusty rangeland. Dust and tears, these are what I remember most about the day of your birth, your mother's weeping, and the dust sifting in through locked windows and bolted doors and the closed draft of the chimney. And at the very last moment before you were born, she said to me when we were alone, "What if the baby is like you. Oh God, help us, my baby and me." Her baby, not mine.

Right from the first she kept you away from me. To protect you. I had germs, she said; I was dirty from working with cattle. I washed and washed, my shoulders ached pumping water from the drying wells, but I was always dirty. She had to safeguard her baby, she said. Her baby, never mine.

I couldn't protest, I couldn't even speak of it out loud to anyone, but I must tell you now before I die. I must claim you, though I swore to her I never would, as my daughter. I die in the hope and trust that your mother will bring you to visit my grave. May God bless you, Daisy, and your children, and your children's children.

Your loving father, Carlos Camilla

AVAILABLE AND COMING SOON
FROM PUSHKIN VERTIGO

Jonathan Ames

You Were Never Really Here

Augusto De Angelis

The Murdered Banker
The Mystery of the Three Orchids
The Hotel of the Three Roses

Olivier Barde-Cabuçon

Casanova and the Faceless Woman

María Angélica Bosco

Death Going Down

Piero Chiara

The Disappearance of Signora Giulia

Frédéric Dard

Bird in a Cage
The Wicked Go to Hell
Crush
The Executioner Weeps
The King of Fools
The Gravediggers' Bread

Friedrich Dürrenmatt

The Pledge
The Execution of Justice
Suspicion
The Judge and His Hangman

Martin Holmén

Clinch
Down for the Count
Slugger

Alexander Lernet-Holenia

I Was Jack Mortimer

Margaret Millar

Vanish in an Instant
A Stranger in My Grave
The Listening Walls

Boileau-Narcejac

Vertigo
She Who Was No More

Baroness Orczy

The Old Man in the Corner
The Case of Miss Elliott

Leo Perutz

Master of the Day of Judgment
Little Apple
St Peter's Snow

Soji Shimada

The Tokyo Zodiac Murders
Murder in the Crooked House

Masako Togawa

The Master Key
The Lady Killer

Emma Viskic

Resurrection Bay
And Fire Came Down
Darkness for Light

Seishi Yokomizo

The Inugami Clan
Murder in the Honjin